TUFF INC PUBLICATIONS PRESENTS

Bad Blood 2

a novel by

Tuffy

The accounts of this book are fictional and in no way represent any person or event.

Library of Congress Control Number: 2011920510

ISBN 978-0-9844285-4-0
Cover Design: www.StricklyGraphics.com
Editor: Ann Marie Escher

Printed in the United States of America

Acknowledgements

First of all, I would like to thank Allah for my everything.

I thank my book world angel Ms. Laquita Adams and her staff. Laquita, thanks for embracing me and my company with open arms. You made Maryland my second home and you helped me get a strong fan base in your town. I would also like thank Toni from OOSA. Thanks for keeping it real in your reviews. I'd like to thank the vendors who pump our books and the book stores, Black & Nobel, Horizon, and Books in the Hood (Divine) just to name a few.

As always, I have to tell my Philly authors to keep their pens moving: Tenia Jamilla, I'm a fan; Raheem, Terri Woods, Kareem Hendson, you're from Chester, but Philly is your backyard; Keon Smith, you're Tuff Ink's next up to bat; and Kenneth Williams and all the others that are up and coming.

I want to shout out to all of my real folks who have been riding with Tuffy and Tuff Ink from day one and still remain a phone call away. Qaseemah is the glue. Thanks for enduring my rants and raves when I get impatient about Tuff Ink. You did your thing with this company in my absence. Thanks, and get your book done. This year is your year to be on that best sellers list.

I want to really acknowledge and thank Nina Moses. It's been fifteen years and you still got my back. You better know that I got yours as well, always did. Linda King, Sheri Hill, Paige Goodin, and Barry Torrence...damn cousin, you really held the Ink down and made sure the stores were stocked. I'm on my way home and you know the Ink will go to the moon when I touch. You will be right there with me.

Now to my family and friends. I forgot a few of y'all in the other books. Shani, Janaya, Keemy, Aunt Nay, Kenny Bump, Eric, Poppa, Micky, Ducky, Sput, Wuda, Marty, Brad, Marty Kool, Rasul, Omar, Jig, Briz, Shiz, Turtle, Gliss, Herb, Yusef (Kenny), Nino Brown (Take Down), China Whyte (my little brother), Black Mann, Cam, Bub, CP, the whole Bottom, 31st to 46th Street, Woody, Littles and Kurt, Lanair, Milton, Butter, Fu, Rashida (twin), Mike Mike, B-Easy and Shahir, Nay Nay, Calvetta, Omar, Doc (Duqeene, Hardcore Publishing) and Sadiq (Wilkensburg), Buck (TJ), Stoney Mike, Gliss, and D.P. To Milton Moore and Laneir Moses, get home soon. I miss y'all!

To my bro Trick from Raleigh, NC. You're the realest dude I met in a long time. You're my bro for life. I'll be to your town soon so we can shut it down.

Shout outs to China Whyte, Reed Dollaz, Sparks, G-Bucks, Barry, and Rell. I appreciate y'all coming together for that photo shoot.

Last but not least, my beautiful Mom and my Aunt Ellen, my second Mom. I love y'all and thanks for everything. Rest in peace Grandmom, Macky Woods (I need you homie), Bra-Strap Smalls, Tyree, Danny Diamonds, and Glow (G-ball). I love y'all.

Mom and Ellen, don't read this part....

Now to you haters...y'all haters can't stop me. If my success hurt y'all that bad then go kill y'all selves because I'm going to keep doing good. I'm a winner so I won't lose. What's funny is that 95 percent of you hating-ass chumps don't even know me because if y'all did, y'all would watch y'alls mouths. How do y'all hate on a nigga that y'all don't even know?

For the cowards that do know me but only rap when I'm not around, but when I'm in y'all presence, y'all be pipe-riding, please know that, at the end of the day, I'll punch one of you chumps in the mouth. I don't report to nobody. I'm my own boss, always have been. That's why you chumps don't got shit because y'all be worrying about all the wrong shit. Whoever don't like what I said, put blood in my mouth when y'all see me.

Chapter 1

Sharon hated the fact that she had to drive all the way back to Delaware from Philly after having dinner with Champ, Thelma, Wanna, Micky, Toot, and Rhonda. She used the time to think about what she was going to do about the baby she was carrying in her womb. Tone was dead, and although she hated the fact that he was the father, the baby was innocent.

"Damn you Tone, I hate you. Ooow, I hate you! You fucking bastard. How could you leave me like this? You fucking abandoned me and now you're abandoning this fucking child. I fucking hate your selfish ass," she hissed to herself, talking to her dead ex-boyfriend who she'd never see again. She was so busy cursing Tone out that she didn't notice Trev following behind her.

Trev was planning to do whatever it took to make Sharon come up off any paper that his cousin left behind. Tone's sister, Nay, planted a seed of hate for Sharon in Trev. She told Trev a lot of bullshit lies and he fell for them. Trev vowed to get his cousin's shit from his no-good bitch, Sharon, especially since she didn't go to the funeral.

Sharon finally hit her exit and pulled off the expressway. It felt good to be minutes away from pulling into her driveway because now she could get some much-needed rest. She pulled in as Trev parked on the street.

She was so caught up in the mess of her life that she didn't notice the amateur trail-home game Trev had put down on her.

By the time Sharon finished gathering her things and her thoughts, Trev had exited his vehicle and crept alongside the house. When she put her keys in the door, Trev ran up behind her, pushing her into the house with his gun in her back.

"Bitch, be quiet and don't pull no funny shit," Trev said, pushing Sharon into the living room and down onto the couch.

"Oh my God, Trev, what are you doing here?" Sharon said, after realizing it was him.

Crack!

"Shut up bitch," Trev said, smacking Sharon on the head with the butt of his gun. "I'm here to get what my cousin left and I'm not here to play games."

She felt her head to see if she was bleeding, and was relieved to find she wasn't; but that didn't mean she didn't get a hickey from being smacked with the gun. Sharon was crying and her head hurt.

"Tone didn't leave shit here with me, and we weren't the fuck together when he died," Sharon cried.

"Sharon, I'm not playing with you. I will kill your pretty ass and leave you here to rot, so you better tell me something," Trev said, with his gun pointed at her.

"The only cash I have in the house is the eight grand I have in my drawer."

"I don't want no funky-ass eight grand."

Sharon began to panic. Something compelled her to lung at Trev. He kicked her in the stomach so hard she flew back down onto the couch.

"Sit your monkey-ass down," Trev said, cocking his gun.

"Ah shit, you fucking bastard," Sharon said, as she fell to the floor and balled herself up into the fetal position.

"Bitch, where the shit at?" Trev said, as he stomped on her repeatedly.

"There's a safe in the floor beneath the carpet under my bed."

"What's the combination?"

Sharon could barely speak.

"I don't know, I don't know, I really don't know," she mumbled through the pain.

"Well bitch, we're going upstairs, and we're going to find out," Trev said, grabbing her by the collar, forcing her to lead the way upstairs with his gun poking her in the back.

Trev didn't give a fuck about the trail of blood dripping from underneath her pants.

"I hope this safe is not in the same room that barking is coming from."

"No, I locked my dog in the guest room."

"Good, I didn't want to have to kill your dog."

As they entered the bedroom, Trev pushed the bed aside with one hand as he pointed the gun at Sharon, who was standing in the corner, with the other. He walked over to her and pushed her to the floor. He motioned for her to uncover the safe. Once exposed, he forced her to try the combination.

"Bitch, use tag numbers, social security numbers, dates of birth, or anything else you can think of. If you play games, we'll be here all night or until you bleed to death," Trev said, now noticing the blood soaking through her jeans. He didn't think he had kicked her that hard.

Micky used his key to enter his mom's house.

"Mom, I've been calling your house phone to let you know you left your cell at the restaurant," Micky said, as he walked through the door.

His senses went up at the sight of blood on the floor leading up the steps, and Cavalli's constant barking. He didn't bother to go back out to the car where Toot and Rhonda waited. Instead, he went into the kitchen to retrieve the gun Sharon had stashed in a drawer. After Ern was killed, Sharon got a license to carry. She had two registered guns; the one she carried with her and the one she left in the kitchen. Micky and Tone were the only other people who knew the location of the pistol. Micky picked up the gun and headed upstairs.

"What the fuck is all this blood?" he said softly, as he crept upstairs.

The plush carpet made it easy for him to travel through the house undetected. Cavalli was barking relentlessly. Trev had gotten used to the noise and was blocking it out of his mind. Micky could hear his Mom crying as he reached the top of the steps.

"I need a doctor, Trev. I don't know the fucking combination. I need a doctor."

Micky could see Trev standing over his mom with a gun pointed at her head as she attempted to open the safe.

Boom...Boom...Boom!

Before Trev knew what hit him, he was slumped over Sharon. He was dead before his body fell over her. Sharon started screaming. She thought the shot was fired from Trev's gun. She was a little confused until she heard her son's voice calling out to her.

"Mom, what's wrong? Where is this blood coming from?"

Micky rushed over to help her up. Sharon was still a little dazed and couldn't answer her son's question. She started crying uncontrollably and embraced her son as Toot and Rhonda came rushing through the bedroom door. They heard the shots fired and immediately came in to see what was wrong. Although Toot told Rhonda to wait in the car, she refused and came in with him.

"My baby, my baby, my baby," Sharon kept mumbling in a daze. She repeated the phrase as she was taken to the hospital by ambulance.

~~~~~

Wanna, Champ, and Thelma weren't in the house long enough to get settled in before the phone call from Rhonda. Wanna was shocked by what Rhonda reported. Although she was upset about not being able to spend the night comforted by her man, Wanna gathered her things to go rescue Sharon, like always. She and Champ got in her Range Rover and headed to Delaware's Christiana Hospital to check on Sharon. They convinced Thelma to stay in the house because she was going to visit Bingo in the morning. She stayed on the condition that they would keep her posted.

Champ was watching Wanna drive. He could tell she was scared, full of questions, and fed up with all the bullshit that seemed to find them. He was fed up as well. Ever since his near-death experience, he'd been questioning if all the street shit was worth it. He made his money a long time ago. Although he had at least six months to a year before he planned on calling it quits, the shit he'd been through lately had him contemplating making an early exit out of the game. That, along with being in love and his belief in the Islamic literature Shaahir had been sending him.

"Baby girl, what's wrong?" Champ asked, as he rubbed Wanna's thigh.

"Champ, all this stuff is getting on my nerves. Y'all are going to give me a nervous breakdown. Sharon is my girl, but she makes some of the dumbest mistakes. How the fuck did Trev come from Atlanta and end up in her house with a gun to her head?"

She paused for a minute before she continued.

"I should have been a friend a long time ago and told her how much of an asshole she was for even dating Tone. If I did, none of this shit would have happened."

Champ was quiet for awhile as he let his girl vent. When she was done he commented, "Baby girl, all this shit will come to an end soon. Sharon's my heart, too, but she seems to always be the victim of bad blood."

He grabbed her hand.

"Wanna, that's why I always find myself schooling you and Thelma. Security is everything. Do you know how many times I asked you today alone if you were sure that you weren't being followed or to check your rearview mirror?"

Champ was always on Wanna and Thelma's backs about staying on point because he knew the streets knew they were his weakness, and he would never want them to be used as pawns or leverage to get to him.

"Champ, you're always on us about that and now it's automatic. The funny thing is that I always tell Sharon to play her mirrors and stay on point because of these crazy niggas in the streets, and especially because of all the crazy shit Tone was into. I couldn't stand his coward, jealous ass," Wanna said, subconsciously looking at the marks left on Champ's wrists as a result of being handcuffed to a metal chair when he was abducted by Tone and Sab.

If Wanna could, she would wake Tone up from the dead and kill him all over again. Her level of hate for him was like no other.

"Baby girl, Sharon will eventually get it together. She just has a black cloud over her head. Did you read the literature Shaahir sent me? If so, what did you think?" Champ said, trying to find out what Wanna thought about the Islamic material.

"Baby, I didn't get a chance to read it, but I'll get to it tomorrow. Why? What do you think?"

"I'm really open to it. I just have to get a clear understanding of a few things," Champ said, thinking of how Shaahir stressed in his letter that he didn't want Champ to die a nonbeliever.

Champ didn't have a religion, but he knew that God had brought him out the hands of his abducters.

They pulled up to the ER and turned the car over to the valet before they entered the lobby. The appearance was different from the lobbies of Philadelphia hospitals. It was clean, spacious, and not as crowded. They spotted Rhonda, Micky, and Toot waiting on the side. When Champ and Wanna approached them, they all exchanged greetings and hugs. Wanna pulled Rhonda aside away from the men to give them a chance to talk.

"What happened, Micky?" Champ said, sincerely concerned.

"Unc, I'm glad my mom left her cell phone in the restaurant. We were the last to leave since Toot had to go to the bathroom. The waitress noticed me and asked if someone from our party left their phone behind. I saw that it was my mom's, so I got it and was going to drop it off to her in the morning. But Toot's joy-riding ass kept insisting that we drop it off tonight. When I got to the house, I saw blood on the floor and the dog was barking like crazy."

Champ stepped back because he couldn't believe what he was hearing. Micky nodded his head at Champ as he continued.

"I went to grab the gat my mom keeps in the drawer and crept up the stairs. I could hear my mom crying, and when I got to her bedroom door, I could see her on the floor fucking with the safe and this nigga, Trev, got a gun to her head. I blacked out thinking how them niggas did my pop, and I aired that nigga out. Toot and Rhonda came running in, and Toot just started stomping that dead nigga," Micky said, demonstrating Toot by kicking his foot in the air as if he was stomping someone.

"Where did this nigga come from? Trev hasn't been in town for years," Champ said, trying to figure out this mess.

"Fuck where he came from as long as his lame ass goes to hell," Micky replied.

"I'm not going to his maggot-ass funeral either," Toot said, talking about his cousin as if he was an enemy.

"What did your mom say happened?"

"Unc, she was bleeding heavy and so spaced out that I didn't ask too many questions. The doctor did come out and tell me that she had a miscarriage."

"Miscarrage?" Champ said, raising his voice.

"Yeah, I didn't know she was having a baby, Unc."

"I didn't either. Wanna come here," Champ said, waving her over.

"What's up baby?"

"Why didn't you tell me Sharon was pregnant?" Wanna frowned.

"Because I didn't know. This is news to me," Wanna said, now curious about Sharon's situation.

"We got to find out what happened. I wonder if Trev followed her home, or if he was already there when she got there," Champ said, now angrier that Sharon was attacked while pregnant.

"I don't know, Unc, but here comes the doctor now," Micky said, pointing to the short Indian doctor approaching them with a clipboard in his hand.

The doctor suggested that Micky come over to speak with him privately.

"This is all immediate family, doc," Micky said, assuring the doctor that he was free to divulge the particulars.

"Okay, I was just checking. Sharon is doing better than we thought. She did, however, have a miscarriage. We are going to keep her overnight for observation and to run some more tests. She has a few bumps and bruises. We expect her to have a full and steady recovery."

"Doctor, when can we go in to see her?" Wanna asked, waiting to see her girlfriend, but tired of seeing her people in various hospitals due to violence.

"Well, she's had a long night, and she needs her rest, so maybe it would be best if you all came back later this afternoon when she's awake," the doctor said with a mild smile but stern face to let them know his request was serious.

"Doc, how about letting us just peek in on her," Rhonda requested.

The doctor looked at their faces and knew they wouldn't take no for an answer.

"Okay, but try not to wake her," the doctor said before he walked away.

The guys let the girls peek in on Sharon while they waited behind in the lobby. Champ turned to Mickey.

"Yo, what did the cops say?"

"The detective gave me his card and said I have to come in to be interviewed tomorrow, rather today at lunch time," Micky said, realizing that it was after five in the morning.

"Do you need to take a lawyer?" Champ asked, concerned about Micky.

"Naw Unc, the detective said as long as the gun comes back clean, I'm good. He said that he just has to get my statement because it's procedure."

"Alright, but if they try any tricky shit, call my phone, shut up, and wait until the lawyer comes."

"Unc, I think it'll be cool. Dude said, off the record, that I did the right thing, and if it was his mom, he would have done the same. He also said that he would never gun after a law-abiding citizen behind a piece of shit like Trev," Micky said with one eyebrow raised and a smirk on his face.

"Damn, if the detective only knew," Champ chuckled.

Micky and Toot joined in on the laugh as Wanna and Rhonda returned.

"What's so funny?" Wanna asked, as she looked at the giggling men.

"Nothing boo, how is Sharon?" Champ asked.

"She was asleep. She looked like herself laying there."

"Cool. Let's get up out of here. We'll come back later," Champ said, as he grabbed Wanna by the waist.

"Unc, we're going to go back to my mom's crib. We've got to clean up and feed Cavalli. After that, I've got to go give that detective my law-abiding statement," Micky said chuckling, as Toot and Champ burst out laughing.

Rhonda and Wanna looked at them as if they were crazy because they didn't get the joke. They all chatted until the valet brought their cars around. Before departing, they shared handshakes, hugs, and good-byes.

Wanna pulled off with Champ leaning back in his seat on the passenger side.

"Baby girl, when Sharon gets out of this jawn, I'm going to have a long talk with her," Champ said, as he turned the radio up slightly.

"About what? Her having a baby by that monster and not telling us? I'm going to grind her up about that so you don't have to say a word to her about it," Wanna said, with her nostrils flaring from the anger she felt toward Sharon.

Champ always got turned on when Wanna's nose flared. He also knew that it was a sign that she was upset.

"It's about more than her being secretly pregnant by nut-ass Tone. He was always a lame, and I don't care if that's what she chose, which is why I never spoke on it. I do, however, have a problem when her choices put Micky at risk. Ern was damn near a brother to me and Micky was his world, so I'll be damned if she puts him on the line because of her fucked-up choice in niggas."

"Baby, Micky's fine and Tone and Trev are dead, so they can't bring any harm to Micky or anyone else."

Champ shook his head and said, "You're right, but suppose he would have killed that nigga with a dirty gun and went to jail for a homicide? That's what my problem is."

"I didn't think of it like that," Wanna said, as she navigated her way through the traffic.

"The cops wouldn't care if dude was on their property or not, they would still book Micky on that bullshit. Sharon can date whoever she wants, as long as she don't put anyone from our circle at risk in the process, especially Micky," Champ said, as he looked over at Wanna, whose nose was really flaring now.

"Did I tell you that you turn me all the way on when you're mad?" Champ said, changing the subject.

He began to rub between Wanna's legs and could feel the warmth of her fat pussy through her jeans.

"Who said I was mad?" she asked, a little distracted by Champ rubbing on her.

"Your nose is flared up so your nose said that you're mad," Champ joked, as he continued to rub on her pussy.

"You better stop before we have to pull over," she said, as she looked over at him and smiled.

"Okay, but Thelma should be out of the house when we get there, and I need to sample this," Champ said, as he rubbed Wanna's pussy one last time.

Chapter 2

Reem was up early in the morning. Although he wasn't related to Tone or Toot, he was Trev's cousin on Trev's father's side of the family. Trev was his favorite cousin, and whenever he came to Philly, he would always holler at Reem. Trev used to beg Reem to come to Atlanta and stay with him. The few times Reem visited Trev, Trev would show him the time of his life. He took Reem to all the hot spots in Atlanta, such as Body Tap, Strokers, Visions, and Justin's. Reem's favorite spots to hang out were Club 112, Bizzy B's, and Magic City. He always felt like a king in Magic City.

Trev would never allow Reem to stay in a hotel when he came for a visit. Instead, he would stay in one of Trev's apartments in Marietta, Georgia, on Bentley Road about fifteen minutes outside the city.

Reem couldn't believe someone killed Trev. Nay called and told Reem that she wanted to meet him this afternoon to give him some details on Trev's murder. Reem was getting money Uptown, and his crew was slowly on the rise. Although he wasn't known for playing with guns, Reem was ready to bust his gun to avenge Trev's murder. He wanted to get some of his daily runs out of the way before he went to meet Nay.

Reem pulled up to the crib of his favorite young bull, Jim, on Sheldon Street, as he called to let Jim know he was outside. Jim came out with a cup of tea in one hand, a muffin in the other, and a Newport behind his ear. Once in the car, he put his tea in the cup holder.

"What's up nigga?" Jim said, as he bit into his muffin.

"It ain't shit. I'm still a little hungover from last night."

"Yeah, Bayhirah and them had you drinking that Patron straight," Jim said, snacking on his muffin and sipping his tea.

"I know. I had about seven double shots of that shit," Reem said, rubbing his head.

"She's finally giving you some rhythm, and you don't know how to act," Jim chuckled, knowing that Reem had been on Bayhirah's head for about a year now.

"Yeah, I had the little chick last night. She would have rolled out with me if her sister, Aliyah, didn't start drawing with all that my little sister ain't going with you while she's drunk shit," Reem said, reminiscing about the scene Aliyah put on outside the Crab House.

"Yo, I heard their pop is this Muslim oldhead named Rafiq, and he be on their head about them messing with street niggas and being out of their overgarments."

"I heard the same thing, but it's like six of them and they are all bad, so what do he expect a nigga to do?" Reem said, pulling onto Huntington Park.

"I don't know, but I heard oldhead used to be on some gangster shit back in the day," Jim said, to warn his friend.

"I don't want no trouble out of oldhead. I just want to stick this whole dick with the mushroom tip up in Bayhirah," Reem sniggered.

Jim joined in and started laughing hard. Reem looked over at Jim.

"Yo, you fucked that muffin up like we ain't getting to a dollar."

"Reem, I'm hungry as shit, and I knew you wouldn't stop to get nothing to eat because it's all work and no play when you're on a mission."

"You're right, but you still didn't have to fuck that muffin up like that," Reem said, as he parked the car.

They both got out after Reem popped the trunk.

"Get that City Blue bag," Reem yelled to Jim.

Jim grabbed the bag and they went into Reem's crib, which he referred to as "the lab." They used the crib to break down their work and cook their coke.

"Jim, let's try to knock this shit right out. I got to go find out about Trev's murder from Nay's fat ass, so I can get right on top of it."

"Reem, you know Nay's always gossiping, and she always hyping shit up. Don't let her have us on no dummy mission."

"You're right, but I'm going to listen to what she got for me," Reem said, pulling the four bricks out of the bag.

"What are we doing, breaking down or cooking?"

"We're going to break 'em down first, but we're going to cook one of these bricks as well."

They got the scale and blender out of the cabinet. They had a system they used that worked very well. Jim carefully measured out 14 grams of pro-cain cut. He laid out twenty-four sandwich bags, and put 14 grams of cut in each along with 14 grams of coke. Reem took each bag and blended the contents with an electric blender. Once he finished the same thing with all twenty-four bags, he put 97 grams of rocked-up fish scale in each bag and tied them up. This was Reem's way of getting an extra 4 ½ ounces off each brick. The extra money he would make off the free 13 ½ ounces was his money to blow on bills, tricking, and buying bottles at the bar. This was what the Philly hustlers who weren't quite brick pushers called the take-out. As long as you had good coke to start with, the 14 grams of pro-cain didn't impair the coke.

"Yo, let's cook this brick so we can get up out of here," Reem said, grabbing the baking soda and his large VisionWare glass pot out of the cabinet.

On cue, Jim grabbed the bag of ice.

"Yo, I'm going to cook half of this brick straight to the oils for the post because our post can't have the same thing that we sell to the young bulls on the other corners," Reem said, putting the pot on the stove.

Jim weighed out 500 grams on the digital scale. He put it all in a big, one-gallon, zip lock bag then crushed it up as much as he could without busting the bag and poured it into the pot. Reem dumped the baking soda over the coke and poured enough water into the pot to cover the coke. He turned the burner to medium. When the water cleared up, he poured a handful of ice into the water causing the cooked coke to gel at the bottom. He took his big spoon and began to stir the gel into a cookie form. Once he had control of the gel and it began to lock up, he poured the water off.

"Damn, this shit is butter. Do you see my cookie?" he said, referring to the coke he molded into a big circle.

Yeah, that thing is oils," Jim replied, as he took a puff of his Newport.

They went through the same routine for the other half of brick; except, once it gelled up and he poured the water off, he put 42 grams of baking soda on top of the gel and whipped it into the coke until it locked up.

"Damn, even the whip looks like butter," Jim said, pulling on his cigarette.

"Nigga, this shit is still butter," Reem said honestly, because 42 grams of baking soda couldn't hurt 500 grams of coke.

They cleaned up the mess once Reem was finished. Jim had a few players lined up to cop off him, so he took five of the 4 ½ ounce bags with him. Reem had a sale for half a brick, which was equivalent to four of the same bags. They put the remainder of the work up and proceeded to go complete their sales.

"Man, once we finish these runs, we got to go get the young bulls so they can come bag this crack up," Reem stated, as he increased the volume of Jay-Z's *Volume One* CD.

They got the young bulls to bag the crack up once they finished making their runs. Jim stayed behind to supervise their work while Reem went to meet Nay.

Reem got a phone call from Bayhirah while he was on the way to meet Nay. He had been waiting on her call all day, but didn't want to seem too anxious when he answered.

"Yizzo," he said, trying to play it cool.

"Hello is the correct way to answer the phone," Bayhirah said sarcastically.

"Yo, I'm not trying to hear that mess. Yizzo is how I answer my phone," Reem said, standing his ground.

"Whatever boy," Bayhirah replied, as if she had an attitude even though she was really turned on by Reem's assertiveness.

"I'm all man. I haven't been a boy in years," Reem chuckled.

"Are you going to get smart, or are we going to talk?"

"I'm just messing with you. Loosen up."

Bayhirah cleared her throat before saying, "What are you doing tonight, Reem?"

"Whatever you want to do, as long as you don't let Aliyah's crazy ass curse me out again."

Bayhirah giggled.

"Let me find out she chumped you. She was just a little drunk off of all that Patron you had us drinking, but she's cool," she said, pausing momentarily before adding, "Actually, she was the one that convinced me to call you."

"Oh yeah?"

"Yeah, anyway, let's go out to get something to eat. I know that all men like that stupid basketball, so we can go to Friday's on City Line Avenue. They're always showing the games."

"Yeah, I'm with that. The Lakers are going to beat the Magic for the championship."

"Whatever, I just want to go out and kick it with you."

"Alright Bayhirah, call me around eight tonight."

"Okay, bye."

"'Bye," Reem said, as he hung up while thinking about Bayhirah's pussy print evident through the jeans she was wearing at the Crab House last night.

He was hoping to get his hands on her in the near future. When he was coming down Ms. Bernadette's block, he called Nay. She was standing outside by the time he parked. He got out and leaned up against the car with Nay.

"What's up Nay? What you got for me?"

"I got a lot for you, Reem," Nay said, trying to be sexy.

Although they were related to Trev, the two of them were no relation themselves.

"I'm talking about what do you have on Trev's murder," Reem said, sensing Nay was on some flirting shit because she was licking her lips.

"Oh, the little boy, Micky, killed him. Trev was fucking my brother's bitch, Sharon, and her son Micky couldn't take it. He shot Trev while Sharon was sucking his dick," Nay said, lying.

"Damn, I didn't know Trev took Tone's bitch," Reem said, knowing that Trev wouldn't cross Tone in that manner.

"Oh, Tone gave the bitch to Trev before he died, and Trev has been fucking her ever since," Nay quickly added, sensing Reem might be onto her.

"Okay, I see, because I know that wasn't Trev's style, to fuck the girl of somebody he has love for."

"I know, but Tone partied the freak bitch with him and let him have her."

"So the little nigga Micky killed Trev because Trev was fucking his mom. I got to ask this little nigga Micky if he has a fucking problem," Reem said, trying to get a reaction from Nay.

"Naw, don't ask him shit. Just blow his motherfucking brains out."

"Alright Nay, I'm going to get at the nigga," Reem said, walking away to get into his car.

Before he could get in, Nay grabbed him.

"Reem, you're grown now, so let me know when you want me to suck a vein out of that dick. I know that dick is good with your little, bow-legged self," Nay said, trying to sound sexy.

Reem jumped into the car and got the fuck away from Nay as fast as he could.

"I got to check this bitch's story out because she's not going to have me on no bullshit. If Micky did this, then it's war. I need a newspaper so I can check this shit out," he said to himself.

~~~~~

Bingo had just come back from a visit. He was glowing as he always did when he came from seeing his wife. He was looking forward to the trial. His lawyer put in for a speedy trial motion and the judge granted it, so the prosecution had 180 days to bring them to trial. When their main witness was killed, the prosecution put in for a two-week postponement. The judge granted them the two weeks, so they had thirteen days to start trial.

Shaahir walked up and shook hands with Bingo, Nino, and Teddy.

"Yo, I'll be down to the bat cave after I offer *Salat*," Shaahir said, referring to Bingo's cell. Shaahir had become like family to them.

"Alright, we'll be there."

"Them Muslims are always praying," Nino said, thinking that it seemed as if Shaahir was always about to offer *Salat*.

"They pray at least five times a day," Teddy butt in, as they all walked into Bingo's cell.

Nino went straight into Bingo's locker and grabbed a Twix.

"Break that down my nigga," Teddy said, with his hand out.

"I'm going to get you one," Nino huffed, as he opened the locker again.

"I don't want a whole one," Teddy yelled.

Nino closed the locker and gave Teddy half of the one he had.

"Yo, we should be home in two weeks," Bingo said, looking out the window of his closed cell door but talking to his two co-conspirators on the other side of the cell.

"Yeah, and I can't wait because I got a few niggas to check," Teddy said, eating the caramel off the top of the Twix.

"Teddy, let's just get past the bullshit first, and then we can worry about all the other shit," Bingo said, knowing his little brother was trigger-happy and dying to get the little niggas who ran off with the paper and the niggas who have been popping shots at their crew by talking a bunch of bullshit.

"Okay bro, but I'm on my loose cannon shit when I touch."

"Let's just get there."

They were quiet for a few minutes until Shaahir knocked on the door with his familiar knock.

"May I enter?"

"Come in Shaahir."

"What's up y'all?"

"Nothing, I told you that you don't have to knock and ask to come in, my nigga. You're family," Bingo said, shaking Shaahir's hand.

"I know what you said, but Muslim's knock and ask permission to enter someone's dwelling."

"I hope this won't be our dwelling long," Teddy replied, looking out of the window at the people walking freely up and down the street.

"Y'all will make it out okay," Shaahir countered.

Teddy and Nino left the cell to play casino in the day room, leaving Shaahir and Bingo there to talk.

"What's on your mind, Bingo?"

"Nothing besides getting up out of here. I got a lot to handle."

"Bingo, I go home next week. My violation time is up, and if you need me to take care of anything, you just say the word. As far you getting out of here, I'm telling you from experience that this shit always works out for the good niggas, and you're a good nigga."

"Thanks man. I have to admit that you have been good to me, Nino, and my brother since we've come through this jawn. I know Champ got you when you touch because he looks out for all his peoples, but I got it going on too. And if I win this trial, I got you."

"Bingo, I'm good. I did all I did because you're Champ's people, and anything we've built after that is because you are a hell of a dude."

"That's what's up. Oh, my wife said that Champ is mad as hell at Sharon because her son had to kill the nigga Trev."

"Who is the nigga Trev, and why do Champ care about the nigga?"

"Champ don't care about the nigga. The nigga is Tone's cousin. He grew up down our way but he moved to Atlanta. Champ is mad with Sharon because she put Micky in danger by fucking with the nigga Tone in the first place."

"Damn, the news said that the nigga was trying to rape Sharon when her son walked in."

"Yeah, that's what the news says, but Thelma said the nigga was there trying to rob her for Tone's shit."

"Damn, the nigga tried to rob his cousin's chick? Niggas are crazy."

"Yeah, but what's even crazier is that the nigga Trev had his own paper and he wasn't a greasy nigga, so I think it's more to the story."

"Damn, that shit sound wild. Is Micky good?"

"Yeah, he's straight. He killed the nigga with Sharon's gun and the gun was registered."

"That's what's up."

~~~~~

Reem and Bayhirah were in T.G.I. Friday's enjoying the game. The whole city seemed to be there. The game was off the hook, and all the little crews were trying to outshine each other.

Bayhirah was feeling Reem. He was a much better guy than she gave him credit for being. He was caught up in the game and talking to some of the hustlers he knew, but he constantly focused his attention on Bayhirah to make sure she was okay.

Reem kept his composure when the hustlers that knew Bayhirah or one of her sisters came over to speak to her. She was always thorough enough to introduce Reem as her friend first; and in return, he was thorough enough to slide to the bar or go kick it with someone he knew to give her some space.

Wuda, from down the Bottom, walked over with his cousin, Barry.

"Reem, this is Wuda and Barry. They are Tuffy's cousins. You know Tuffy, my sister's baby's father. Wuda and Barry, this is Reem."

Reem said his what's ups and slid off to talk to Danielle and Tanya at the bar.

"What you doing here, Bayhirah?" Wuda asked.

"Minding my business and being grown. Where is my nephew's father at?" she asked, knowing that Wuda and Barry were normally with Tuffy.

Wuda turned to point at the TV.

"Look at the TV...he's at the Orlando game with Jig and Omar."

She looked up at the TV and back to them.

"Why didn't y'all go with them?"

"Because they took some chicks," Wuda concluded.

"Them niggas are always on the go with some chicks," Bayhirah said sarcastically.

"They outgrew this nut-ass city years ago," Barry said, speaking for the first time.

"Tell Tuffy to come get his bad-ass son when he gets back," Bayhirah said, as Wuda and Barry went to finish watching the game.

Reem came back and checked on Bayhirah. She was impressed that he wasn't on any insecure shit. The Lakers won game five for the championship on Orlando's home court, 99 to 86.

"Let's get out of here before these niggas start drawing and these cops start tripping," Reem said, taking Bayhirah's hand and leading her through the pushing crowd.

"Damn, Kobe finally did it without Shaq," Reem said, as he let Bayhirah into the car.

"Reem, I don't really care for basketball. I just wanted to come out and spend some time with you. If I didn't have school in the morning, I would hang out with you a little longer."

"It's cool, we'll have more time to hang out; that's if you want to see me again after tonight's little outing."

"Reem, you're cool, and I think you're a little cutie."

Reem was blushing from the compliment. He drove her to her car and made sure she was safe. Before getting into the car, Bayhirah gave Reem a hug and a peck on the cheek. She promised him she would call him when she got in the crib.

Chapter 3

The week went by quickly. Champ had his talk with Sharon. Although he had intended to be hard on her, he was rather sensitive. He really loved her like a sister. He did let her know how he felt about putting Micky in harm's way. She assured Champ that she never intended to compromise her son's safty. She informed Champ that Trev must have followed her to the crib and that she was happy Micky showed up when he did. Champ was glad he got that conversation out of the way, and now he was thinking of his exit plan.

He told the connect he was going to bring Ducky through so he could deal directly with him when he retired. He was hoping that Bingo won his trial so he could sell him and Thelma the house he shared with Wanna in Marcus Hook. He planned to keep all the businesses and properties he had in Philly, but he was going to move to New Castle, Delaware, in the bushes. Brooks Brothers had just built a gated community complex down there.

Along with his age, the reality of death or jail at the end of the game, and falling for the Islamic literature Shaahir had been sending, Champ was really on the verge of calling the quits in the next few weeks. He even felt bad about giving Ducky a hundred bricks yesterday.

Ducky was by far his main man and Micky was his favorite nephew; but no matter how much love and admiration they had for him, they didn't understand the retirement shit he was talking, and they didn't see what was wrong with him being Muslim and hustling. They all came up in the streets of Philly where some of the most hardened criminals were Muslim. Champ told them that he didn't want to be like that, and that what they were doing was blemishing Islam; that hustling and murder were totally against the teachings of Islam. He made it clear that if he was going to be Muslim, he was going to be done with the streets. He did let Ducky and Micky know that he'd always be a call away if they needed him.

As he sat in the passenger side of the Bentley GTC with the top down with Ducky and Raheem parked behind him in Raheem's Range Rover, Shaahir came out of the front door of the jail smiling hard. They all jumped out to give Shaahir hugs and handshakes. They busted on the tan khakis the jail gave him to wear when he left.

"Yo, look six windows up right there and wave," Shaahir said, pointing to where Bingo's cell was.

Champ, Raheem, and Ducky waved, and within seconds they heard Bingo banging on the window with a cup. That was how inmates let people know they see them outside the window.

"Yo, let's go to South Street so you can get out of them bullshit khakis," Champ said, jumping back in the passenger seat of the Bentley while Ducky and Raheem got into the Range.

"Damn, I guess I'm driving," Shaahir said, jumping in the driver's side of the Bentley.

"Yeah, you have a license and South Street is right around the corner. You want me to take you to buy some of them throbes that the Muslim boys up Germantown *Masjid* be wearing?"

"I'm going to get some throbes made from Naeemah, but right now we are going to get them Prps, Cavilli, Seven, True Religion, and things along those lines. Don't get it messed up, Champ, you can still be fly and be Muslim," Shaahir said, hoping that his dear friend didn't feel as though, once he became Muslim, he had to shut his whole life down.

"Okay, I'll remember that. I do know one thing though, if what I've been reading is correct."

"What's that brother?" Shaahir said, turning off Eighth Street onto South Street.

"All the criminal activity that I see the Muslims we know get themselves caught up into is totally against the teachings of Islam," Champ said, as they drove down Fifth and South.

Shaahir was quiet. He pulled in front of Platinum's clothing store and parked.

"I'll have this talk with you when we leave from down here."

They went into the store with Ducky and Raheem following them. They got all the latest shit out. They went down the street to Fushions clothing store and did the same. Of course, they went into Dr. Denim and got all the thugged-out shit. They put all the bags in the trunk and got back into the car. Before they pulled off, Shaahir spotted his young bull, Dawud, from Price Street. Shaahir got out and Dawud ran right over to him

"*As Salaamu Alaikum*, Shaahir," Dawud greeted him.

"*Wa Laikum Salaam*, Little Uzi," Shaahir said, hugging his young bull and calling him by the nickname he gave him years ago.

"Damn oldhead, when did you get home?"

"Stop with the oldhead stuff. I just got home today. How have you been?"

"It's been rough without you, but I've been holding on."

"Yo, I appreciate you going around my Ummi's house, taking the trash out, and checking on her from time to time. You scored big with me by doing that, Little Uzi."

"Shaahir, that's the least I could do for you. I really didn't have any extra money to send you, so I tried to let you know that I'm still with you through the small stuff."

"That was more sacred than any amount of money you could have sent."

"Damn, I see you in the Bent with the bull, Champ. Price Street is wide open," Dawud said, letting Shaahir know he was still ready to get it down.

"Yeah, that's my man. Give me a few days and I'm right at it."

"I'll come past your wife's house and holler at you then."

"That's what's up."

"I need you, big bro."

"I got you."

They shook hands, and Shaahir jumped back into the car with Champ. They pulled off. They were headed to the Germantown *Masjid* so that Shaahir could meet his wife who was driving the car he had before he got locked up for the nine-month violation. He had the CL 63 before he was locked up, and although he could still get away with the one-year-old machine, he elected to let Champ help him get the GT.

"Yo, are we still on for tomorrow, Champ?"

"Yeah, we're good. I got Mike at F.C. Kerbeck on deck for tomorrow. He's going to take the CL and some paper and put you straight in a GT."

"That's what's up. I'm going to the *Masjid* to offer prayer then go home and enjoy my wife for the rest of the night."

"That sounds like a winner. What about what we were talking about before we parked on South Street?" Champ asked, refusing to let Shaahir out of his sight without getting an answer to his question.

"Champ, it's like this. Everything that you see Muslims doing in the street that's a crime definitely goes against the religion."

"So does that mean that they are fake Muslims?" Champ asked, with one eyebrow raised.

"No, no, Champ, they are still Muslim. They are just weak and living in sin. Hopefully, they won't die while doing the forbidden things that Allah has warned them about in the Qur'an and through his prophet, Muhammad, may peace and blessing be upon him."

"So they are basically gambling with their souls?"

"In a sense, yes. I'm not perfect and I truly believe in Allah and the last day. I'm not the best Muslim but I try my best. I'll never deny that Allah's religion is perfect, but I'm not perfect. Maybe one day I'll give the streets up as a whole. But I'm being honest, I'm not that strong right now," Shaahir said, speaking and feeling like damn near every Muslim that came up in the streets.

"I appreciate your honesty, and I'm glad I have you to talk with and to walk me through these things."

"Champ, I've been honest with you since I've known you. Furthermore, I'll never lie about Allah or his prophet, may the peace and blessing be upon him, to justify my wrongs."

"Shaahir, I'm really thinking about taking my *Shahadah* and becoming Muslim, but if I do, I'm done with these streets completely."

"Champ, I want this religion for you because it is pure, it's the truth. I swear, it's the truth. On the other hand, I don't know what I'll do without you in these streets. I'll probably have to kill one of these niggas out here," Shaahir said, knowing that no one would treat him as his man Champ has treated him over the years.

"Well, I'll be around for a couple of weeks to get you where you need to be."

"And then what? I can't deal with none of these suckers out here, Champ."

"Shaahir, I'm done, but you'll be good because Ducky will have the connect."

"Damn, that's what's up. We're going to miss you out here."

Shaahir was happy that Ducky would have the connect; it was just like him getting the connect himself.

"You won't miss me because you know y'all will be at my restaurants. I'll still see you in the *Masjid*, and we'll still go out to eat and things of that nature, right?" Champ asked Shaahir.

"Yeah, but that's different."

"Well, that's the way it will be. I know you got your mind made up, so I won't push you, Shaahir; but you should leave the streets alone too, and we can do some legit things."

Champ was trying to entice Shaahir to follow what he knew was right.

"Champ, you're right and I'm wrong. Maybe one day I'll get it together," is all Shaahir could manage to say, as they hopped out and got Ducky and Raheem, who followed them up to the *Masjid* to help put the bags in the trunk of his CL.

His wife patiently waited in the passenger seat until he finished with Ducky and Raheem. Champ was in the driver's seat of his car by the time Ducky and Raheem got back into the Range. Champ just stared at the *Masjid* as Shaahir and his wife disappeared through the doors of the Muslim house of worship.

~~~~~

Reem was really starting to feel Bayhirah. She cleaned his cut up the other day when he came from Trev's funeral.

Toot decided to go to Trev's funeral to see what was being said among his distant family. Everything was cool until Nay started pumping Reem's head up about Toot; saying he had no right being there, and that Toot was with the little nigga that killed Trev. Reem, who fell for her bullshit, stepped up to Toot and asked him to leave. They had a big argument that turned into a brawl inside the funeral home. Toot was a little too much for Reem. Toot had Reem on the ground punching him until Jim jumped in and kicked Toot in the face. They jumped on Toot until a few family members broke it up.

After the funeral, Reem went to see Bayhirah. She cleaned up his cuts with peroxide and spent the rest of the day with him talking about life. Reem didn't even hit the pussy yet, but he seemed to be catching feelings for her. Today they planned to get something to eat from Devon's after Bayhirah got out of school, so Reem wanted to get done early. He picked Jim up so they could get their running around out the way before Reem's schedule was clear.

"Damn nigga, you drink more tea and eat more donuts than a damn cop," Reem said, pulling onto Huntington Park Avenue.

"Ha ha, you're a fucking comedian. It ain't a cop in this world that is as hard as me, my nigga," Jim said, sipping his tea.

"Nigga, you ain't hard."

"I was the only one hard enough to get your cousin off your ass when he was pulling that Floyd Mayweather ass whipping on you. I heard your punk ass screaming," Jim said, hitting below the belt.

"That nigga ain't my cousin. That's Trev's cousin, and I'm going to kill his faggot ass soon I get a chance. Plus, since you're dick-eating them, let their asses feed you, nigga!" Reem screamed.

"Aw nigga, stop!"

Boop...Boop...Boop! Blaat...Blaat...Blaat!

The sound of gunfire was suddenly heard along with the cracking of glass being shattered. They were so busy arguing that they never saw the guy on the back of a motorcycle raise the baby SK and let loose on their car. The motorcycle pulled off Huntington Park with the shooter and the driver.

Reem let off the brake after the first slug hit him and ran straight into the Puerto Rican store on the corner of 19th and Huntington Park Avenue. People started coming to their aid. They were both hit and hit bad. The cops where on the scene in minutes, but the ambulance hadn't arrived yet. As always, no one was talking to the police, at least not on the scene.

Starsky and Hutch pulled up. They jumped out and walked over to the uniform cop.

"Who was the first on the scene?" Officer Hutson said to the officer.

"Smitty was here first."

"Yo Smitty, what do we have here?"

"Right now we have two John Doe's. Both of them are dead, but I didn't search them for ID yet."

"Is anybody talking?"

"Naw, but I overheard through the so-called whispers that a motorcycle pulled up at the light and the passenger on the bike let loose."

"Pop the trunk on this baby," Hutson said, while Officer Starks searched the dead bodies for ID.

"Hey Hutson, come back here," Starks yelled, after shuffling through the trunk.

Hutson hurried to the trunk at the sound of the urgency in his partner's voice.

"What we got?" he asked.

"We got work to do," Starks said, holding the gym bag open, exposing four kilos of cocaine.

"Damn, find out these little motherfuckers' real names and street names," Hutson said to Starks, as if he was the boss.

The ambulance finally arrived. Reem and Jim were already dead by the time it got there, but they did the typical procedure shit anyway to make it look hopeful. They were actually able to pump life back into Reem for a minute by shocking him. Starsky and Hutch were on a mission now, and they lived for these kinds of missions.

~~~~~

Micky pulled the black motorcycle into the garage on 38th and Mt. Vernon.

"Damn nigga, you riding this dumb-ass motorcycle like you was trying to make me fall," Toot yelled to Micky.

"Nigga, shut up and put the hammer up so we can get out of here," Micky said, playfully pushing Toot.

Toot did as Micky told him. He put the SK in the ceiling. They went back outside and jumped into the new Escalade Toot got two weeks ago.

"Damn my nigga, you really put some work in this time. This wasn't no vehicular homicide shit that you're used to pulling off," Micky said referring to the time Toot ran over Dave.

"Micky, I had to get that pussy-ass nigga A.S.A.P. Who did that nut-ass nigga think he was dealing with?"

Micky never saw Toot so hyped.

"Fuck it main man, you got that nigga and that's all that counts. I told you to let me hit the nigga because I sent you to the funeral," Micky said, remembering how badly he felt when his best friend came to the house with his face all swollen and busted up.

"Micky, I told you I had to do that because the shit was personal. Them bitch-ass niggas jumped me. Jim bitch-ass knows I used to fuck him up when we were little, and he kicked me in my face," Toot said, rubbing his face.

"The pussy won't kick nobody else, him or your cousin."

"That bitch nigga ain't my cousin."

"You know what I mean."

"No, I don't know what you mean. That bitch nigga is Trev's cousin. In fact, fuck all of them, and when I see fat-ass Nay, I'm going to smack her ass," Toot said, thinking of the smirk Nay had on her face when he got up off the floor.

"Nay is harmless and she is your cousin for real."

"Man, fuck all of them. Her fat ass instigated the whole shit."

"Well, if you smack that fat bitch, I'm smacking her fat ass, too. I'm with you, homie, and don't ever forget that."

"I know Micky, and I'm with you too."

They pulled up to their loft on Delaware Avenue. Micky jumped out and Toot drove off to meet Quiana. He met her at Club Onyx one night when they were in there balling. He noticed Quiana throwing more money at the white stripper, Bubbles, than the average nigga was throwing. Bubbles was by far one of Toot's favorite strippers, so when she took the stage, Toot was always on deck. The night he met Quiana, he damn near forgot Bubbles was in the building. When he spotted the brown-skinned, thick chick rocking Dior open-toed sandals with the neatly pedicured, pretty feet, he wanted to know who she was. She had on a Dior shirt, carried a Dior pocketbook, and wore a pair of white Lucky jeans that exposed the gap she was blessed with.

After making sure he was intact, he went right up to her. After they talked a while and she let him know she wasn't gay, he took her and her crew back to the VIP section with his crew. Micky, Ducky, and Raheem all made sure Quiana and her crew were good. She was feeling Toot and Toot was feeling her. Toot was used to fucking all the hood rats in the city, but Quiana was different.

She was a RN and worked for the University of Penn hospital at 34th and Spruce Streets. Toot remained himself around her, although he made some adjustments to let her know he had a classy side. He'd been getting little pointers from Rhonda who had become like a sister to him. Since the night they met, he and Quiana had been out on a few dinner dates.

Toot was going to meet Quiana on her break. He was having a feeling about Quiana that he never had about any other woman in his life, and he hadn't even smelled the pussy yet, let alone hit it.

When he pulled up to valet parking, he hit the attendant twenty dollars to keep his truck right there. She was already standing outside. He walked over to her, and she gave him a hug and a peck on the lips. They were both feeling each other, but they weren't letting each other know just how much.

"What's up baby girl?"

"You're what's up, baby boy," Quiana said, as they walked to the food court.

"Is that right?"

"Yes, that's right. Do you want something?" Quiana said, ready to place her order.

"Yeah, but it ain't on the cart," Toot chuckled.

"Is that right? Be careful what you ask for because you just might get it. Can I have a turkey BLT and a cup of coffee with extra cream and sugar?" Quiana said, placing her order, but staring at Toot.

"Quiana, my play-brother Micky and his girl want to go to the harbor in Baltimore this weekend and I want you to go with us."

"Sure, I'm down. Why don't you come by my house tonight? I just got the new Katt Williams stand-up on DVD and I need someone to laugh with," Quiana said, shooting her shot at Toot because she was tired of playing games.

"I'm down baby girl, what time?"

"About eight, if that's good?"

"That's cool."

"I'll go to the Bottom of the Sea and get us some food before I come over."

They waited for Quiana's food. He walked her back to the entrance where her newsy co-workers looked on. He gave her a hug and a kiss and was on his way to hook back up with Micky who was waiting on him at the loft.

Chapter 4

Ducky was in front of Champions waiting for Champ to arrive. He was caught up in his thoughts. Champ meant the world to him, always looked out for him, and accepted him, flaws and all. He couldn't believe Champ was giving it all up.

"Damn we got a tight system. We're living it up. We're getting so much cash that we can wipe our asses with it. We got every bitch in the city chasing us; the bitches the average hustler in the city takes personal, we're smutting them bitches. Well, me and Raheem are because the rest of the crew done got booed-up. Damn, I think that's what it is. The nigga done fell in love, and Wanna is begging the nigga to get out of the streets. He's blaming it on religion when, in fact, it's all about being in love. He can give it up, but I'm turning it up. I'm not falling in love because bitches always trying to change a nigga. I'm fucking all the bitches, but I'm only loving my niggas and my money. There is no way a religion could make me give this shit up. I'm just glad he's giving me the connect," Ducky said, stuck in deep conversation with himself until he saw Champ pulling up.

He jumped out of the car and walked over to Champ. Ducky had never been late when he was supposed to meet Champ.

"What's up Ducky Raw?" Champ said, shaking Ducky's hand.

"The price of pussy, and when you retire, the price of coke," Ducky said, joking.

Champ had to laugh at that. They walked in and went straight to their booth in the back with the manager, Gail, following them.

"What are you having today, boss?" Gail asked Champ, knowing that even though he owned the store, he hated being called boss.

"Iced tea and two orders of our regular, and you're the boss, Gail, not me," Champ said, smiling at the old lady who was more like an aunt than an employee to him.

"Okay, I'll be right back."

When Champ was abducted and on his deathbed, Gail ran the restaurant and made sure everything was intact. She went by the hospital every day to see Champ. She prayed for him and kept Wanna posted on the affairs around the restaurant. She loved her some Champ and he knew it. That's why he always looked out for her.

"Ducky, I'm done in two weeks for real. I'm talking about completely done with the streets. I'm walking away. I've convinced Juan to deal with you direct. We all have a meeting next week. I told him that you'll be the next best thing in Philly. He said, although I'm retiring, I'm still responsible for you. Ducky, I put my stamp of approval on you. Don't let me down. No matter what, keep Juan's money straight. Follow his instruction and you'll be straight. Keep your circle tight. Micky, Toot, Raheem, and Shaahir are all you need. You're the new me, so play the cut and don't trust no niggas," Champ said, running down his instructions.

"Damn homie, I guess I'm going have to step all the way up and show you that you've taught me how to win in this shit."

"Just follow what I gave you and you'll be good. Remember, it's two things in this world that will make you cry, and that's niggas and onions."

"I'm ready Champ. Yo, are you sure you can just up and walk away from all this shit? We've been brought up in this shit."

"Yeah, we've been brought up in this shit, but it's not the only shit I know of to get by. I got to walk away, and I wish I could make y'all walk away with me, but y'all will walk when y'all are ready. I can't risk myself anymore to the bad blood that comes with dirty money."

"Yeah, but who retires from the game? It ain't like you can get benefits or a 401K," Ducky said, trying to lighten the seriousness of the meeting.

"Jay-Z, Baby, Jay Prince, Jeezy, and cats like that all allegedly played in the game and up and made it another way," Champ said, as Gail approached their table.

"Let me know if y'all need anything else," Gail said, setting their food down.

"We're fine," Champ said, waiting for her to walk away before continuing.

"All I'm saying, Ducky, is that I'm done. Sure, I want you to be done as well, but ultimately, that's your decision. I won't be selfish and force your hand to quit because I'm quitting. Ducky, you know that's not my style."

"Champ, you've done all you could do for me. I got to take it from here. I won't disappoint you."

"I know you won't."

They sat quietly for a while eating their food. Ducky had to give it to Champ; it took a lot to walk away from the game. The average nigga could never walk away from the game, especially while they were on top; but then again, Champ wasn't the average nigga.

"Damn Champ, I never tried to compare you to Ern because I love both y'all the same, but you're the best nigga all around, and that comes from the bottom. I know I'm a little rough around the edges, but I'm going to pattern as much of my game as possible after yours," Ducky said, as he pushed his plate to the side.

"Ducky, be you and you'll be fine. Trust me," Champ said, flagging Gail down to come get their plates.

"Do y'all want anything else?" Gail asked, placing the bill on the table.

"Naw, we're good," Champ said, placing a fifty dollar bill on the table before leaving with Ducky.

When they got out of the store, Champ stopped at a stand a Muslim brother had and bought some oils. He probably would never wear them; he was just giving the brother a play.

"Yo, why do you always pay for food we eat in the restaurant when it's your restaurant?"

"Because one thing has nothing to do with the other. If I get service from Champions, I have to pay for that service to ensure my business can take care of itself."

"I hear you, but I still don't understand."

"You know I get too deep for myself at times," Champ said, not wanting Ducky to feel like he was on some deep shit.

~~~~~

Wanna hadn't seen Sharon in a few days, so she called and told her to meet her at the mall. Wanna and Thelma decided to do a little shopping, and she figured Sharon could use the outing. Wanna wasn't ducking Sharon, but she'd been on the phone and out with her cousin, Aminah, as of late.

Aminah is Muslim and had been helping Wanna understand Islam. Aminah was thrilled that her cousin was even interested in the religion. She was patient with Wanna, and because of their family ties, Wanna was comfortable asking her all she needed to know.

Aminah wasn't the type that accepted Islam because her man accepted it, and she didn't want Wanna to accept it because Champ was leaning toward accepting it. Aminah was pretty sharp with her knowledge of the religion. Wanna was sitting in the passenger seat of her Range while Thelma drove. Wanna was thinking of how pretty Aminah looked in her garbs.

"What are you so spaced out about, Wanna?" Thelma asked, startling Wanna.

"Nothing, I'm just thinking how pretty Aminah looked in her garbs when we went out to lunch the other day. Aminah always looked good in her garbs."

"You know, I got to flaunt this big ass up in a pair of jeans, but I see a lot of sisters styling in them garbs."

"Thelma, you know I'll be getting my garbs made, and I got to keep a big bag and a mean shoe on."

"Wanna, these chicks know that you're Mrs. King of Prussia so they won't be tripping if you tone it down and garb up.

"You and cousin Champ are really serious about this Muslim stuff, huh?"

"Yeah, but the funny thing is I wasn't really with it at first. I was like Champ...just going through a phase, and not being no Muslim. But when Aminah started walking me through it, I started leaning more toward Champ."

"Wanna, whatever makes y'all happy and is going to keep my cousin out of the streets and out of jail, I'm for it."

"I know that's right."

"What's up with Sharon's crazy ass?"

"She needs a God-fearing man to keep her dingy ass from getting herself or one of us hurt."

"I know Sharon is naïve to be fucking with that piece of shit nigga, Tone, but he played her from the start."

"He killed Ern, and deceived her into thinking he was her shoulder to lean on."

"Yeah, that's crazy that he did that to Ern. I always defended Tone's punk ass when people would say he did it, and come to find out he did it."

"Did they tell Sharon yet?"

"Naw, Micky is supposed to tell her when she gets over losing the baby."

"Wanna, that nigga Tone was vicious. How could he kill Ern? That was a smooth, bow-legged nigga. That nigga was a ghetto hero," Thelma said, thinking of Ern, and lusting over a dead man.

"Yeah, Sharon went from ghetto hero to ghetto zero," Wanna said, smacking hands with Thelma as they shared a laugh.

"Micky looks like Ern. I think him and Rhonda is the cutest couple," Thelma said, turning onto Mall Boulevard.

"Yeah, Micky and Rhonda are a sweet couple. Micky is all that. I admire how he stayed by that girl's side when she got raped," Wanna said, thinking how much it must have meant to Rhonda to have Micky by her side through all of that.

"We should have called Rhonda and brought her shopping with us."

"I called her, Thelma. She has class, and she was pissed that she couldn't come with us. That's my niece right there."

"That's our niece."

"That young girl has an old soul and is sweet," Wanna said, dialing Sharon's number as they pulled into valet parking.

"Yeah, we just pulled up," Wanna said into the phone, listening for Sharon's response before hanging up.

"She said she's in Neiman Marcus right at the exit," Wanna said to Thelma, who had just passed the keys to the valet.

"That's good. I want to grab some new Gucci sneakers from their men's shoe department," Thelma said, grabbing the ticket from the valet.

They walked into Neiman's, and Sharon was at the door like she said she would be. All the ladies exchanged hugs and hellos.

"Come on over here," Thelma said, pointing and leading the way toward the men's shoe section. "Gucci has a brand new pair of white, high-top sneakers with their signature red and green stripe going down the side of them. I love this right here. I'll take these and the all-black Prada's in a size ten," she continued, directing the salesman who was watching them as if they were about to steal something.

"And give me the same two pairs in an eleven," Wanna said, deciding she'd get Champ something while she was out.

"Okay," the salesmen said, as if he were happy even though he was really mad that these fly chicks were ordering over a thousand dollars in sneakers for their men.

From the looks of them, he was sure they could afford the sneakers because they had on Rolexes. Sharon and Thelma both had their Louis Vuitton bags, and Wanna had her Hermes spy bag out. The salesman and everyone else looking on knew that the three of them looked like they had and came from paper.

"Thelma, Bingo starts trial next week, right?" Sharon asked.

"Yup, and my boy will be home. The lawyer said he'll beat every charge."

"That's what's up."

"I'll be there to support y'all."

"I appreciate it, Sharon. We need all the support we can get."

"How do his brother and Nino's chances look?"

"They should all be okay," Thelma said, thinking of how hard the time had been on their relationship.

She wasn't built for the jailhouse relationship shit. Before she got caught up in her thoughts, the salesman was walking toward the register to ring up their purchases. They walked up to the register.

"Will that be cash or credit?"

"Credit, and I'll pay for both orders," Wanna said, putting her American Express card on the counter.

"Do you have ID?" the salesman asked, feeling something shady going down.

"Yes, here's my driver's license," Wanna said, putting her license on the counter and feeling irked knowing that the salesmen had stereotyped them.

"Okay, let me go get the manager to show me how to run this card," the salesmen said, using the stall tactic to hold them up while he checked them out.

"Yes, you do that. In fact, tell your manger Wanna is out here and that I would love to speak to her."

"Sure will," he said, thinking he was on the bust of the day.

He left and came back following behind Nancy, the store manger. Nancy had Wanna's ID and credit card in her hand.

"Tawanna, I'm so sorry for the hold up and your inconvenience," Nancy said, hugging Wanna, then Sharon and Thelma.

"Nancy, you have to tell him he can't come to Neiman's with Strawbridge's service. The stereotyping and stall tactics are for those kinds of stores."

"He's new, Tawanna. I almost flipped when he handed me your credit card and ID. I told him you've been shopping here for over fifteen years. In fact, I sold you your first Gucci bag," Nancy said, engaged in conversation with the girls as if the salesman wasn't even there.

"Joey, I'll ring them up," Nancy said, brushing Joey off, not even waiting for an answer. She talked to Wanna and the girls for a while and even gave them a 15 percent manager's discount.

Wanna, Sharon, and Thelma continued their shopping and girls' day out. They grabbed Rhonda a few things and called her to let her know they wished she were there. Sharon felt good. She needed the outing. She hugged Thelma and Wanna tightly and let them know she loved them. She thanked Wanna for always being a sister to her no matter how good or bad she was doing.

She left to go home, and Wanna and Thelma left to meet Champ at Outback Steak House on Henry Avenue. Wanna invited Sharon to come with them, but she said Micky and Rhonda were coming to her house to get something to eat.

"Wanna, I feel so bad for Sharon and what that rotten-ass nigga did to her life," Thelma said, sitting in the passenger seat of the Range this time.

"Yeah, that bastard took my girl through it. In fact, he took us all through it. Sharon is my girl though, and I'm glad she's getting over it," Wanna said, turning off a back street that cut through Norristown onto Main Street.

"Yeah, she seemed to loosen up after we were in the mall for awhile. She's even looking like herself again."

"Yeah, she's looking good."

"You seen the young bull trying to crack on her?"

"Yeah, he was a little cutie too."

"Don't make me tell Champ you was all on the young bull," Thelma said, joking.

"All that ass that Champ looks at? Girl *please*. I was just looking at the young bull with his jewelry and his fresh cut stepping to Sharon, not knowing she got a son his age."

"Sharon was gleaming as if she was going to call young bull."

"Sharon is not that desperate, Thelma."

"That don't mean she doesn't want a little dick here and there. Bingo better win this trial next week because I need about a yard of dick myself," Thelma said, laughing hard.

"Girl, you are crazy."

"Wanna, I'm real."

"Yes, you are and no one can take that from you."

They drove the rest of the way talking about the events that went on in their lives and the events to come.

~~~~~

Bingo had been calling and waiting for his trial to start next week. He only really kicked it with Teddy and Nino. When Teddy and Nino were out in the day room playing cards, Bingo would chill in the cell and listen to the radio. He missed kicking it with Shaahir. Shaahir used to be the nigga he could talk to about life. Shaahir had basically become his go-to man who kept him from stressing while he was in jail. Shaahir had a way of keeping true to his religious beliefs while still being grounded enough to relate to those different from him.

"Damn, I miss Shaahir with his silly-ass laugh, always knocking on the door saying 'May I enter?' as if he was a Jehovah Witness or something. I owe Champ big time. He really sent dude to make sure I was good. He took my wife in although she's his cousin, and he paid for me, Teddy, and Nino's lawyers. I got the paper, but I couldn't send anybody to get that paper with the feds all up my ass," Bingo said, talking to himself.

Teddy and Nino came into the cell.

"What was y'all doing?"

"Nothing," Nino said, heading toward Bingo's locker to get a Twix.

"Yeah, he's right. He was doing nothing, but I was busting his ass in casino," Teddy said, waiting for Nino to open the Twix so he could get half.

"Nigga, you ain't beat shit and you be cheatin'," Nino said, opening the Twix and giving Teddy half, as always.

51

"Yo, trial will be here before you know it. Are y'all ready?"

"We don't have a choice," said, Nino.

"That's crazy how they got bitch-ass Jay-Baby to start cooperating," Teddy said, looking at Bingo, knowing that the only person he could hurt was Bingo.

"Yeah, that's cool though. Perry said that means they are reaching," Bingo said, repeating what the lawyer told him.

"I knew that pussy was snitching when they put that separation on us," Nino spat.

"Naw, I got the paperwork. He just gave a statement last week."

"I'm telling you, if I ever run across him, he's going down on sight," Teddy said.

"The lawyer said that's all they got. We're good because he's going to make him look like a fool up there."

"Yeah, I hope that's right 'cause we got to get back to living. I can't get jiggy with this shit," Teddy said, tugging on the green jumpsuit inmates are issued.

"Brother, you ain't lying. They got us rocking these string bean jumpers," Bingo said, causing Nino and Teddy to laugh with him.

They were all they had to get one another through their sticky situation.

Chapter 5

Weezy had Price Street all to himself since Reem had been killed. Reem was his man, and Weezy was the only one who could post up or have someone post up on Price Street besides Reem and his people. Weezy grabbed work from Reem who always gave Weezy the best coke he had at the best price because of their history. When the New York niggas came through Price Street about three years ago, Weezy was the first one on the front line. Rumor was that Weezy shot one of the niggas, dragged him into an alley, and set him on fire. Of course, none of the Price Street niggas told on the nigga who held the hood down.

After they ran those NY niggas out of their hood, there was no way anybody would be able to tell him he wasn't hustling out there. With Reem dead, all the money on the block was sure to be his. His little cousin, Dawud, was his right hand man, and Dawud knew that Shaahir was home and that Shaahir promised to get them prices they couldn't refuse. Weezy was cool with Shaahir, too, but Dawud was really Shaahir's main young bull and everybody knew it.

Weezy would have thought Shaahir was bullshitting if Shaahir didn't make the promise to Dawud. Dawud was always talking about Shaahir this and Shaahir that.

"Yo Dawud, I hope Shaahir don't bring us no bullshit by here tonight," Weezy said, sitting on Dawud's steps, petting Dawud's puppy.

"Weezy, you know my oldhead do right by me. He always did."

"Yeah, I have to agree with that."

"He would have come this morning but he had something to do."

"Yo, you sure this a puppy? This a big damn puppy."

"Yeah, he's five months. Fila's get big as shit," Dawud said, petting the dog.

"I might have to get one of these jawns. Can they beat a pit?"

"If you get the pit in the right spot. But pits, real pits, are built to fight 'til death. Fila's are protection dogs. Like if one of these climbing through the window ass niggas come in the crib when we're not around. Bricks is going to eat they ass alive."

"That's a fly name for him, Bricks. I got to get one of these jawns, but first I got to see if your man, Shaahir, is going to come through with the real white bricks," Weezy said, wanting to see what Shaahir had for them.

"Man, I told you he was in the GTC Bentley with the bull, Champ, and Shaahir was driving that thing."

"Damn, if he fucking with the nigga Champ like that, I know shit must be easy for him. Word is when the nigga Champ got kidnapped and was in the hospital, his absence caused a drought in Philly, Delaware, *and* Jersey. They say oldhead had that paper for real," Weezy said, wondering if he would ever reach that level of success in the streets.

"Yeah man, the nigga got his nephew, Micky, driving a brand new Maserati, and that nigga Micky is only eighteen or nineteen years old. All the little bitches be talking about the young bull like he's a hood star."

"Yeah, I heard Micky got that Maserati. You know Micky's father went to school with my Aunt Joy. His name was Ern, and they say that nigga really had that paper. I heard on All-Star weekend he came through in a Bentley and shut shit down. They said all the out-of-town niggas that came to the All-Star the year it was in Philly thought that the nigga was a rapper or something."

"Yeah, I heard about oldhead. I heard he told one of the little Philly rappers in the club that weekend 'Nigga you rap, but I'm the nigga the rappers rap about' and pulled out fifty thousand cash, daring a nigga to try him," Dawud said, gesturing with his hands.

"Yo, do you think we could get to that level of paper?"

"Weezy, all it takes is the right connect."

"Do you think Shaahir can get us there?"

"No, but I think he is a hell of a stepping stone. Let's put it this way, he's the best shot at a fair shake we got in this city."

"I'm telling you, Dawud, ain't nothing or nobody stopping us from getting this paper this summer. I'm on my grind, and either a nigga is with me or against me."

"You know I'm with you, my nigga."

"Oh, no doubt we are family. Guess what else I heard about the nigga Ern?"

"What's that my nigga?"

"I heard his best friend killed him, and they say that the nigga that killed Ern is the same one that kidnapped Champ."

"Yeah, they said he started messing with Ern's girl too. They said he was a grimy nigga."

55

That's crazy. What's even more crazy is the fact that Reem is supposed to be the nigga's distance cousin. The thick bitch at Reem's funeral that kept saying she had to holler at me is supposed to be the nigga's sister. His name was Tone or something like that."

"Man, that's why I don't trust niggas, Weezy. I only trust you and Shaahir. Outside of that, I don't trust niggas as far as I can throw them and I'm not strong enough to throw a little nigga."

"Dawud, it's different when niggas love is genuine. That motive love is a motherfucker."

"I agree. Yo, I'm about to go offer *Salat*."

"Okay, my nigga. I'm about to slide around the corner and see if Tameeka can suck this dick. Pray for me, my nigga."

"You need to take *Shahadah* and pray for yourself," Dawud said, shaking Weezy's hand, untying bricks, and going into the house to pray.

~~~~~

It was the second day of the trial, but it was really the first day of arguments. Yesterday, they picked the jury and recessed until today. Bingo, Teddy, and Nino were ready to rumble. Their lawyers were ready as well. Everyone came out to support them. The trial was held in one of those big courtrooms that you see on TV, but there were so many people in the courtroom it appeared small. Champ, Thelma, Wanna, Micky, Sharon, Toot, Ducky, Shaahir, and Rhonda were in the front row showing their support. Bingo, Teddy, and Nino were brought in first. Once they were seated at the defense table, the bailiff brought the jury out and seated them. When the judge came out, the bailiff told everyone to rise. He introduced Judge Hart to the courtroom then told everyone to be seated.

"Good afternoon ladies and gentlemen of the jury. I appreciate you being here. I would like you all to bear with me as I prove that these three men possessed five or more kilograms of powder cocaine. They conspired to sell five or more kilograms, and they intended to deliver five or more kilograms of powder cocaine.

"We have audio of the leader, Brandon "Bingo" Grant, talking to our star witness who is also their co-defendant and who pled guilty to these same charges last week. He will be the key in breaking down the conversation between him and Mr. Grant, which will help you break down the coded conversation between these three dealers. Their conversations are very short, but Mr. Rivara will tell you what was being said because he was part of the conspiracy, and who better to inform us about what was being said in code than the person who helped develop the code?

"Thanks again, and I'm sure you will see it for what it is and see that the government has charged the right men for these crimes," the US attorney said, before taking his seat at the prosecutor's table.

It looked bad for Bingo. The US attorney sounded very convincing. Bingo, Teddy, and Nino, along with their lawyers, elected Fortunato Perri to do the opening and closing arguments. Perri approached the jurors as cool as a fan. He looked like an Italian mobster himself with his tailor-made suit draping perfectly over his shoes and sleeves so perfectly stopping at the edge of his wrists to expose his Rolex every time he moved his arms.

"Ladies and gentlemen of the jury, good afternoon. Thank you for your time, which the government has elected to waste. I believe in the justice system, and please don't think I'm saying that our decent government will waste your time purposely. The government has good intentions, but they've been deceived by an admitted drug dealer whom the US attorney said himself has pleaded guilty to the charges against these men."

Perri turned and pointed to the three co-defendants before looking back at the jury. Although they were not all his clients, he was determined to get them all off. His swag was through the roof and he used it to his advantage. The women in the courtroom were entranced by how dapper he was. He flashed a smile then walked toward the jury as he adjusted the platinum cufflinks that peeked from under his blazer.

"Mr. Grant's only conspiracy with his brother, Teddy Grant, and their dear friend, Nate Powel, was to sell tires. Mr. Grant is an entrepreneur. He owns a pool hall and a tire shop. He employs neighborhood kids. Teddy Grant and Mr. Powel here are employees at the tire shop. Mr. Grant and his wonderful wife, whom I've had the pleasure to meet, are active in the community, and they have a non-profit organization called Kids First, which caters to underprivileged children. They hold fundraisers and provide food, clothing, and shelter to these kids who would otherwise have to do without.

"If your civil duty is to uphold justice, you will see that Mr. Grant is a taxpayer and a decent citizen. Communities suffer without men like Mr.Grant. Please don't throw his life away for the lies of a disgraceful, admitted drug dealer trying to snake his way out of a sentence by making innocent phone conversations into fairy tale drug transactions that never existed. The government has no drugs or paraphernalia. All they have is a snake, and I intend to cut the grass and expose him for Mr. Grant and his co-defendants' sakes."

Perri was walking to the defense table, changing the mood in the courtroom. Champ smiled and winked at Perri who he had seen beat many cases.

"You show off," the US Attorney whispered to Perri when he walked passed his table.

Perri just smiled and kept walking to his seat. Much whispering could be heard throughout the courtroom.

"Your Honor, if I may, the prosecution would like to bring forth our star witness, James Rivara," the US attorney said, as the bailiff appeared at the back door with Jay-Baby.

Jay-Baby's knees buckled when he saw all the people who came to support Bingo. He was seated in the witness stand. The court official asked him to stand and he complied.

"Would you say and spell your name out loud for the court, please."

"Yes, my name is James Rivara, J-A-M-E-S R-I-V-A-R-A," Jay-Baby said in a shaky voice.

"Do you swear to tell the truth, the whole truth, and nothing but the truth so help you God or stand affirm?" the court official asked, holding the Bible in his hand stretched out toward Jay-Baby.

"Yes, I do."

As soon as this routine was over, the attorney was out for blood. He was hyped. He knew that if Jay-Baby said what they went over this morning, he was sure to get a conviction.

"Mr. Rivara, good afternoon."

"Good afternoon," Jay-Baby responded.

"Do you know the Grants and Nate Powel, and if so, would you please be kind enough to point them out?"

Jay-Baby pointed at Bingo first, then Teddy, then Nino.

"Before we go any further, did you plead guilty to possession of five or more kilograms of cocaine and conspiracy to distribute them?"

"Yes sir, I did."

"Do you remember making this statement? Take your time, and go over it carefully to make sure that these are your words and that is your signature."

Jay-Baby read the statement for about five minutes before answering.

"Yes, this is the statement I made."

"Your Honor, I'd like to present this statement as Exhibit A to the court."

The US attorney passed the judge a copy of the twenty-page statement.

The judge said, "Please mark the statement as Exhibit A. You may proceed," he allowed, looking over his glasses at the statement.

"Do you remember here on page five in the second paragraph where you said that you and Mr. Grant conducted drug transactions in front of Teddy Grant and Nate Powel several times, and that when you called, and Brandon Grant said he was at the shop, that meant he had the drugs at the shop with him?" he said, handing the jury a copy of the statement and showing Jay-Baby the statement.

Jay-Baby was quiet for a while with his eyes watering. The whole courtroom was quietly waiting for Jay-Baby to answer.

"Are you okay? Do you feel threatened by someone in here?"

"Yes, I'm okay, and yes, I made this statement but I lied. I lied to protect my mom. You and your agents are the only ones I feel threatened by. You threatened to lock my mom up who was totally unaware of the fact I had drugs in her house, and you threatened my freedom."

"Do you understand that by going back on your word I could charge you with perjury, and perjury carries a five year sentence?" the US attorney said, turning red from knowing his case would go down the drain if Jay-Baby didn't cooperate.

Before Jay-Baby confessed, he actually was leaning toward dropping the charges.

"See, there you go with the threats again. Your Honor, I don't care how much time this guy tries to influence you to give me, I can't sit here and lie on these guys. Bingo is a hard worker and tried time and time again to pull me out of the streets by offering me a job at his shop, and only because of my own cowardice I made them tapes say whatever the US attorney wanted them to say."

The US attorney was pissed.

"I'm done with this witness, Your Honor."

"Before we dismiss this witness, does anybody from the defense have anything to ask him?"

"Yes, Your Honor," Perri said, seizing the moment to knock the government's case right out of the ball park.

"Go ahead, counselor."

Perri took the floor.

"Mr. Rivara, I just want to be clear on two things. Mr. Grant never dealt drugs to or with you, and you only made the tapes to interpret what you thought the government wanted them to interpret to save yourself?"

Perri said in a mild manner, not wanting to push Jay-Baby too far.

"Yes, I told them what they wanted to hear. Bingo never sold drugs to me, and the drugs they found in my mom's house was mine, all mine," Jay-Baby said, now crying uncontrollably.

"Thank you, Mr. Rivara. Your Honor, I move to strike Mr. Rivara's whole statement, and if the government doesn't have anything more than some tapes of my client telling his brother and employee to meet him at his tire shop, I move to have the case dismissed," Perri said, then took his seat next to Bingo.

"I take it you are done with this witness," the judge said, looking back and forth from the defense to the prosecution.

Once both parties agreed that they were done with Jay-Baby, the judge had him removed from the courtroom. Jay-Baby looked at Bingo before he left and Bingo winked at him.

"Does the government have any more witnesses?" the judge asked, looking over the top of his glasses at the US attorney, as if he was a school teacher.

"Yes, we have an expert drug conversation interpreter, but we cannot use him without Mr. Rivara's cooperation."

"Do you know that if the government does not have anything else, I will be forced to dismiss all charges?"

"We don't have anything else, Your Honor."

"On that note, I, Judge Hart, in the case of the United States versus Brandon Grant, Teddy Grant, and Nate Powel, dismiss all charges."

All of Bingo, Teddy, and Nino's supporters broke out in cheers. Bingo, Teddy, and Nino all shook hands with their lawyer. The marshalls told everyone to keep their cheers down. Thelma stood and stared at her husband with tears in her eyes. The marshall let Bingo and the others go hug and talk to their loved ones, but told them they would have to go back to the processing room to make sure they didn't have any warrants, and to get them officially released.

Bingo leaned over and whispered in Champ's ear, "I owe you big time, homie."

"Bingo, I'm good. I am happy for you. You don't owe me nothing. Just be good to my cousin. Our relationship is bigger than any amount of paper."

Champ stepped back and smiled at his friend.

"Champ, I know what you're saying, but right is right, and I have the paper, so I'm giving it to you," Bingo said, and went to hug his wife before Champ could go back and forth with him.

"I'm so happy baby. Let's go home," Thelma said with tears still in her eyes.

"I got to wait until the release is official so it will be about an hour or two."

This is some BS. The Judge said free, and it don't get no more official than that," Thelma said, not understanding all of the things the marshall explained to Bingo.

"Boo, it's only an hour or two. It's procedure," Bingo said, giving his wife a kiss on the lips and rolling with the marshall who was patiently waiting to take him back to the processing room.

Raheem, Toot, Shaahir, Ducky, Micky, Champ, Wanna, Rhonda, Thelma, and Sharon all waved at them and shouted comments of love and congratulations as Bingo, Teddy, and Nino were escorted out of the courtroom. The US attorney also watched them go out the doors as he gathered his papers, and wished that things had turned out differently.

"They'll slip up again, and I'm going to retire all of their black asses, especially Mr. Motherfucking Community Service Bingo," he said to himself, as they disappeared from the courtroom.

"Damn, I've never seen a witness break down like that in the ten-year history of me being a marshall," the marshall said to Bingo and his boys, as he put them in a cell.

"Yeah, he broke down because he couldn't lie on a guy that's been good to him ever since he's known him," Bingo said, without putting the marshall too far in his business.

"Yeah, and I've never seen so many people come out to see and support suspected drug dealers like that. I know that US attorney like a book. He's mad as all outdoors right now. He is going to do everything in his power to get James Rivara the max time he can get. I'm going to get right on top of your paperwork so I can get you all out of here as soon as possible," he said, noticing that they were basically brushing him off.

He locked the door and left the three men there to talk among themselves.

"We fucking did it, big bro. We fucking beat the feds," Teddy said, hugging Bingo.

"Yeah, we pulled it off. But Perri said that they will be on my heels for a lifetime. I got to chill," Bingo said, knowing he was getting too old for the bullshit.

"You can chill, but I'm going right at it."

"Yeah, I'm with Teddy," said Nino, shaking Teddy's hand.

"I'm not done. I'm chilling and I'll talk to y'all at the crib," Bingo said, cutting off the conversation, not trusting the room they were in.

"Damn, Jay-Baby fucked their whole case up."

"Yeah, I got a new respect for him. He should not have shit in the first place, but I'm glad he made his wrong right," Bingo said, thinking that he was still going to check on Jay-Baby and send him money here and there while he was doing his bid.

He knew that Teddy would try to convince him not to send Jay-Baby a dime, but Bingo had love for Jay-Baby, and he knew that not everybody was built to go to trial.

Chapter 6

Dawud and Weezy couldn't believe Shaahir was giving them good coke at such a good price. After three days, they were selling at a pace at which neither one of them had ever moved.

Weezy decided he would let the young bulls in the hood sell their coke hand to hand on Price Street on the condition that they got the weight from him and Dawud. The coke was moving fast now that Weezy and Dawud provided the young bulls with the raw that Shaahir gave them.

At first, Dawud thought it was a bad idea to give up the block; but after he realized it was less risky and less work, and that he would profit just as much by selling weight, he was happy with the idea. In those three days, their clientele grew, and they were serving a lot of people throughout the Uptown area.

"Damn Dawud, Shaahir really came through for a nigga with this break he gave us," Weezy said, counting through the piles of money he and Dawud made last night.

"Nigga, I told you that if he gives me his word, then that's what it is. On some real shit, if Shaahir say a mosquito can fly the plane, I'm goin' to put the mosquito in the cockpit," Dawud said with a dead-serious face.

"I don't know about that, but dude got my loyalty from here on out. How could I not ride with and for the nigga who's feeding me?"

"Yeah, he got us eating and it's only been days."

"Yeah, he got us munchin' for real. I used to think Reem was looking out for fronting me a brick at that high-ass number," Weezy said, putting a rubber band around the money in his hand.

They were counting the money into $5,000 stacks. Reem had a good price; $23,000 was a good number for someone on Reem's level to front a nigga.

"Yeah, but Shaahir is hitting us with five bricks of fish scale at nineteen thousand a joint."

"Yeah, I agree that Reem was higher and Shaahir is showing us love, but Reem's nowhere near the level Shaahir is on. Shaahir got Champ behind him, and in this city it don't get no bigger than Champ."

"Yeah little cousin. We're on deck now and we're rolling with the right team."

"Get Shaahir on the phone so we can clear our tab," Weezy said, putting a rubber band around the last stack.

Dawud went into the kitchen, got the prepaid phone off the table, and dialed Shaahir's number. Shaahir picked up on the second ring. Dawud greeted him and asked him where he wanted to meet. He gave him greetings again and hung up. The call didn't even last a minute.

"He said to meet him at John's, the breakfast store on Germantown and Chelten Avenue," Dawud said, opening the cage so he could put the dog in it while they were gone.

"Okay, we're out," Weezy said, putting the money in a plastic shopping bag.

Dawud put Bricks in his cage and they left. When they got into the car, Weezy popped in Young Jeezy's CD, *The Recession.* They pulled off with Young Jeezy pouring out of the speakers.

"Damn Dawud, it's going to be a hell of a summer, and I owe it to you."

"Shit, we owe it to Shaahir."

"Yeah he looking out, but I know if it wasn't for his relationship with you, he would never have looked out like this."

"Yeah big cuz, but it don't matter where we get the work from or who had the connect, we always held it down together. Reem never put an ounce of coke in my hand, but I ate off of every brick you got from him. You always said, between me and you, there's never any little-I's or big-U's, and it will remain like that until the end," Dawud said, leaning back in the passenger seat.

"That's what's up cuz."

"Yo, did you read in the newspaper about the bull Bingo?"

"Yeah, he beat the feds a few days ago. They was talking about it in the barbershop yesterday. This chick in there said she was in the courtroom," Weezy said, turning onto Chelten off Germantown Avenue.

"Yeah, you know that's Shaahir's man too."

"Damn, Shaahir knows everybody. The chick said it was like a party up in there with his whole crew."

"Yeah, the boy Bingo is married to Champ's sister or cousin."

"It's hard as shit to beat the feds," Weezy said, parking across the street from John's.

"I know, and if you don't have no paper, you don't stand a chance."

"Chains are cool to cop, but more important is lawyer fees," Weezy said, quoting a little Jay-Z, as they hopped out of the car and walked across the street.

When they walked into John's breakfast store, the smell of cologne, perfume, and greasy food mixed together polluted the air. It was packed in the dimly lit, sit-in or take-out breakfast store. There were many hood chicks there wearing the typical smallest shirt and tight jeans they could find. Shaahir was in the back sitting by himself talking on the phone.

Weezy and Dawud headed toward the back, excusing themselves as they squeezed through the packed restaurant full of attitudes. When they finally reached Shaahir, they sat in the two seats he was holding down for them. He continued his phone conversation, and they could tell whoever it was had his full attention by the way he was smiling, almost glowing.

The waitress brought three plates of turkey bacon, cheese eggs, and home fries. Shaahir had ordered their food before they got there.

"Do y'all want plastic or silverware?" the waitress asked, knowing that many people don't like to eat off the silverware.

"We want plastic," Dawud said, answering for all of them.

Two minutes after the waitress brought their plastic forks and knives, Shaahir hung up the phone.

"What's up Weezy?" Shaahir said, speaking to Weezy who had already started eating his food.

"What's up Shaahir? Damn, this food is crazy. Good looking on putting our order in."

"*As Salaamu Alaikum*, Little Uzi. Slow down, that food ain't going nowhere."

"*Wa Laikum Salaam.* Yes, this food is going somewhere…it's going right in my stomach," Dawud said, shoving a piece of bacon in his mouth and pouring ketchup on his home fries.

Shaahir laughed and started eating his food as well. They sat there eating and engaging in minor chitchat. Weezy insisted on paying for the food. He paid the tab and tipped the waitress. On their way out, Nay stopped Weezy. Shaahir and Dawud walked outside and left Weezy to talk to Nay. Once outside, Shaahir jumped into his car with Dawud and made a U-turn so they could park directly behind Weezy's car."

"Yo, Uzi, y'all moved that thing faster than I thought you would."

"Shaahir, that thing is all that you said it was."

"Yo, we got plenty of this shit. As long as y'all keep the paper straight, it's no limits on what we can do. Uzi, it's pedal to the metal."

"Shaahir, I'm glad you're home oldhead."

"Cut that oldhead stuff out."

"Damn, I see whoever was on that phone had you open."

Shaahir started blushing.

"Uzi, that's my weakness. I love women. In fact, Friday we are giving my man, Bingo, a coming home party. I want you and Weezy to come out so I can introduce you to my peoples," Shaahir said, getting out of the car to talk to the chick that had just pulled up behind him.

Dawud could see the light-skinned chick seated behind the steering wheel. From what he could see, she didn't have on garbs, so he knew she wasn't Shaahir's wife, and she was pretty. Shaahir had his head in her passenger window, talking to her. Weezy came across the street and stood next to Dawud.

"Who is that?"

"I don't know, but she looks good from here."

"Dawud, I just got a close up look at her when I walked across the street. She bad as a motherfucker."

"Yeah. Yo, who was that big girl that stopped you? Was that your new jawn?" Dawud said, chuckling hard.

"Man, you know I don't mess with no big jawns. That bitch was tripping. She said she was trying to catch up with me since the funeral because she heard how I ride."

"Ride what? Fat bitches?"

Dawud laughed at his own joke, but Weezy didn't find shit funny.

"Naw man, that's the bitch that was at Reem's funeral. She just told me some wild shit, but I don't know that bitch to be taking info from her, especially no info that would fuck our thing up."

"What did the bitch say?" Dawud said seriously.

"The bitch goes into all this shit about how Reem fucked Toot up at Trev's funeral for hanging with the nigga, Micky, who killed their cousin, Trev. She said that Reem and Toot wasn't cousins, but they was Trev's cousins."

"Damn, where the bitch know you from to be dropping this shit on you like that?"

"The bitch don't know me at all. I guess she was asking questions at the funeral, and they directed her to me. I'm not getting in that shit. She said she almost sure it was Toot. The fat bitch's breath was hulking, so I was trying to get away from her."

"Damn, we got to let Shaahir know what's being said about his peoples."

"As soon as he's done boo-loving, I'll tell him."

"Man, it's crazy how people can put a man's name in a murder, and they didn't witness the shit."

"Dawud, I'm trying to get this paper. This is our break. Reem was cool, but I'm not fucking our opportunity up because a bitch I don't even know with halitosis says she almost sure somebody did it. There's no such thing as almost sure. It's either you're sure or you're not."

"Sure or not what?" Shaahir said, walking up on the end of the conversation.

"Man, that fat bitch that stopped me when we was leaving John's is talking reckless about Champ's nephew and his man."

"What did she say and where is she at?" Shaahir said, looking over at the resturant.

"She said that Toot murdered my man, Reem, and Micky rocked his cousin. She said she's almost sure about Toot killing Reem. I don't know homegirl from nowhere. I'm with you, Shaahir. I'm just letting you know to let your man know that his cousin, Nay, is running around talking crazy."

"Where is the chick at?"

"She pulled off in that grey Magnum."

"Don't repeat that shit to nobody. I got to put my folks on point. We don't need no shit like that right now."

"I just told you. What's crazy is that we don't know who else she told."

"Cool, let me get that paper, and I'll get with y'all in an hour or two."

Dawud got the bag and put it in the back seat of Shaahir's car. They pulled off to go finish the work they had left and to collect the rest of the paper. Shaahir left to meet Ducky at the car wash.

~~~~~

Thelma was happy to have her man home. She was so happy that she smothered him everyday for the last three days. If he said he had to make a run, she would want to gun with him. He let her go with him damn near every time she asked to go.

They made love four to five times a day for three days. She was happy to be back in her own house. She loved Champ's house and was even comfortable there, but there were nights when she felt so lonely faced with the reality of Bingo's absence. She would sit up some nights and cry herself to sleep and on other nights, she would masturbate until she drained herself. She sometimes thought of how good Wanna had it to be able to do simple things like lay in bed every night with Champ.

Thelma's worst nights at Champ's house were when he attempted to sneak and fuck Wanna quietly. It used to start with Wanna's head lightly tapping on the headboard; then it would get louder and louder. Thelma would hear her cousin dicking Wanna down and trying to muffle her moans at the same time. Wanna would try her best to be quiet but would end up moaning louder and louder. Thelma was happy to be able to do some moaning herself now.

"What's up baby? What do you have planned for today?" Thelma said, in her red Victoria's Secret bra with matching boy-shorts hugging her fat ass.

"I'm going down to the tire shop to meet the insurance adjuster, so he can cut me a check to get the shop repaired from the fire damage. Teddy is supposed to meet me there," Bingo said, noticing how the darkness of Thelma's skin made the red boy-shorts look as if they were actually painted on her.

"You know we're suppose to meet Wanna and Champ for dinner tonight," Thelma said, walking over to Bingo, who was standing near the dresser putting on his deodorant.

"Yeah, I know," Bingo said, as Thelma began rubbing his chest and kissing him on the neck.

"Baby, I got to meet this insurance adjuster at the shop," Bingo said through clenched teeth.

Thelma ignored him and continued sucking on him and feeling his body. Before he knew it, she was on her knees pulling his dick out of his pants.

"Baby, I got to...damn, this shit feels good," Bingo said between breaths.

Thelma was sucking the head of his dick nice and slow, twirling the top of her tongue around the head and in the hole to taste his pre-cum. Bingo was leaning up against the dresser, as Thelma started sucking his dick longer and harder. He started squeezing her titties. She was so turned on from sucking his dick that her pussy was soaking wet. She was definitely in control. She took his dick out of her mouth, stood up, and dropped her boy-shorts to the floor before stepping out of them. She bent over the dresser and guided Bingo's fully erect nine and a half inch dick, which felt like eleven inches, right into her neatly shaved, soaking-wet pussy.

"Damn daddy, I missed this dick," Thelma said, throwing her ass back on him, matching his every motion with every inch of his dick inside her.

"You like it when daddy beats this pussy up? You wanted daddy to be late to his meeting so you could cum all over his dick? Huh, bitch, huh?" Bingo said, fucking her with long, quick, powerful strokes as he watched himself in the mirror.

Thelma loved when he talked dirty to her. Her pussy was throbbing, and she was near her climax.

"Yes daddy, beat this pussy up. Make me cum all over that big dick. I feel it in my stomach, daddy, don't stop," Thelma moaned in her sexy voice.

"I'm about to cum, too. Cum with me bitch...cum with me. Oowww!" Bingo said, as his body began to tremble while shooting his load into her.

"Damn daddy, I'm cumming, too. Don't take it out," Thelma said, cumming on his dick, her body shaking.

"I got to go wash up and get out of here," Bingo said, heading for the bathroom.

"I know I made you late, but it'll only be ten or fifteen minutes late, if that. Call Teddy and tell him to stall the adjuster, or call the adjuster and tell him you was caught in traffic and you'll be a little late," Thelma said, following him with his cell phone in her hand.

Bingo turned on the hot water, soaped up the rag, and was about to wash himself off, but Thelma took the rag and handed him the phone.

"I'll take care of the cleaning. You call Teddy."

Bingo hit Teddy's number on speed dial as Thelma lifted his balls gently and started cleaning them.

"Yo, you might get to the shop before me. Let the insurance guy in so he can look around. Tell him I'll be there in ten minutes. Okay? Peace."

Bingo hung up the phone. Thelma finished cleaning his private parts. She bent over as if she was about to suck his dick again.

"Yo, stop. That's why I'm late now," Bingo said, trying to push her head away.

"Shut up punk. I'm kissing my friend good-bye," she said, planting a kiss on his dick.

She stayed in the bathroom running her bath water while he quickly got dressed. She walked him to the bottom of the stairs without one piece of clothing on.

"Be careful, and come back on time so we can meet Champ and Wanna for dinner. I would ask you if I could go along with you to the shop, but you're already late. And since you showed me such a good time this morning, I won't crowd you today."

"Give me a kiss."

They kissed and said good-bye. Thelma went upstairs to get into the tub. She was happy to have her life back.

Bingo went outside and jumped in his new S65. He called the all-black Benz with black interior and 22-inch black, deep-dish Ashanti rims his grown man machine. He really understood the blessing of being a free man: no more recall for count; no being forced to be around a bunch of lying, fairy tale story telling niggas; no more eating slop; no more living off Oodles of Noodles soup; and no more taking orders from a bunch of CO's that are younger than the average man they like to boss around.

It was back to his lavish, two-car garage, and four bedroom, two and a half bath home with his beautiful wife, plasma TV's, and the king-size, pillow-top mattress; no more half of a twin, flat mattress with the tiny pillow. He could never understand how inmates that claimed to be the boss on the street could argue over the thirty-nine dollar K-Mart TVs mounted on beams facing the dayroom. It was times like that he realized jail was new army; dudes could be all they wanted to be. He vowed never to put himself around a bunch of lames again. His thoughts were interrupted when his phone started ringing. He saw Teddy come up on the caller ID.

"What's up little bro?"

"Nothing. I just let a dude in to look at the damages."

"Yeah, how long has he been there?"

"He just got here. How far are you?"

"I'm about ten minutes away."

"Alright, I'll be there waiting on you."

"I'll be right there," Bingo said, as he hung up the phone.

Bingo didn't know if he could retire from the game all at once like Champ was going to, but he planned on falling way back. He was too old for dumb shit. Everyone in the streets of Philly at all the hot spots was talking about how he beat the feds. They were talking as if it was a walk in the park; what they didn't understand was the stress of the actual trial and standing to lose your life to the government for fifteen, twenty, or thirty years, and in some cases, people get life sentences. He knew that he made out and knew that the second time would be twice as hard. He knew that they would gun for him next time. He planned to get with the connect on the weekend. He made up his mind to only give work to Teddy. He would push the entire load off on Teddy and play the background.

When he pulled up, Teddy was standing outside talking to Nino who had just pulled up.

"Yo, what's up y'all? What's happening?" Bingo said, jumping out of the Benz.

Teddy said what's up, followed by Nino. They shook hands and gave each other hugs.

"Damn, the chrome lip on that Ashanti got this S 6-pound sitting criz-zazy," Nino said, running over to the Benz.

"Yeah, I still love my GT, but this is my baby right here."

"It must be nice to get such a lovely coming home present," Nino said, joking but feeling jealous of the boss.

"Yo, let us spin this around the corner while you talk to dude," Teddy cut in.

"Go ahead," Bingo said, tossing him the keys without a second thought. Bingo never cherished cars or any other material shit.

He walked into the building and saw the adjuster poking at the charred ceiling with a metal pole. When he was done, Bingo went over to where he was standing. I'm sorry for running late, but traffic was crazy."

"No problem, Mr. Grant. Your brother let me know that you would be late. I'm pretty much done assessing the damages. I just have to check the last room down there. Your brother said that was your office. Is this correct?" the short, Italian adjuster said, all in one breathe.

"Yeah, that's the office down there. This place looks like a tornado hit it."

"Yeah, the fire did damage, but the firefighters did the most damage. They always trash a place when it comes to putting a fire out. They really enjoy busting windows out. They never fail to bust windows. I still haven't figured that one out," the adjuster said, opening the office door.

"Maybe they wanted to bust out windows since they were children. One of my houses caught fire before when my tenant left the stove on. The kitchen was the only spot that the fire consumed, but they busted windows out on the second and third floors. The fire commissioner told me that they bust the windows to air the smoke out, but he didn't know why they busted the upstairs windows when they could have just opened them. All he gave me was an apology and a speech on how the firefighters are overworked, underpaid, and hardly appreciated," Bingo said, looking into the room, as the adjuster looked over the room with a sharp eye.

"My boss told me that they invested in window stocks," the adjuster said, now writing in his notepad.

"Damn, they messed this office up."

"Yeah, the fire didn't get back here, but there is water damage, and you need a new computer," the adjuster said, winking at Bingo, knowing damn well there was no damage done to the little office.

"Mike, you're alright with me," Bingo said, calling the adjuster by name.

"Yeah, just know that this will cost you lunch," Mike said, smiling.

"How about you have lunch on me for a week?"

"That's what I love to hear."

Bingo walked outside and let Mike finish conducting his appraisal.

He leaned against the wall of his tire shop thinking how the game had become so watered down. When he was coming up, a dude had to really be somebody to be in the game. But nowadays, everybody was in the game. The young bulls didn't even start out in the trenches anymore. They eased right to the top.

He thought of how Tone had fucked up the whole team. He knew Tone was the one who set the pool hall and tire shop on fire. He wasn't sweating that because he knew Tone was a hater, and that's the type of faggot shit he expected out of a hater; but he despised the nigga for killing Ern and kidnapping Champ.

Before he could get wrapped up in his thoughts, Teddy pulled up in the Benz with Jay-Z's *Streets Is Watching* pouring out of the system.

"...♫ kidnap ♪ niggas ♪ want to steal ya ♫, broke nigga want ♪ want no cash, ♫ they ♪ ♫ just wanna ♪♪♪ kill ya ♪♫..."

The music caught Bingo's attention before Teddy turned off the ignition.

"Yo cuz, them niggas was sick on 39th and Fairmount Avenue seeing us come through in this with the seat leaned back, windows down, sunroof back, and temp tag big as day in the window. I know them niggas are like, damn, them niggas just beat the feds and already came home and grabbed a wide-body Benz," Nino said, not letting Teddy or Bingo cut him off.

"Bingo, you got to let us push this to the party now you're all on some lovey-dovey shit with Thelma, so y'all can roll in the GT, and we'll follow y'all in this thing," Nino said, a little too hype for Bingo.

"Nigga calm down you act like we ain't been driving Benzes and shit," Teddy said, not believing how hyped Nino was about going through the hood spinning in a Benz.

"Yeah, we never did it three days after beating the feds. Niggas know we beat those people with a bat," Nino said, beads of sweat popping out on his forehead.

"Yo Nino, we're not trying to entertain these streets. If you didn't learn nothing from the feds, you should have learned that the government got the paper and resources to take any nigga to trial at anytime. Dawg, y'all can drive the car to the party. Y'all can even drive it to the moon, but please know that the car don't make the nigga, it can only break a nigga," Bingo said, realizing that Nino could possibly be dead weight and the cause of them all going back to jail.

He vowed to privately talk to Teddy about Nino. He loved Nino, but he was not going back to jail because he was reckless.

"Yo Bingo, my nigga, on some real shit, I want these chumps to see me this time around. Fuck laying back and doing the Park Avenues and shit. I need a big body, too. When we was in the feds, some nights I would be like, damn, I'm about to do fifteen maybe twenty years. My life would have been lost to that prison, and all I've been out here is the bull Nino that rides for Teddy and Bingo. Of course, I drove your Bentley and shit, but I got to get my own shit this time," Nino said, sniffing and wiping his nose.

"We'll all talk about this later," Bingo said, looking at Teddy with a your man is tripping expression on his face.

"What's later, my nigga?"

"After the party?" Teddy said, cutting the conversation short.

The adjuster came out. Bingo walked over, leaving Nino and Teddy talking by the Benz.

"So what did you come up with?"

"Well Mr. Grant, there's about $56,000 in damages, but I squeezed $62,000 out. I got a brother that will do the work for $51,000. You can give him $56,000 though; $5,000 for you know who, and you can keep the extra $6,000 to treat yourself to something if you know what I mean," Mike said, seeing the hustler up in Bingo and trying to cash in some of the money that Bingo was sure to get from Allstate Insurance."

"Listen Mike, I have somebody to do the work, but if you get me that $62,000, I'll give you five grand cash. I don't play games, and you can ask Sharon if I am a man of my word," Bingo said, using Sharon as a reference because she referred Bingo to the crooked adjuster.

"You know, once I have my supervisor sign off on the appraisal, we normally mail a certified check out, and it takes three to four days to get to you. How about, instead of me dropping the baby in the mail, I hold onto it, and you can come by the office to get it tomorrow at noon? Or you can phone me and I'll bring it out to you."

"That's cool."

"Mr. Grant, please have my $5,000 with you."

"I will."

They shook hands and the adjuster left. Bingo did not care about giving him $5,000 because he knew that he could get the work done for $40,000. He wondered how many times Mike had pulled this shit off.

Chapter 7

Nay was acting like a nut. She blamed everybody for Tone's murder except Tone. She hated Champ, Wanna, and Micky, but she really hated Sharon and Toot to another degree. She blamed Sharon for the murders of Reem, Trev, and Tone.

She told her mom that Sharon and Champ were fucking and that they staged the kidnapping in order to kill Tone in cold blood and take his money and properties. She tried her best to convince her mom that Sharon didn't love Tone, and she used the fact that Sharon didn't come to the funeral to prove her point.

Ms. Bernadette knew that Nay was jealous of Sharon. She knew Nay could never understand how Sharon had Tone wide open, which is why she didn't buy Nay's story about Sharon fucking Champ and staging Tone's murder. She read the newspapers, and she saw the case of Champ's kidnapping and Tone's murder several times. She also remembered how crazy Tone talked to her during the two weeks before he died. The last time she talked to her son, he really broke her heart. Tone was so high off power and agitated because his mom told him to get some help that he called her all types of no good bitches and hung up on her. She cried for two days straight. If Tone weren't her only son, she probably would not have come to his funeral either. Nay was full of shit talking about Sharon staging the murder so she could rip Tone off for his money and properties, and Ms. Bernadette knew it.

Sharon had called Ms. Bernadette a week after Tone's funeral and had a long talk with her. She told her about how Tone wasn't himself anymore, and that despite all the heartbreaking stuff Tone put her through, she still loved him. She also told Ms. Bernadette that he left eight properties and arranged to give Ms. Bernadette three of them. Nay didn't know anything about Sharon voluntarily giving her mom the properties. Nay tried so hard to sell Ms. Bernadette on money being Sharon's motive for staging the murder that Ms. Bernadette knew she was full of shit and jealous of Sharon.

Nay started to feel that her mom was onto her, so she stopped talking to her mom and accused her mom of siding with the bitch who killed her brother. Nay wouldn't rest until Sharon fell flat on her face, but she decided she would handle Toot first for betraying their family.

Nay pulled up to Monroe's Diner on Passyunk Avenue. She entered, told the waitress her name, and was escorted to a table in the back where a white man wearing dark shades sat. Even with the shades on, anyone who knew detective Hutson knew it was him from a mile away.

"What's up Reenay? How are ya'?" Hutson said, getting up to pull Nay's chair out.

"I'm fine Hutch," she said, calling him by the name she heard Tone and all the hustlers she knew call him.

She sat down in the chair he pulled out for her. The waiteress took their order and then left the two of them alone. Hutson stared at Nay as if she was a pork chop.

"What's the problem, Hutch?" she said, feeling good at the thought of him lusting after her.

"Oh, nothing. I'm just amazed at how much you look like your brother," he replied, not lusting after her; in fact, he was turned off by how she had let herself go.

She was always a thick girl. In fact, when he and his partner first started investigating Tone they had labeled her as Tone's thick, pretty, fly sister. Now she was a total mess. Her hair was pulled back in a ponytail. She had gotten bigger, and her clothes seemed to be getting tighter and cheesier. She had bags under her eyes and she seemed to be getting high. Before, she would have been perfect for an unmarried cop to throw his dick in, but now, all she was good for was getting the information she said she had for him.

"Tone was never this pretty," Nay said, swinging her head to the side as if she was sexy.

"Yeah, you're right. What did you have to tell me about the murder of Kareem and Jim," Officer Hutson said, cutting Nay off from the flirting shit.

"My little cousin, Toot, is behind that shit. Even if he didn't squeeze the trigger, he was the one who paid to get them killed."

"Why would your cousin kill your cousin's cousin?" Hutson said, not understanding where Nay was going with all this.

"Because he is a dick-rider that turned on his family so that Sharon and Micky could accept him as one of their own. When Toot's coward ass came to Trev's funeral, Reem and Jim beat his ass up, and I laughed in his face," Nay said, then hushed up as the waitress came and placed their food on the table.

As the waitress left, Hutson began to talk.

"Reenay, I can't arrest Toot because he was fighting with Kareem. Did you see Toot shoot Reem or anybody else?"

"No, but I know for sure he killed Reem and Jimmy. Hutch, you don't know how sneaky Toot and that damn Micky are. Them young bulls are selling a lot of drugs and they are killing niggas," Nay said, slopping down her food in a trifling manner

Hutson was disgusted by the way she was eating and how she used the word nigga.

"Reenay, if you don't have any proof of this stuff I can't move on it. If you can't do a control buy and get addresses where there's some drug activity, there's nothing I can do," he said, getting up and placing a twenty-dollar bill on the table to pay their check. He was so disgusted by the way she ate that he didn't even bother to eat his own food.

"Let me see what I can come up with, and I'll get back to you. Okay, cutie?" she said, pinching his butt before he walked off, leaving her there to eat by herself.

"I might have to give a white man some of this pussy. I have to get Toot to trust me enough to get the evidence I need to get his ass busted or get the boy, Weezy, to blow his motherfucking head off," Nay said, finishing the food on her plate and starting in on the food Hutson left. When she finished all the food, she handed the waitress the twenty that Hutson left to pay the $18.65 bill. She waited for the change, stuffed it in her pocket, and left without tipping the waitress.

~~~~~

Micky and Toot were on their way to meet Ducky and Raheem to discuss a few things and pick up some work. Toot wanted to stop by Quiana's workplace first. He had been staying over at her house of late and was really digging her. Micky liked her for his boy, and she was becoming cool with Rhonda. Quiana had been by the loft to hang out with Toot, Micky, and Rhonda.

When they went to Baltimore, they all had a ball. They stayed the weekend and came back on Monday. They went to the ESPN-Zone, Cheesecake Factory, and, of course, to Phillips to get best crab cakes in the world.

It was as if Quiana had known all of them for years because she blended right in. They went to the bar on top of the Hyatt at night and partied the night away. They really enjoyed that weekend, and from that point on, Quiana had become like family.

"Yo Toot, I think you're open. Quiana got you hooked," Micky said jokingly, trying to see if his friend would deny his feelings for Quiana.

"Homeboy, I'm not even going to front she is a bad bitch, and she got me right now."

"I know, but at least you know too," Micky said, laughing at his friend's honesty.

"Yo man, the bitch sucks my dick with Halls in her mouth. My dick felt like vapors was shooting all through it. Have you ever had that done?"

"Naw nigga, my dick don't have a cold, so it don't need Halls," Micky said, laughing at his own joke.

"Alright, you think it's a joke, but when Rhonda pulls them Halls out on that dick, don't start bitching my nigga. That shit had a nigga walking on the ceiling," Toot said, pulling into valet.

When she saw them, Quiana walked over to the car. Toot got out, and Micky rolled down the window, spoke to her, and rolled the window up so they could talk privately.

"What's up with you, Qui-Qui?" Toot said, hugging and kissing her.

She loved when he called her Qui-Qui simply because he had given her a nickname.

"You're what's up with me. I'm following your lead, young man. Do you know what direction we're going in?" Quiana said, holding Toot's hand.

"I don't know exactly, but plan on going to the top, and as long as you're with me, it don't matter how long it takes me."

"Is that right? I hope you don't hurt me. I swear I've never fallen for a man this fast. I'm not going to hold you up. I just wanted to see your face. I'll call you at three this afternoon when I get off," she said, leaning over to kiss him.

"What are you doing today?"

"I'm supposed to go with Rhonda to the mall. She said she wants to introduce me to the girls, and we're going to get something to wear to the party tonight."

"What girls?"

"Micky's mom, Wanna, and Thelma," Quiana said, looking at her pager, which was going off indicating she had to go attend to a patient.

She kissed him again and ran off. He jumped back into the car.

"She told me to tell you good-bye because she has a patient."

"I like Quiana, Toot. She good peoples."

They rode over to Ducky's detail shop listening to Lil' Wayne's *Tha Carter III.*

"Micky, this is going to be a hell of a year," Toot said, pulling up to the detail shop.

"Yeah, we're going to show these little niggas how to get down," Micky said, jumping out of the car.

They both walked into the detail shop, where Ducky and Raheem sat at a table eating donuts and talking shit.

"What's up little niggas? Eat some donuts little niggas," Raheem said, sounding like Pinky off Ice Cube's movie *Friday.*

"Nigga, you always offering shit out like you paid for it with your hype ass," Ducky said, playing with Raheem.

"Nigga, I just want my little niggas to see what these Boston cream joints is hitting for. I'm telling you little niggas right now, these jawns are crazy."

Toot grabbed a donut and bit into it. Micky just sat there looking at Raheem, trying to figure out why he was hyped.

"Toot, that's what I'm talking about. You know a good free donut when you see one, but this little pretty nigga with the Maserati don't know shit about free shit. I'm going to start calling you Maserti Micky," Raheem said, playfully pushing Micky.

"Raheem, you're tripping about these nut-ass donuts as if you're getting paid for advertising them," Micky said, grabbing one of the donuts, thinking to himself that Raheem must be getting high or something. The last few times he had seen him, he had been hyped whether it was late at night or early in the morning.

"That's what I'm talking about little nigga, Boston motherfucking cream," Raheem said, pumping his fist in air.

They all laughed.

"Yo, this nigga has been tripping all day long," Ducky said, drinking his tea.

"I'm not triz-zipping. I just want my niggas to have the best of the best."

"What, the best donut? Nigga, you tripping for real," Ducky said, gesturing Micky to follow him to his office at the back of the shop.

They could hear Raheem's voice booming behind them as Ducky closed the door.

"Boston motherfucking cream!" Raheem screamed at Ducky and Micky, who were long gone down the hall with the door to the office closed behind them.

"That nigga is tripping for real, Ducky. If I didn't know any better, I would think he was high," Micky said, leaning backing in a chair.

"Naw Micky, you know we don't do any getting high in this crew," Ducky said, shooting down the accusation that his right-hand man was getting high.

"Yeah I know. Raheem is my oldhead and I love him. I just never seen him act that way."

"Yeah, because you're not around his crazy ass all day. Anyway, I left thirty bricks in the work van out front," Ducky said in a low voice, as if someone might be listening.

"Ducky, the money's in the stash box of the car I'm leaving to get detailed, so you can take it out when you get a chance."

"Yo, you know it's official...after this weekend, Champ is done."

"Yeah, he told me that he was done, but you will treat me the same way he did," Micky said, wanting Ducky to

92

agree to what Champ promised him; that shit won't change.

"Yeah, he gave me strict instructions to make sure you're super good at a super price, little homie. Even if he hadn't told me to look out, I would have still looked out for you," Ducky said, as he chewed the last piece of his donut.

"Damn, can you believe Unc is going to walk away from all this?" Micky said, waving both hands in the air.

"Micky, at first I thought he was just shook from the bullshit that Tone pulled off on him. I talked to him several times trying to convince him that we need him out here with us, but he still flat out said it's over. I believe him."

"Well, I guess we have to hold it down, ya' dig?" Micky said, picking up the flier to Bingo's coming home party.

"Yeah, and he said this last night out in the club."

"Damn, he's tripping with that shit," Micky said, not understanding that Champ was tired since he'd been in the game before Micky was even born.

"We got to party hard tonight."

"Ducky, say no more. I'm bringing some paper out to blow tonight."

"I'm bringing out something crazy tonight too."

"Well, I'll see y'all down at the club," Micky said, getting the keys to the van from Ducky.

They walked into the detail shop, where Raheem was sweating and slap-boxing Toot. Raheem was ducking and dodging, animated like a real boxer.

"Yo, chill out. You're drawing. You got all the customers looking in here like y'all are fighting for real," Ducky said, grabbing Raheem by the arm.

"Nigga, fuck them customers. I'm trying to show our little homie how to throw his hand in a fight."

"Throw your goofy ass down on the couch."

"Nigga, as soon as I catch my breath, we are going to body-box," Raheem said to Ducky, breathing hard.

"Nigga, you're going to fuck around and get your body in a box fucking with me," Ducky said, looking around to make sure none of the customers could see him show Raheem the butt of the gun at his waist.

"Oww, nigga, you know I love them burners," Raheem said, all hyped, sitting down on the couch.

"We're out. We'll see y'all down Onyx," Micky said, grabbing Toot by the shoulder.

They jumped into the van and headed to their stash house.

"Yo, Raheem is hype as shit. He is really burnt out," Toot said, looking in the mirror.

"Nigga, you crazy too, slap-boxing that old-school nigga. Nobody do that slap-boxing shit no more," Micky said, turning onto the expressway.

"Man, what was I supposed to do? We were watching ESPN and they showed Mike Tyson, then he asked me what I know about boxing. I said a little something, and then he hauled off and smacked the shit out me."

Micky busted out laughing, imagining Raheem smacking the shit out of Toot.

"Man, you laughing. I was about to shoot that nigga until I noticed he was playing and wanted to slap-box. What's up with that nigga?"

"I was just telling Ducky that he might be getting high or something."

"His nose kept running, and it was too early for him to be so hyped."

"I think he's snorting that coke," Micky said, as they got off the exit.

"Micky, you know Champ don't play the gang using drugs."

"I know, but Ducky is the man now, and he's probably so close to Raheem that he can't see the fact that Raheem is getting high or don't want to accept the fact. We got to watch that, though, because that shit can really get one of us hurt."

~~~~~

Champ had just finished dicking Wanna down and getting dressed. He waited for Wanna to get dressed and come down the stairs. She came down with an Emilio Pucci, cutout mini that hugged every curve on her body. She had on a pair of $1,200 Christian Louboutin Galaxy Pass 100 sandals. Her hair was pressed straight and hung down past her shoulders. She was mind blowing.

"Damn, you make me want to stay home and enjoy my future," Champ said, hugging Wanna, inhaling the Miss Dior Cherie L'Eau perfume.

"I'm down with staying in with my Champ," Wanna said seriously, willing to take her clothes off and chill in the house with Champ.

"Baby, if this wasn't Bingo's coming home party, I wouldn't even go out. You know Thelma wouldn't speak to us for a year if we missed this party," Champ said, grabbing his keys, turning out the lights, and setting the house alarm.

They took Champ's cream Bentley GTC since it was just the two of them. He pulled out of the driveway and called Ducky on his cell phone.

"Ducky, I'm on my way. I'll meet you at the Sunoco station at the bottom of the Pratt Bridge, and we'll ride over together. Okay, peace," Champ said, hanging up the phone.

"That was Ducky. He'll be waiting on us."

"You're driving, so they will be waiting on you," Wanna said, putting on her favorite song "Cater To You" by Destiny's Child.

Champ was feeling good about going out with his whole crew and the woman he loved. They drove down the expressway talking about life as they always did. Every once in a while, Wanna looked at the scars left on Champ's wrists from the handcuffs Tone and Sab had squeezed tightly on him during the kidnapping. She hated Tone more and more as she pictured Champ being tortured by Tone's evil ass.

"I'm glad you are getting out of the streets. Do you know that I didn't know how I was going to make it without you when you were in that hospital bed? Did you hear me crying my heart out to you at the side of your bed? Do you know any tears I left on your bedside?"

"Yeah, I heard you at my side. You and Thelma talked me back to life. Thelma used to be tripping. Wanna, real rap, it's crazy because I used to hear y'all clear as day. I decided after that faggot-ass nigga Tone pulled that bullshit off, that I'd take what I've been blessed with and enjoy my family and my beautiful girl. I'm too old, and I did everything in the streets that there is to do. I know my crew thinks I'm getting soft because of the kidnapping, but, Wanna, I swear I'm all man and I'm not scared of pussies like Tone. I'll meet anybody anywhere to shoot it out or fight it out when it comes to me and mine, but it has to be worth it. I've made more than enough money to last us two lifetimes, so there's nothing in the street that's worth me putting me and mine on the line for at this time," Champ said, pulling up to the light at the bottom of the Pratt Bridge.

"I know your immediate circle knows you're not getting soft. They probably question you leaving the game because they know they will need your assistance. I know you're all man. There's nothing in the world could make me believe any different."

They pulled into the gas station. Micky and Rhonda were in his Maserati, and Ducky and Raheem were in Ducky's CL63. Sharon was driving Toot's Escalade, and she let Toot and Quiana drive her GT Bentley. Champ pulled in and hit his high beams, signaling them to follow him around to the club. When they pulled up, all eyes were on them.

Although there were Maybachs, Phantoms, and other high-powered cars out front, all eyes were on Champ, who was by far the biggest nigga in the city, and after the abduction, everybody had been waiting on his next move. This was his first time out on the party scene since he'd been home from the hospital.

Ducky and Raheem jumped out first to escort the rest of the crew to the door. It was nice out. The players were out in their jewels with pockets bulging. The chicks were out half-naked, flaunting their asses, cleavage, and pussy prints. The line to get in was around the corner. Champ's crew didn't stand in line. Instead, they walked to the front of the VIP line. One of the bouncers got to Champ before another bouncer could cash in what was sure to be a good tip from the well-known boss of the city.

"What's up Champ? How many do you have with you tonight?" Brother Abdul Akbar, the senior bouncer, asked.

"It's twelve of us all together," Champ said, pointing at his crew which included Shaahir, Dawud, and Weezy.

"Alright, come through and let me know y'alls last man," Abdul Akbar said, lifting the rope and letting them through. Ducky stood there, and once everyone was in, Abdul Akbar put the rope back as Ducky slid him a stack.

When they walked in, it was the same as when they pulled up; all eyes were on them and they could feel it. They all walked up to the VIP area that Bingo and Thelma had secured for them. After they all said their what's ups and exchanged handshakes and hugs, they began to branch off into smaller groups.

The women with their crew sat and talked among themselves. Champ chitchatted with a lot of different people, but the person he was eager to talk to surprised him by being in town. Jab, who used to run with Ern's cousin, Jinz, was already in the VIP section with Bingo when Champ came up. After Jinz was killed, his immediate circle moved out of town. Jab was his main man. There were rumors floating around Philly that Jinz was still alive, but nobody had any proof. Jinz was Ern's cousin, but he was like family to Champ as well.

"Damn Jab, what's up baby boy? I thought you moved out of town?" Champ said, hugging Jab.

"Yeah, but I'm allowed to come hang out with old friends, right?"

"Jab, I miss you homie, and I miss Jinz."

"Yeah, we miss Jinz too, and I miss you, Champ."

"What have you been up to, and who all came out with you?"

"Man, I came with Lips, Ben, and Uncle Sput. I tried to get my wife to come, but she don't ungarb in public no more," Jab said, drinking tonic water.

"Ungarb? Kirah took *Shahadah*," Champ said, thinking of Kirah and how thorough she was.

"Yeah, we took *Shahadah*."

"Damn, you know I'm about to take *Shahadah*...me and Wanna."

"Wanna? Your sister Wanna?"

"That's not my sister. We're together now."

"Damn, I know y'all used to be on y'all play-sister and brother tip. Yo, *Shahadah* is where it's at. This is not the spot to talk about it, but let's get together tomorrow with Kirah and Wanna for lunch."

"That's what up. I hope that's not liquor in that cup."

"Naw homie, this is tonic water," Jab said, holding his cup up.

They kicked it a little bit then Jab got his crew and left. He just came to show Bingo love, not to party the whole night. That was not the case for Raheem, Teddy, Nino, and Ducky. They were pulling chicks left and right.

"Yo Teddy, tell her to come here," Raheem said, pointing to a brown-skinned chick. Teddy grabbed the girl by her shoulder and sent her over to Raheem.

"What's up miss? What's your name?" Raheem said, with a bottle of Ace of Spades in his right hand, half-eaten raw lemon's in the other.

"Hi, I'm Shanice, and you are?" she said, holding her hand out to shake his hand.

"I'm Raheem, a.k.a. your ticket to Hollywood. I'm going to make you famous," Raheem said, as he took her hand, raising it up to kiss it.

Shanice chuckled.

"So, you are my ticket to Hollywood, huh?"

"Naw, not *Hollywood* Hollywood, but I will make you famous in this city."

"Is that right? And how do you plan to do that?"

"You're blossoming into a star as we speak. Look at the all chicks and haters. They are asking themselves who is that right there talking to the boy Raheem up in the VIP?" Raheem said, drinking the Ace of Spades right out of the bottle.

"I think I like you with your cocky self. Why don't you get a cup and stop drinking out the bottle boo?"

"Because my whole crew is bosses, and bosses drink straight from the bottle."

"Okay boss, suppose I would have wanted some, then what?"

"I would have bought you your own bottle," Raheem said, swigging on the champagne.

"I think I really like you, but I don't drink champagne."

"What do you drink?"

"I drink Patron."

"Ducky, give us a bottle of Patron," he said, leaning over the VIP table.

Ducky passed him a bottle, which he gave to Shanice. He kicked it with her for a little bit before he put his number in her phone and let her go back to her girlfriends.

He went to catch up with Nino. They were on their way back to the bathroom for the third time. They each went into their own stall. They were sorting the raw that Raheem provided. Raheem and Nino had been kicking it for the last few days getting snorted.

Ducky, Teddy, Nino, Raheem, Micky, and Toot had all met down Scooters Bar three days ago. Nino and Raheem started kicking it heavily since they found out they both liked to snort that nose candy.

As soon as Champ's crew came in Onyx, the first person Nino ran over to was Raheem. He wanted to know if Raheem had brought the coke as he promised. Once he gave Nino the package, they both went into the bathroom, and ever since then, they had been in and out of the bathroom.

"Yo, that shit was crazy right there. I'm talking about straight fish scale," Nino said, exiting the stall, and looking in the mirror to clean his nose.

"Yeah nigga, we got that shit. I'm the life of the party," Raheem said, snorted out of his mind.

"Yo cuz, I'm feeling all of this party shit, but I'm not feeling the entire underdog shit. Like I told you earlier, this nigga Teddy, talking about he got a new connect, and the connection don't want to meet nobody. I know Bingo is still giving him coke. I don't believe he's retired. He's just talking that retired shit because Champ is talking that shit. That bitch Thelma is too money hungry to let a nigga retire," Nino said, as they walked back to the VIP.

"Nino, chill. We'll talk about the bullshit these niggas are trying to do tomorrow. Right now, let's get these hoes," Raheem said, high as a kite, dancing off beat like a white boy to R. Kelly and Juiceman's song "Superman High."

Champ and Bingo were kicking it most of the night. The night was going smoothly. Ducky, Micky, and Toot were standing at the edge of the VIP throwing money in the air. All eyes were on them. Raheem and Nino joined them after they took two bricks of dollar bills off Champ and Bingo's table. While the crew was having fun throwing up the money, Champ and Bingo were trying to see what they could do to get off, and stay off, the scene.

"So, Champ, you really think you can step away from the street shit?"

"Bingo, after seeing you almost lose your life to prison and learning that nigga Tone was really behind Ern's murder on top of kidnapping me, I'm a fool to stay in these streets. I've made my money, so I can blow out."

"I heard that, but you can play background and still get your paper."

"I don't want nothing to do with these streets. I'm done. I'm going to become a Muslim and enjoy all that I have earned while building a new, legit empire," Champ said with a straight face.

Their conversation was cut short when Wanna and Thelma came and jumped in their laps. They enjoyed the rest of the night, kicking with the niggas in the crew and the hustlers trying to reach out to them in hopes of getting in with either of the bosses. The party was a smash. They bought a lot of bottles of champagne, they threw a lot of money in the air, and they exchanged a lot of numbers with both players and chicks with promises of getting with them soon.

Of course, after the party was over, the car show began. Every foreign car and every set of rims imaginable was in front of the club. The players were plotting on how to get their weight up to play a little more major. The haters were plotting to take something and hoping for the real players' downfalls. The hoes were plotting how to get a player's dick in their mouths so they could get paper in their pocket.

Chapter 8

It had been a week since Champ retired from the game. Now that he was focused on being legit, he felt good about taking his *Shahadah* with Wanna. He kept his birth name on his businesses; but around the *Masjid* and amongst his peers, his attribute was Saleem. Wanna selected the attribute, Fatimah, meaning "one who abstains," because she thought it was fitting for their new lifestyle. The two were married at the *Masjid* As Sunnah An Nabawiyyah on a *Jumu'ah* Friday. The *Walimah*, the celebration of marriage, was three days later and was open to all who wanted to come celebrate their union. The event was catered with a wide selection of food and beverages. Champ made sure there was enough for any Muslim who came.

Champ was at peace with himself and ready to enjoy his life outside of the game. The crew missed his presence already. Micky didn't have any complaints, except that Raheem was starting to get reckless. He was talking to people in the street about their crew's business. Ducky seemed a little too passive with him because of their history. Micky told Ducky time and time again about what was being said about Raheem running his mouth on the streets, but this latest incident was Micky's breaking point. It was reported that Raheem was telling people that he and Ducky had a connect and that he was serving

Micky fifty bricks at a time. Micky was so pissed he told Ducky to keep Raheem out of his business and decided to stay clear of Raheem. He would have killed Raheem if he weren't so close to Ducky.

Micky and Toot were starting to kick it with Shaahir on a daily basis. Shaahir bought the seafood store up on Chelten and Chew Avenues. Micky and Toot were up there regularly chilling unless they were serving one of their customers.

Chicks started spreading the word that all the players were hanging in Shaahir's Sea What It Is seafood store. After awhile, Shaahir's spot became the happening spot. On the weekend, chicks would flood the store before they went to the mall or the club. Shaahir didn't mind his spot being a hang out as long as they spent money there.

One day, Micky, Toot, and Shaahir were sitting out front kicking it when, to their surprise, Champ and Wanna pulled up. Champ stood out front kicking it with his boys, who he hadn't seen in weeks and barely talked to, while Wanna went inside to get some food.

Shaahir's food was so good that even the people at the *Masjid* were talking about it; that's how Champ got the word of it. He not only wanted to be supportive of his good friend's store, but he also wanted to see his man. He was still human and missed his homies. When he saw Micky and Toot out there with Shaahir, it made him happy. They all kicked it, and although they wanted and needed him back in the streets with them, they respected what he was trying to do.

When he pulled off, it hurt them; little did they know it hurt him too. Champ didn't miss the streets, but he missed his whole crew, each and every one of them. They were more than just a bunch of niggas that he was supplying; they were his extended family.

Ducky kept the price the same for Micky, and he tried his best to fill Champ's shoes, but that was like getting Gary Colemen to fill Shaq's size twenty-twos. Ducky tried his best, but Champ was the best at what he did. Micky was actually moving more work than before, but he missed having Champ around. Ducky was like family, but there was no one alive that could compare with the admiration Micky had in his heart for Champ. Champ had shown Micky love from day one, and he taught him the game. He was Philly's champion, but he was Micky's hero.

"Damn, Unc is really done with the game," Micky said, as he followed Toot and Shaahir into the store.

"Yeah, he had his *kufi* on and everything," Toot said, as Shaahir went behind the counter, leaving Micky and Toot at the table alone.

Toot's phone rang and he answered it after looking at his caller ID.

"Hello. I don't know what you're talking about. Yo, I'll talk to you face to face," he said, before hanging up.

"Yo, who was that?" Micky said, seeing that Toot was upset.

"That was nut-ass Nay talking reckless on my phone. I think that bitch is working with the cops."

"Why do you think that?"

"Because the stupid bitch said on the phone, 'Let me get half a brick of that shit that you and Micky used to sell for Tone.' Micky, that bitch knows better than to talk like that on the phone, plus she knows I don't fuck with her like that. I wish she would have come to meet me the other day when she called me talking that shit about people saying I killed Reem."

"Yo, I'm telling you that we got to put that bitch down. She's going to be a problem," Mickey said, as they got ready to leave.

As soon as they said their good-byes to Shaahir, Dawud and Weezy came in, so they decided to stay a little while longer to kick it. Shaahir had introduced them all to each other one night when they were popping bottles at the Crab House. Dawud and Weezy were holding down the Summerville section of Germantown for Shaahir. Since they were all in the same age bracket and basically eating off the same plate, all the young bulls were cool with each other. Dawud and Weezy were pressed for time, so they got their pre-ordered food, said their good-byes, and promised to hook up with Micky and Toot later.

"What's up with y'all two niggas? Where are y'all about to go?"

"We 'bout to go down the Bottom," Micky said, as he grabbed spring water from the soda box for him and Toot.

"Yo, all the little chicks be leaving their numbers here for y'all. I be telling them that y'all are married."

"Damn, you be hatin' us out like that? Shaahir, you're supposed to be lining them up so we can knock them down," Toot said playfully, pushing Shaahir.

"I'm just playing. I don't tell them that, and if I did, they wouldn't care anyway. Dawud and Weezy told me the other day that, since the little bitches learned that y'all are all on the same team, their pussy rate has skyrocketed," Shaahir said, as he nudged Toot's back.

Shaahir looked at Micky and Toot as if they were his little brothers.

"Yo, Weezy and Dawud be passing us off all the Uptown chicks when we're up in that Crab House. I rock with them two niggas like that," Micky said, sipping his water.

"I'm glad y'all are getting along. Y'all need to be each other's eyes and ears."

"No doubt, we got them Uptown, and they got us down the Bottom," Toot said, sipping his water and thinking about killing Nay's fat ass.

~~~~~

Raheem and Nino had been riding together on a regular basis. They were cool before, but they had gotten closer of late. They both felt like underdogs, and with a little bit of cocaine in their system, they felt as if they were getting the short end of the stick.

Raheem would vent and say how Ducky had been fronting with the coke and how Champ was wrong for giving Ducky the connect and not him. He complained about how Ducky and Champ used him when there was drama but just spoon-fed him with coke. He would never take responsibility for all the money he fucked up. Bottom line, he was not a hustler, but Champ and now Ducky both gave him big money daily. He had is own crib and car, but it wasn't enough.

Nino would vent about the same thing with Bingo and Teddy. He told Raheem that he thought Bingo was bullshitting about being out of the game. He said that Teddy was raising the prices because they didn't want him to make any money. He was also mad because he didn't feel as though Teddy and Bingo rode hard enough about Dawud's murder.

Raheem and Nino would ride and talk for hours, snorting coke and making plans to take Ducky and Teddy off some paper and start their own business. Nino had some clientele and a couple of crack houses down the Bottom. They both agreed to stick with their crew until they got the break they needed to start their own shit.

"Yo, where the fuck did you get all of these fucking guns from?" Nino asked, sitting on the couch in his apartment, looking at the military bag full of guns that Raheem brought over.

"These are the guns we had at our stash house, and since I'm the one that was doing all the shooting, it's only right that when I roll out on them suckers the guns do too," Raheem said, as he stuck a rolled-up dollar inside the quarter ounce of coke he had in a zip lock bag, prepared to snort.

"Damn, what did Ducky say when you asked him for all these hammers?" Nino asked, watching Raheem snort the coke, impatiently waiting his turn to snort some of the raw himself.

"I didn't ask that goofy nigga shit. I just went to the spot and took the burners. Ducky got soft. He doesn't bust his gat no more. He is the new Champ. That nigga just wants to sell bricks and suck up to the connect," Raheem explained, as he passed the coke to Nino.

"Raheem, we don't want them niggas to know we aren't feeling them until it's too late," Nino said, pinching the coke, feeling an instant rush.

"The nigga won't know the hammers are gone. We don't mess with these jawns unless we are really beefing. Since we've been chilling, there is no reason for him to go to that crib, and if he do go and come to accuse me without any proof, I'm going to shoot the nigga in his face."

"Damn Raheem, you must hate your crew as much as I hate mines."

Nino snorted some more of the coke and passed it back to Raheem.

"Fuck them niggas because they said fuck me. I've been holding this shit down forever and look at the thanks I get. How the fuck this nigga Shaahir opening up a seafood store and shit? That nigga's from Uptown. He got a store called Sea What It Is. They all are going to see what it is."

Raheem paused for a moment and shook his head as he became angrier. He balled his fists up as veins popped out on his forehead. He blew out air before he continued.

"Little fucking Micky is getting more money than me. This little, pretty-ass nigga is driving around in a fucking Maserati and had the nerve to ask me do I want to drive his whip. I said no, and I was thinking I wanted to whip his ass. I'm going to show these nigga about shitting on me," Raheem said, talking so fast that he got it out all in one breathe because he was amped up off the coke.

"Yeah, that's crazy. I just told Teddy yesterday that I ain't on no yes-man shit. I done bust my gun too much for our crew to be spoon-fed. He kept saying that the new connect don't want to meet nobody. I know Bingo is giving him the load and letting him be the front man. I'm going to get mines one way or the other. If we have to snatch Bingo, Thelma, and Teddy's asses, they are going to give me my cut. It's me and you, Raheem. Fuck everybody else."

Nino took the bag back from Raheem and snorted some more of the raw.

"Yeah, I'm with you, baby boy. First, let's get this free money that I told you about last night. That's a sure-shot payday for us," Raheem said, as his phone rang.

"Yeah, what's up? I'm trying to let my man, Nino, hit that too. Oh yeah, you know Nino? Okay, cool. I'll pick you up tonight."

Raheem hung up the phone with a smirk on his face.

"Who was that?"

"That was Nay fat ass. I told her we are hitting that together on the party tip. I had that bitch in the bathroom at Scooters snorting this flavor with me. She sucked my dick in the stall and swallowed all of my babies that I shot in her mouth."

"Me and Teddy partied Nay a couple years ago. She do have some good pussy. We can chill and let her eat these dicks up," Nino said, thinking of how he and Teddy almost killed the bitch when they shot up Tone's Benz and killed her boyfriend on the Boulevard while she was driving.

"Yeah, but let's go handle this business first, and then we can handle Nay with that good head she got," Raheem said, as he headed for the door.

They jumped into Nino's Buick Park Avenue. Raheem drove out to Penrose. When they got to 72nd and Dicks Street, he pulled over on the corner and parked. They jumped out of the car together and walked up the street. When they got to the door they were looking for, Raheem tried a few keys off his ring until he got the one he wanted and opened the door.

"Yo, we got to hurry up. We're in and out baby," Raheem said, as he began searching the house.

After ten minutes, they found seven bricks of cocaine in a book bag. They left with the seven bricks and headed back to Nino's crib. They were happy that they just got the takedown that they needed.

"Damn, that was sweet," Nino said, thinking of the money they would make off the work.

~~~~~

Ducky definitely had more than seven bricks that he could front Raheem, but Ducky knew that Raheem wasn't a hustler; he was a shooter. Because of that, Ducky decided to follow Champ's lead by throwing Raheem a few stacks here and there. He was also allowed to be the middleman for the few customers that he had.

"Yeah Nino, I told you that we are going to get what these pussies owe us. How the fuck do they got this nigga Shaahir with enough bricks to leave seven of them in a stash-crib like they're furniture? When I be trying to make my little three and five brick sales to my players, they be all over my back with that Raheem you're a shooter not a hustler bullshit. We'll see how much of a hustler I am now."

Raheem felt like he was on top of the world.

"How did you get the key to his spot?" Nino asked, a little confused by how smoothly the hit went.

"'When the goofy nigga came by to drop his car off to get washed, he left the house keys on the key ring. I already knew where the crib was because it used to be Ducky's stash house."

"The nigga didn't notice his keys missing when he came to pick up his car?"

"Naw, after I got the keys copied, I put them back on the ring, so he never knew they were missing."

"Nigga, you're a borderline genius."

111

"You know you'll have to move the work because they will be calling me to help find out who robbed the spot," Raheem said, knowing Ducky would call on him to ride as soon as Shaahir called with news of the robbery.

"I got it Raheem, and I'm lining Teddy up as soon as I can so we can take his punk ass off'," Nino said, rolling up a dollar bill to use as a straw to snort some more of the coke.

They drove back to the crib snorting and talking shit with each other.

~~~~~

Bingo had been falling back on the street shit a lot, just as he planned. He would get the work from the connect and give it directly to Teddy. He was firm with Teddy about keeping his involvement strictly between them, and Teddy did as he was told. He took the load every time and pushed it off on his customers while keeping Bingo's involvement to himself. Although it hurt him to bullshit Nino about Bingo still giving him the coke, he had to follow Bingo's instructions. Bingo was even more firm with Teddy about not letting Nino know that he was still the one passing off the bricks.

Bingo didn't like Nino's last conversation at the tire shop. He felt as though Nino was acting as if he never received a fair break from him now or in the past. He also could tell that Nino was getting high by the way he was acting at their coming home party at Onyx. He didn't know what he was getting high off of; but what he did know was that Nino seemed to be someone totally different from the dusty nigga that Teddy brought around several years ago. The Nino from that night wasn't the same person he cleaned up and put on paper. Bingo couldn't put his finger on what it was, but something urged him to watch his back around the nigga. Bingo started to think he was tripping until Nino made a statement that turned him off.

Nino had stood in the middle of the VIP saying, "Everybody keeps saying this is Bingo's coming home party, but what about me? I went to trial too."

That statement played over and over in Bingo's head for days. He knew that, although Nino was drunk and high off something, he really felt some jealousy and hatred toward him. Since then, Bingo had been keeping tabs on Nino through Teddy.

"So what's good with you, little bro? Are you being careful out there?" Bingo said, walking into the living room with Teddy following him, leaving Thelma in the kitchen to clean up the mess from the meal she prepared, which they had just eaten.

"I'm good, Bee. I'm only fucking with the select few people and I'm moving at a slow pace."

"That's cool. What's up with Nino?"

"He's cool. He's been on a bunch of complaining shit as of late, so I just pass him the work and let him go about his business. His block is still jumping, though."

"What is he complaining about now?"

"He said the prices are getting too high."

"It's a drought right now, so he got to pay more just like we're paying more. When the drought is over, the prices will go back down."

"I tried to explain that to him, but he wants to argue, so I be on some take it or leave it shit because I'm not catering to him or nobody else."

"Dude turned into a nut."

"I know but that's my boy."

"You need to keep an eye on him though, because I'm not feeling him and I don't trust him like I used to."

"He's cool. He is just going through it because he thinks he is the underdog and that you've been ducking him."

"I ain't ducking that nigga. You duck a nigga when you owe them something, and I don't owe him shit. I've been avoiding him, not ducking him. There's a big difference," Bingo said, as he turned his 56-inch, liquid, flat screen TV to ESPN.

"You know what I mean," Teddy said, as he grabbed his keys off the table.

"Teddy, be easy out there, and don't let none of the niggas you're serving know nothing about our operation they don't need to know," Bingo said, wondering to himself if the street shit was even worth it.

"I'm on it, bro. I'm in and out, and we can fall back after we build the paper back up from our losses with that trial," Teddy said, walking into the kitchen to give Thelma a hug and say good-bye.

"Yeah, once we get back, I'm done with this shit. I thought Champ was tripping to walk away, but I'm seeing why he let go of this shit."

Bingo shook his little brother's hand before Teddy walked out. Bingo locked the door and went back to lie on the couch to watch "Sports Center." When Thelma was done in the kitchen, she joined her husband on the couch.

"What's up with the tire shop and the pool hall? Are you really selling them?"

"Yeah, I got some Jewish investors that I met through Sonya, and they want to buy both of them," Bingo said, putting his arm around his wife.

"What's up with Sonya? I haven't seen her or her bad-ass son, Sajid, since they came down to support you at your trial."

"Sonya's cool. She's doing what she's been doing since she was a teenager. She's fighting to get her dad back on the streets. I've never seen a chick ride for their man or dad like she rides for Shakour."

"I know. She rumbles hard for her father. I don't know him but I've heard of him."

"Shakour is a good dude, and all the cats that go through Graterford State penitentiary from Philly either get up under Shakour, Sharif, Black Sam, Dawud, little Clark, or oldhead Rickens. The crazy part is that them dudes took care of niggas for years, and when the niggas they took care of get home, they don't check back in on the cats that held them down.

"I tell Sonya all the time to tell Shakour to throw niggas to the wolves when they come through because niggas don't pay homage when they get on the street," Bingo said, thinking of how Shakour kept his sanity and still stayed tuned to the streets after being in jail for over twenty years.

Bingo and Thelma talked a little more then went upstairs to get in bed. Thelma's period was on, but that didn't stop her from pleasing her man by sucking his dick until he exploded in her mouth.

Chapter 9

Ducky didn't know that Champ's former position as boss of the crew would come with so many headaches. He began to have a new respect for Champ and the way he maintained his composure as the boss no matter what was going on. Ducky was a hustler without question, and no doubt he was a gangster; but being a boss took a special leadership quality, and above that, it took a special type of patience.

With all the shit going on, Ducky began to question his ability to lead the crew. If it wasn't for his pride, he would have begged Champ to come back to take over the crew. He was beginning to feel overwhelmed by everybody who wanted him to fix their problems on the spot. His phones rang so much that he would often just sit looking at them as he considered throwing them in the nearest dumpster. The latest event with Raheem really had him stressing.

Raheem was Ducky's right hand man; they'd been close since elementary school. They started hustling together, and they were in countless shootouts together. Their bond was so strong that they understood each other. Ducky understood how Raheem was feeling about not being placed in charge along with him; he also knew that Champ knew Raheem's biggest weakness and the part that weakness played in him not being chosen to run the crew.

The last time Raheem and Ducky were together at the detail shop, Ducky listened to Raheem go on and on about how he felt that Champ was wrong for not choosing him to run the crew or at least be co-captain. Ducky desperately wanted to explain Champ's reasons to Raheem, but he couldn't bring himself to tell his main man it was because he couldn't count and had poor money managing skills. Raheem didn't understand that dealing with the connect on the level that Champ was dealing with on every shipment could cause you your life, your family's lives, or the combination of them both.

The connect doesn't want to hear that you're a million or two short because you miscounted, tricked, or mishandled their money or product. Instead of getting into the details of why Raheem wasn't chosen, Ducky simply told Raheem that, although he was not chosen, he would always be co-captain as long as Ducky was boss. Raheem felt better at that moment until he got back around Nino and started snorting coke again. Ducky always stuck up for Raheem and always gave him the benefit of the doubt even when his gut feeling was telling him that Raheem was wrong.

This latest incident with Shaahir's stash house being robbed without any forced entry was pointing to Raheem being the one that did it. Besides Ducky, Champ, and Shaahir, Raheem was the only one who knew about the house. Raheem was the only one who had access to Shaahir's keys, and the fact that he hadn't answered his phone in weeks made him look even guiltier.

Ducky pleaded with Shaahir to let him catch up with Raheem first to make sure it was actually Raheem that did it. Shaahir agreed with Ducky, but secretly told Dawud and Weezy to call him if they saw the nigga Raheem.

Shaahir wasn't sweating the work; he just wanted to get rid of Raheem because he felt he was a snake.

When Ducky discovered that the house he and Raheem stashed all their heavy artillery in was robbed without any signs of forced entry, he knew that Raheem was behind both houses being robbed. He didn't tell Shaahir that his crib was robbed too, because he didn't want Shaahir to go after Raheem. He still felt obligated to find Raheem first; he wanted to find out what was going on with him, and why he would steal when he had access to any amount of coke, guns, and money.

Ducky was going to meet Shaahir at the detail shop, then slide passed Raheem's girlfriend's house to see if he could find him there. He had been calling twenty times a day since everything happened, and he drove past Raheem's girl's crib frequently. One day she told him he had just missed Raheem. That was the closest he came to hearing from him.

Ducky noticed Shaahir sitting in the car when he pulled up to the detail shop. He pulled alongside of him, beeped the horn, and flagged Shaahir to get in the car with him. Shaahir locked his car and got in with Ducky. Ducky pulled off so they could drive around a few blocks to kick it.

"What's up Ducky-Baby?" Shaahir said, as he smiled, flashing his white teeth.

"It ain't shit man. I'm just trying to get this paper and stay in my lane," Ducky said, trying to sound as smooth as Champ.

"Did Raheem get back to you yet, or is his phone still off?"

"His phone is off. I went past his girl's house a few times, but she said she hasn't seen him. I told her to call the county jails and hospitals to see if he's listed," Ducky said, as he pulled up to a light.

"That nigga ain't in no hospital or no fucking jail. He's running around with that nigga, Nino, and they just robbed Teddy's crib for ten bricks," Shaahir said, shocking Ducky with the news.

"What? How you know that's true, and when did that shit happen?"

"Teddy told me this morning when I seen him. He said he was going to come by the shop to holler at you today because he's not talking on the phone."

"Damn, Shaahir, what's up with them niggas? They're on some bullshit."

"Ducky, I'm being honest. If I see them niggas, I'm busting their ass on the spot."

"Fuck it! As bad as I want it to be different, we have to handle this shit," Ducky replied, knowing Raheem wasn't going out without a fight.

The thought that Raheem had all the heavy guns assured Ducky that Raheem was prepared for this war.

"Ducky, I know that's your boy, and this shit will be hard for you to be in the middle of. With that being said, I'll handle the whole situation. Teddy is supposed to get his peoples on it too, but I'm moving on it with my own peoples on my own time," Shaahir said, letting Ducky know he had the option to fall back but being firm about his intentions of rocking Raheem.

"Shaahir, I don't know what happened to Raheem. He's been talking and acting crazy. Micky told me that he thought the nigga was getting high, but I wouldn't believe it. Now, as I think back on his movements and conversations, I believe he was truly getting high. Yo, do what you gotta do. Just do it quietly and get it done fast."

Ducky's heart was broken as he pulled up to the detail shop to drop Shaahir off. Ducky couldn't believe he actually gave someone, anyone, the green light on Raheem's life.

"Ducky, be easy and I'll get at you later."

Shaahir jumped out of the car and got into his own. Ducky sat there as he watched Shaahir pull off. As much as he wanted to give up and just say fuck Raheem, he couldn't. He decided to try to catch up with Raheem at a few spots he knew Raheem frequented. He called Raheem's phone, knowing Raheem wouldn't answer. He was shocked by Raheem's voice on the recording saying, "Fuck the world and all the bitch niggas in it. This goes for everybody. Stop calling my phone, you fucking cocksuckers! See me when you see me." After the message, all Ducky could hear was Raheem's wicked laugh in the background.

This fucking nigga done lost his mind. I got to catch up with this nigga before he fucks around and gets himself killed, Ducky thought, as he drove to Raheem's girlfriend's house on Reno Street down the Bottom.

When he pulled up in front of her door, Tammy was sitting on her steps with dark shades on. He beeped the horn, and she ran over to the car after she noticed it was Ducky.

"Get in Tammy."

"What's up Ducky?" Tammy asked, as she got into the car.

Tammy wasn't tripping when Ducky put the car in drive and began to ride around the block to avoid holding up traffic. She was more than comfortable with Ducky. She had known him all her life and he always looked out for her.

121

"What's up lil' sis? Did Raheem come past here?"

"Yeah, that pussy just left. He punched me in my face because I told him that he needs to give you a call."

Tammy took her shades off so Ducky could see the black eye Raheem had given her.

"Damn sis, did he say where he was going?"

"No, he just went up in my room to get the stuff he had stashed in the closet. He said that you don't give a fuck about him, that nobody gives a fuck about him except his man Nino."

"His man Nino? He didn't even like Nino years ago until I told him Nino was family."

Tammy turned toward Ducky and looked at him sincerely. She shook her head as she continued.

"He don't even look like himself lately. He really let himself go. He stinks and he looks like he's been up for days. The last time we had sex, his little, dirty-ass dick wouldn't even get hard."

Tammy was now sitting facing forward with her shades on. She put them back on while she was talking in an attempt to hide the tears that were now streaming down her face.

"Damn, I don't know what's up with Raheem, but I got to catch up with him. I got to get him away from that nigga, Nino. I want you to call me the minute you see him," Ducky said, as he pulled up in front of Tammy's door.

Tammy paused for a moment to gain her composure.

"Okay Ducky, just please get with him before he gets himself killed out there fucking around with Nino."

Tammy leaned over and gave Ducky a hug before she got out of the car. Ducky drove off with mixed emotions. One part of him was saying fuck Raheem and that

Raheem was better off dead; but the other side of him struggled with the thought that it was his duty to save his friend's life. His mind was racing with thoughts on the situation. He felt as if he at least owed his friend a chance to explain.

"This nigga is fucking my whole day up. I can't believe he blacked that girl's eye like that. He is tripping," Ducky said to himself, as he picked up the phone to call Teddy.

~~~~~

Wanna had been so wrapped up in her Islam that she hadn't been out with the girls in awhile. She still conversed with them on the phone, but she was becoming a homebody of late. Her focus was on trying to be the best *Muslimah* she could be. She wore the traditional overgarments that Muslim women wore, but she was no doubt the flyest sister in town with her tailor-made garments.

She accessorized her style with the latest handbags and shoes. Today was the first out to meet with the girls in about a month. They planned to meet at Shaahir's seafood store. Wanna thought it would be good to meet there, so she could patronage Shaahir's business while reconnecting with her girls in comfort. She had on a black overgarment with brown stripes racing down the sleeves coupled with her brown Gucci slides and chocolate Gucci bag. She had to admit she was excited about linking up with the girls even if it was for something as simple as lunch. They all had a lot of catching up to do.

Champ decided to have a chat with Micky, Ducky, and Toot while Wanna was out with the girls. Wanna actually encouraged him to catch up with the boys because she knew he missed them. Wanna called Champ's phone as she got off the expressway at the Germantown and Wissahickon exit. Champ answered his phone with the proper Muslim greeting.

"*As Salamu Alaikum.*"

"*Wa Laikum As Salam.*"

"What's up Fatimah?" Champ said, addressing Wanna with her attribute.

"I'm just calling to ask if you want me to get you something from Shaahir's store for tonight and to see what time you want me to head back to the house Saleem."

"Uh, yeah, can you bring me some of them jumbo shrimp they have stuffed with crab meat and some French fries? Baby girl, I ain't tripping. Enjoy yourself with the girls. I know y'all have a lot to talk about, so don't rush. Just be home at what you consider a respectable hour."

"Okay, I'll see you at the house later, *Insha Allah* (if Allah wills)."

"*Insha Allah,* Fatimah. *As Salamu Alaikum.*"

"*Wa Laikum As Salam.*"

Wanna hung up the phone in awe of her husband. She loved Champ for a lot of reasons; one of them being because he was always considerate of her feelings and her comfort. She knew she had a prize in her husband, and she wanted him to feel the same when he thought of her, which is why she always showed her love and respect for him even in his absence. She was so lost in her thoughts of Champ she hadn't realized she arrived at her destination. When she pulled up, she noticed that the girls were already standing outside waiting on her. Rhonda, Sharon, Thelma, and the latest addition to the crew, Quiana, were all glad to see Wanna pull up.

When Wanna got out of the car, all the girls said their what's ups and hugged her tightly. There was no question how much they missed their girl. They all went inside the store to the booth in the back that Shaahir had reserved for them.

Once seated, one of the waitresses took their orders. They all talked and enjoyed their food. It was a known fact among the community that Shaahir's food was not only *halal* (lawful) but also delicious. Some people even labeled it as the best food in the city.

Shaahir made sure his employees kept the place clean. He was also quick to let them know that the customers were the ones that kept their bills paid, so they were to be treated with the utmost respect. There were always one or two hardheads that came through being disrespectful, but Shaahir always took the honor of putting them in their place so, for the most part, Sea What It Is ran smoothly.

After an hour of catching up with one another, Wanna was ready to drop the news she had for the girls on them.

"I have an announcement for y'all, and I know y'all are going to love it," she said, as she took a sip of her homemade strawberry ice tea.

"What, you and Champ are treating us all to a shopping spree at the Short Hills Mall?"

The girls all laughed and gave high fives for Thelma's statement.

"No, no, Miss Thelma. It's deeper than that."

"Well, spill it out then. You know I'm not good with all that guessing what someone's secret is," Sharon interrupted, wanting to know Wanna's secret bad as hell.

The girls stared at Wanna, waiting for her next word. She looked at them and smiled before she continued.

"We have a new addition to the family. I'm two months pregnant," Wanna finally said, as she patted her stomach.

The girls broke out in cheers as they rushed to Wanna's side. They began to hug and kiss her as they rubbed on her stomach. Wanna had made it her business to get to know her Muslim sisters in the *Masjid*, but this was her family sitting with her at the table. She felt good being around them and sharing her news with them. These were the women that she knew she could call on for anything.

"Ahem…" Rhonda cleared her throat to get the ladies' attention.

They all turned to look at Rhonda.

"Y'all know good news comes in pairs."

"What, you finally learned that sucking-wood trick with a Halls in your mouth I was telling you about?" Thelma said, ignorant as ever, causing the girls to laugh.

"Ewww, no girl! I don't do all that."

Thelma looked at Rhonda, shaking her head in disappointment.

"Anyway, as I was saying before I was so rudely interrupted, I'm two months pregnant as well!"

The girls immediately rushed to Rhonda's side, rubbed on her stomach, and showered her with kisses.

"Y'all must be trying to give me a heart attack, making me a godmom and a grandmom at one time."

Sharon was happy for both Wanna and Rhonda, however, the thought of them being pregnant made her think about the loss of her baby.

"Let me find out Champ and Micky synchronized their watches to get y'all pregnant at the same time," Quiana said, finally speaking.

"Fuck it, Quiana let's get pregnant tonight."

Thelma nudged Quiana in the side then gave her a high five. She had an ignorant sense of humor you just had to love. The girls engaged in conversation for the rest of the evening. They laughed, cried, and even argued over who would be godparents to the kids.

Wanna drove home feeling good about her afternoon. Her mood did not stop her from being on point. She noticed a black, tinted-up Impala trying to put an amateur tail game down on her. Once she peeped the game, she called Champ and put him on point. She then bucked a U-turn on Wayne Avenue and sped back past the car trying to follow her. She tried to get a peep at who was in the car, but the windows were too dark. She hit the little back streets off Pulaski Avenue and jumped onto the expressway. The person inside the Impala knew she busted him, so he didn't bother to give chase.

Wanna knew that she shook them, but she still decided to take an alternate route home. She wasn't scared because she had her licensed gun on her lap as she pulled into her garage. Champ stood in the doorway with a smile on his face.

"Saleem, what are you smiling at?"

"The sight of you holding that gun in your hand."

"I told you that somebody was trying to follow me."

"That was Micky and Toot. I told them to follow you to see if you were on point when you left the store. You know a lot of dope boys be up there, and where there are dope boys, there are robbers."

"You almost got Micky and Toot blasted," Wanna said, putting her gun away, doing a bad job at trying to sound gangster.

"You're not going to shoot nothing, Fatimah. You wouldn't jump at a Chris Cross concert."

"Whatever," Wanna said, as she pushed past Champ.

Champ was proud that she was on point.

~~~~~

Weezy and Dawud had stepped their hustle game up. They had the blocks open twenty-four hours a day and they were selling weight. They were not responsible for the blocks, but anybody that was out there hustling had to get their coke from either Weezy or Dawud. Life was good for them. They now had money to blow on shopping, cars, and partying.

They became real close with Micky and Toot as well. All four of them would hang out from time to time. Whenever they were out, it was obvious that they were the future bosses to run the city. They were always dressed in the flyest shit and jeweled out. The players on the scene would try to cut into them, the haters would hate, and, quite naturally, the chicks would flock to them. On the young bull tip, they had the city in a chokehold.

Weezy was driving up Upsal Street with Dawud in the passenger seat. They were on their way to meet Micky and Toot at Onyx Night Club when they spotted Raheem and Nino driving past them in the opposite direction.

"Damn, did you see that?" Weezy yelled out, as he made a U-turn to follow the car.

"Yeah, I'm about to call Shaahir," Dawud said, picking up his phone.

"Naw, we can handle these niggas and let Shaahir know when the shit is done," Weezy said, grabbing Dawud's hand to stop him from dialing Shaahir's number.

"Okay, fuck it. We can get at these niggas, and then we can go to Onyx to celebrate their death."

Dawud pulled out his burner as they followed the car to the Sedgewick Station apartments. They were sure to stay a block away, so Nino and Raheem wouldn't notice them tailing them. When Weezy spotted the car, Raheem was driving. He parked in front of the complex; Weezy parked behind an empty car.

"We'll wait right here, and when they come out, we'll air them niggas out and keep it moving," Weezy said, with his burner on his lap.

"Yeah, that's crazy that this nigga is staying in these apartments right around the corner from our post."

"Yeah Dawud, we could have been staying up here laying on these chumps. If they don't come out in an hour, we're going to Onyx, and we'll catch them first thing in the morning. We know where they live and what they're driving."

"Yeah, Wee…" Dawud couldn't even get the rest of Weezy's name out before the AK-47 shells ripped through him.

Blap…Blap…Blap…Blap!

The sound of the automatic rifle filled the air as its triggerman riddled the car, hitting Weezy and Dawud inside.

"Who the fuck y'all niggas thought y'all were following," Raheem spat, as he closed the sliding door on the minivan Nino was driving.

"Damn, them little niggas didn't stand a chance dog."

Nino calmly pulled off and headed to the apartment they had in Jenkintown to switch out the van and get another car. The car they left near the murder scene would have to stay there for a couple of days.

"Them little niggas were so busy watching the car we pulled up in that they never noticed us creeping up behind them in the van. They probably thought we went in them lame-ass apartments."

Raheem paused for a moment then became even more upset. He felt somewhat disrespected and underestimated.

"How the hell could Ducky, Shaahir, Teddy, Bingo, or whoever the fuck sent these niggas think that some nut-ass amateurs like that could take us out?"

Raheem laughed then took a sniff of the coke he pulled out of his top pocket.

"Fuck 'em! It's me and you against the world," Nino said, reaching for the bag of coke, as they heard all sorts of sirens in the background going toward the two bodies they left behind.

Chapter 10

No one knew exactly what happened with Weezy and Dawud, but Shaahir knew it had Raheem written all over it. When the young girl described the features of the guy shooting out of the van, Shaahir knew it was Raheem. Raheem and Nino had parked under her window and then ran through the parking lot of the complex to get the van. She saw Weezy and Dawud parked behind the car that Raheem and Nino exited.

She was being newsy; she look out the window when the van crept up with the doors open and noticed Raheem holding a big-ass gun. When the police came, she told them that she didn't see anything. But when she found out that it was Weezy and Dawud, she called her girlfriend, Penny, and told her that she needed to talk to Shaahir.

Penny was one of Shaahir's chicks, so she got him right on the phone. Shaahir has been on tilt ever since. He only told Ducky, Micky, and Toot about the information he received. He promised himself that he would be the one to kill Raheem. Weezy was his man, but Dawud was really like a little brother to him.

Weezy had a Christian funeral. Everyone came out to see him off. Shaahir had to beg Dawud's mom not to have his funeral in a church. Dawud's mom was Christian, and she didn't understand Islam; but she knew Dawud was Muslim and that he would have preferred to be buried islamically, so she let Shaahir set everything up for Dawud to have a *Jannazza* (Muslim funeral).

Shaahir paid for everything. He personally prepared Dawud's body by cleaning him and wrapping him in a shroud. All the Muslims were there as well as the non-Muslims.

Champ and Wanna attended the funeral. Even though they didn't know him personally, they were there for Shaahir; plus it was obligatory for the Muslims to go to the *Jannazza* of their fellow Muslims if they were able.

It'd been a week and Shaahir still couldn't shake the sight of Dawud's dead body. He'd been up each and every night trying to catch up with Raheem, but he couldn't seem to do it. He was about to meet up with Micky and Toot, so they could all exchange some information about Raheem and Nino. Shaahir pulled up to Champions breakfast store where Micky and Toot were already waiting for him in Toot's truck. When Shaahir walked up, they all shook hands, said their what's ups, and walked into the store. They were seated in the back booth where Champ normally held his meetings.

"What's up Shaahir? Are you good?" Micky asked, knowing how much he loved Dawud.

"Naw, Micky Mouse. This one here is a hard pill to swallow. That faggot-ass nigga Raheem killed Uzi-Boop," Shaahir said, calling Dawud by the nickname he had given him years ago.

Micky could hear the hurt in Shaahir's voice.

"It's going to be all right, big homie. We're going to put the dirt on them niggas Raheem and pussy-ass Nino."

"Naw young bucks, I got to get this nigga. He's a little too experienced for y'all. I got the nigga though," Shaahir said, not knowing how much work Micky and Toot had put in at their young ages.

"Damn, I should have shot Raheem's ass when he smacked me that day. I really fucked with Weezy and Dawud," Toot said.

They were quiet when Gail approached their table to take their order.

"What's up Ms. Gail?"

"Hey sweetie, how have you been? What's up with Rhonda?" Gail said, shocked to see Micky there without Champ.

"Rhonda's fine and I'm okay," Micky said, smiling at Ms. Gail.

She took their orders and was gone.

"What do y'all got for me?" Shaahir asked, as soon as Gail left.

"Yo, the nigga Raheem might be sliding in and out of his grandmom's house down the Bottom on 38th and Wallace Street. We can't do him on Wallace Street because the whole hood knows us, and they'd be right in court like 'Him did it,' " Micky said jokingly, trying to lighten the mood.

Shaahir and Toot shared a light laugh at the joke.

"You might have to get some unfamiliar faces to come down and squat on that jawn to see if he slides through," Toot said.

"What's the address to the spot?" Shaahir asked, wide-eyed.

Micky slid him the address. They ate their food, shot the breeze for a little bit, and left. Shaahir decided to take a trip down the Bottom to see what was up. He was deep in thought when the phone rang. It was Champ checking on him

133

"*As Salaamu Alaikum*, brother Saleem."

"*Wa Liakum Salaam*, brother Shaahir. What's up with you?"

"I'm chilling. I'm just taking it one day at a time."

"That's what's up. I'm just checking on you. I would like to meet up with you tomorrow if you're not busy."

"Saleem, I'm never busy when it comes to you."

"Okay, how about around six p.m. at the *Masjid?*"

"That is cool."

"Okay, I'll see you there. *As Salaamu Alaikum.*"

"*Wa Laikum As Salaam*," Shaahir said, as he hung up the phone.

Shaahir slipped his Tupac *Machiavelli* CD in and drove down the Bottom. He parked at the top of Wallace Street, where he could see all the people running in and out of Raheem's grandmom's house. He sat in his car for about two hours, then left.

"I'll slide back down here tonight and see if I can catch that nigga," Shaahir said to himself, as he drove past Raheem's grandmom's house.

Toot and Micky had just finished counting and rubber banding their money so they could go meet Ducky at his apartment. Micky and Toot didn't give a fuck about the fact that Raheem has been tripping, but because of it, Ducky decided that the detail shop was not a safe meeting spot for business. Micky and Toot wanted to run across Raheem themselves, so they could air his ass out. Everybody was sleeping on Micky and Toot, but they had put a lot of work in within the last year. They moved smoothly, they always got the job done, and they never talked about it afterward.

"Yo, put the one-counters up while I go put these rubber bands in the drawer," Micky said, as he put the last

$10,000 in one of the three shopping bags they had the re-up money in.

"Alright Micky. Bring me some lotion to put on my hands," Toot said, unplugging both money counters.

"I got you," Micky said, disappearing into the bedroom.

They cleaned up their mess and went out to the car. Once they were in the car, Micky turned on the dome light switch, hit the break, and pushed the electronic window switch up to open the hydraulic stash box behind the back seat. Toot put the money in the stash box and Micky closed it back up. They always tried to use this Buick LaCrosse when they were transporting money and drugs because it had a safe hydraulic stash box that could only be detected if someone told the police it was there.

"Let's go meet Ducky, and when we get back and move the shit we got lined up, we are going to pay Nay a visit with her rat ass," Toot said, putting in Jay-Z's "Blue Magic" track off the *American Gangster* soundtrack. Micky pulled out of the garage and they were on their way to meet Ducky.

"Yo, what's up with you and Quiana? You know I don't get in your business, but she called Rhonda crying last night, and you stayed at the crib for the last three nights," Micky asked, trying his best not to offend his boy.

He knew that something had to be wrong because Toot had been spending every night at Quiana's house for a couple of months but was at the loft for the past three nights.

"Micky, I fucked up, main man. I had the bitch Muff sucking my dick in the bathroom when we were in the Crab House the other night, and I didn't notice that the bitch left her lipstick all over my dick. When I got home and got in bed, I didn't noticed the lipstick smeared all over my drawers. When Quiana got up for work that morning, she must have noticed it. She woke me up snapping, screaming, and crying," Toot said, still not believing how stupid he was for slipping like that.

"Damn Toot, that little, brown-skinned, bow-legged bitch. Muff, is bad, but she's not so bad that you fuck up with your girl," Micky said, looking into his rearview mirror.

"I know, but I was careless, so it's my fault, not Muff's."

"Toot, you're my brother and we are one and the same. I'd be a fake-ass nigga if I sat up here and told you that I'm any better than you. I fuck bitches and get my dick sucked just as much as you do. It comes with being in the game, but I always wear a condom, and I always make sure that there are no traces of another bitch on me when I go around Rhonda. Toot, I'm not risking her for none of these cum-dog bitches on the scene. I'm telling you because I love you, baby boy. Get Quiana back. and don't let these little tricks we be out here piping come between y'all again."

"You're right Micky. I'm going to get her back, but I'm going to give her some space right now."

"Whatever you do, Toot, don't wait too long," Micky said, now answering his phone which had been vibrating on his hip.

"Hello. Oh, I didn't look at the caller ID. What's up Unc? I miss you. Sure. What time? I'm with Toot. Okay, I'll holler at you tomorrow. One," Micky said into the phone, leaving Toot full of questions, listening and only able to hear Micky's side of the conversation.

"Who was that?"

"That was Champ. He said what's up, and he wants to meet up with us tomorrow."

"Damn, I miss Champ. That's the best thing that happened to us," Toot said, as Micky pulled into Ducky's driveway and called Ducky on the phone.

Ducky came down and let them pull into the underground garage connected to the complex by swiping his parking card across the scanner, causing the gate to open. They went up to Ducky's two bedroom, spacious, luxury apartment.

Ducky had a few chicks, but he didn't have a main girl. He had a different chick damn near every time they visited. Today's chick was about the baddest chick they had ever seen with Ducky. She was a mix of Korean and black. She was picture perfect lying across Ducky's white leather sofa. Her long, jet-black hair hung over the side of the couch. She had perfectly pedicured feet.

Ducky told her to go into the bedroom and finish watching the "Wendy Williams Show." She turned off the 56-inch flat screen mounted to the wall. When she got up to go to the bedroom, it became clear that she was by far the baddest bitch Ducky ever had. She stood about five two with perky breasts that stood up with perfect brown nipples teasingly showing through the pink, silk, YSL robe. When she walked to the bedroom, her perfect, apple-shaped ass swung from side to side damn near hypnotizing all three men.

"Damn, y'all young niggas don't know nothing about that," Ducky said, as the door closed.

"You got one right there, Ducky. What's her name?" Micky asked, still looking at the closed door as if he were hoping she would reappear.

"That's the bitch, Shaletta, from Bristol. She don't hang out much, so you niggas won't know her," Ducky said, grabbing a duffle bag from the closet.

"I knew that I knew her from somewhere. Tuffy brought her and about six other chicks to a barbeque that Omar had out in the park," Micky said, never forgetting a face.

"Damn, Tuffy had her?"

"Naw, I didn't say that. She was actually chilling. Tuffy was hugged up with the real light-skinned one with the long hair," Micky said, not wanting Ducky to mix up what he was saying.

"Oh, because you know Tuffy and that horny nigga Omar be trying to get at every chick."

"Nigga, stop bitching. You told me you was a super-player," Toot finally spoke up.

"Naw Tiz-zoot, I'm thinking about marrying this one. Not no rings and shit, just a personal chick to call mines and fall back off of all these other bitches for a while. But I got to make sure that I'm the first boss who ever had the chick in Philly."

"Not you, pliz-zayer," Micky said, using the same Philly slang that Ducky used.

"Yeah man," Ducky said, stacking the bricks on the table.

"When are you getting some more work?" Micky said, knowing that forty bricks wasn't going to last him long.

"In a few days I'll park a car outside your loft with a hundred bricks in it, and I'll give you a call once it's here," Ducky said, as Micky and Toot began placing the bricks back in the bag.

"Yo, what's up with Raheem? Have you heard from him?" Micky said, once they were ready to leave.

"Naw, dude is a nut and he's tripping. I know it was his hating ass that set the detail shop on fire, too."

"Ducky, we got to track that nigga down."

"Micky, you and Toot stay away from that nigga. He's too much for y'all to handle. I got somebody on it."

"Okay, but y'all need to handle that nigga fast then," Micky said, leaving and knowing that he and Toot were more capable of handling Raheem than anybody.

Once they secured the bricks in the stash box, they pulled off en route to handle their business.

"Yo, we got to bust this nigga's ass as soon as possible because he's on some bullshit that will get in the way of us getting this paper," Micky said, thinking about what could have possibly made Raheem go left-field on their crew.

"After we put this bitch Nay down, we can start on the faggot niggas Raheem and Nino," Toot said, as his phone rang.

"Yo, what's up with you? I'll meet up with you in a few. Maybe around seven thirty," Toot said into the phone.

"Who was that?"

"That was Nay crab-ass. She's on some fishy shit," Toot said, as Micky jumped on the expressway.

"We got to get this dusty bitch out of your hair," Micky said, as he turned up the radio.

~~~~~

Raheem and Nino had been partying Nay on the regular. Whoever was up to it, would fuck her first. Sometimes they would fuck her together. They would get high, party, and fuck all day, every day.

139

They had their money up, but they had to find a new town or new section of the city to get money in because Ducky, Shaahir, and Teddy had all of Raheem and Nino's blocks robbed, shot up, and shut down. Their workers, or anyone believed to be a customer of theirs, caught hell. There was a lot of gunplay, which, in turn, drew a lot of heat. They had their stash apartments, but they stayed over Nay's house most of the time. Raheem was down the Bottom plotting on one of Ducky's old cribs, while Nino was at the crib with Nay.

"Pass the bag," Nay said to Nino, referring the bag of coke out of which Nino was snorting.

"Here," Nino said, passing the bag to her and watching her as she snorted the coke.

"What's up with the nigga Toot? Is he going to bring some coke with him when he comes?"

"I don't think so. I told him I had somebody that wanted to get something, and he cut me off saying he'll meet me face to face. You know how y'all niggas are about talking on the phone when y'all think y'all are on baller status," Nay said, half regretting trying to set Toot up to get robbed instead of setting him up with Detective Hutson like she first intended to do.

"Yo, after you finish that bag, let me get some of that big, pink pussy," Nino said, feeling horny and high as shit.

"Daddy, as soon as I finish, I want to suck that dick," Nay said, getting amped and horny as well off the raw powder.

Between her, Raheem, and Nino, there were several STD's being passed around. Because of constantly getting high and the trifling lifestyle that came with being a functional junkie, none of them bothered to go to the clinic.

"How long do we got before Toot's little, punk ass comes to meet you? I hope you told him to come alone, so I can kidnap his little, punk ass."

"We got about an hour before he comes, and he knows not to bring nobody to my house."

"Yo, I'm going to hide in the bedroom. As soon you get him on this couch facing the opposite direction, I'm going to creep up behind the little nigga and bust him in his motherfucking head with this gun. I'm going to make the little nigga see stars, and I'm not talking about TV stars."

"That's right daddy, make his punk ass see stars," Nay said, dick-riding as usual.

She finished the last of the coke she was snorting and turned up the music. Maxwell's "Pretty Wings" came bombing out of the speakers.

"Ahh, that's my shit, girl. Flap them pretty wings," Nino said with a chuckle, causing Nay to put on a performance.

She started singing and undressing like a stripper grinding her hips. To any real player, she was a major turn off; but Nino was high off the coke and horny as hell, so Nay looked like a bad bitch. Nay grabbed Nino's little dick, lifted it up, and started licking his balls gently, causing Nino to grab onto the bed. She licked all over his balls, giving him a tingling sensation and making his toes curl.

"Damn bitch, I love this dick-suck."

Nay remained quiet and began deep-throating Nino's whole dick. After about ten minutes, he exploded his load into her mouth. She sucked every bit of it off his dick.

Because of the coke, his dick remained hard. He laid
Nay on her back and spread her big, pink pussy open with
his fingers. He had become so accustomed to the scent of
her trifling house and body odor that the dead fish smell
of her pussy didn't turn him off. Nino slid his dick in
Nay's wet pussy and started pumping fast. Every time he
tried to long-dick her with his little dick, it slipped out, so
she grabbed his ass cheeks and held him steady up in her.
He was pumping as hard as he could.

"You like this big dick, don't you, bitch," he said,
between clenched teeth, knowing that Nay loved to be
called all types of bitches when she was being fucked.

"Yes daddy, I love this big dick. I want to cum all
over this dick."

"Yeah bitch. Well, cum on this dick. Tell me this dick
is better than Raheem's. Tell me, bitch," Nino said, hatin'
on his homie as always when Raheem wasn't around.

"Oww daddy. This dick is better than Raheem's dirty
dick. This is the best dick I ever had," Nay said, lying
through her teeth, just wanting to get her nut off.

"Bitch, tell me I look better than Raheem."

"You know you look better than Raheem. Oww daddy,
I'm about to cum."

"Cum bitch, cum."

"Oowww!" Nay screamed, with both of her legs
trembling as she came all over Nino's dick.

Nino pumped harder and faster until he came.

"Ahhh bitch, this pussy is good."

"Daddy, this dick is good."

They laid in the bed for a few minutes, talking shit
before getting up to wash up. Nino went into his pants
pocket and got another bag of coke. He opened the bag

and snorted two lines before he passed the bag to Nay and disappeared into the bathroom.

Nay was snorting the coke and singing, waiting until Nino was finished in the bathroom before she went in to freshen up. In the middle of her singing and getting high, she heard a knock at her door. She looked at the clock.

"Toot won't be here for another forty-five minutes, so that damn Raheem is back. What do he think I gave his nut ass a set of keys for?" Nay said to herself, upset that the knock at the door disturbed her from her nose candy.

"Use your fucking keys, nigga," Nay said, swinging the door open.

Her jaw dropped and her eyes bulged out of her head, as she looked into the eyes of the man holding a gun with a hood draped over his head. Although the hood hid his face, his build and eyes were familiar. It was clear that she knew this man.

"To...Too...Too...Toot," she managed to get out, before the gunman raised the gun.

He shot her five times in the face and upper chest then fled. Nay dropped to the floor. When Nino heard the shots, he came running out of the bathroom. He grabbed his gun and ran into the living room only to see Nay on the floor leaking blood all over the carpet, dead as a doornail, with the door open. He closed the door before his instincts kicked in.

He knew that the neighbors probably heard the shots and that it would only be a matter of time before the police came knocking. He knew he couldn't explain the guns, coke, and a dead woman that he just fucked. He got his things together, grabbed Nay's car keys and was out.

He felt bad that Nay was dead and he had to leave her like that; but he also knew that by staying there he would be in a jam. He called Raheem and told him that it was urgent that he meet him at the crib in Jenkintown. Raheem could hear the urgency in Nino's voice, so he told him that he'd be right there.

Nino was trying to figure out what happened and who wanted to kill Nay in cold blood. He always ended up with one suspect, Toot; but he didn't think that Toot had the type of heart to kill in cold blood. Whoever did it, he vowed to go at him non-stop.

Chapter 11

Shaahir was tired of plotting against Raheem. It seemed like he had been looking for a ghost. Today was just like any other day; he spent hours riding around trying to catch up with Raheem. He pulled up and stopped in front of Raheem's grandmom's house. He double-parked, walked up the steps, and knocked on the door. A pretty, brown-skinned lady answered the door.

"Who is it?" she said, opening the door to see the most handsome stranger she had ever seen.

"It's Shawn. Is Raheem in?"

"No, Raheem has not been here in weeks. If you see him before we do, tell him that his grandmom needs a couple of dollars," the lady said, with her hands on her hips.

Shaahir could hear that the house was full of people, so he knew he couldn't force his way in.

"If I see the nigg…I mean, if I see him, who should I say told me that his grandmom needs a couple dollars?" Shaahir said, as he gained control of his anger.

"I'm his Aunt Jamillah."

"Tell Raheem I said to hold this."

Boom…Boom…Boom!

Shaahir shot Raheem's aunt, ran to his car, jumped in, and sped off. He drove onto the expressway and was Uptown before the law began to swarm around down the

Bottom. He didn't want to shoot a woman, knowing it went against his Islam and his gangster, but his patience was wearing thin. He wanted to get Raheem badly, and he hoped that this would flush him out.

Shaahir called Micky and Toot so they could meet him at Sea What It Is. He switched cars before driving around to the store to meet Micky and Toot. He went into the store and told his manager, who was just opening up for lunch, to send Micky and Toot straight back to his office when they arrived. He went into his office, turned on the news, and sipped on his coffee, which he grabbed from the Dunkin' Donuts. He turned the news up when they flashed a live scene of Raheem's grandmom's house with cops all around.

"Hi, this is Dan Quail. I'm live in Mantua at the scene of a shooting that happened just moments ago in broad daylight at this house on 38th and Wallace. The police are not commenting, but a couple of people who were in the house at the time of the shooting said that someone knocked on the door and fired shots at the woman who answered. It's still unclear whether it was an ex-lover of hers or someone with the wrong address. Whatever the case may be, we'll get to the bottom of it and get the news straight to our viewers. This is Dan Quail, and this has been an 'Eyewitness News' break."

Shaahir hit the mute button.

"Damn, I'm on some other shit, but fuck it. I got to get this faggot-ass nigga Raheem out from under the rock where he's been hiding," he said to himself.

Shaahir picked up his phone to call his man Shakour from Camden. Shakour was locked up in the feds with Shaahir. He came home last week and had been leaving voicemails on Shaahir's phone every day. He dialed the number. Shakour answered on the third ring.

"*As Salaamu Alaikum.*"

"*Wa Laikum Salaam*," Shaahir said, thinking of how Shakour tracked the nigga Sab down for him when Sab and Tone did that foul shit to Champ.

Although Shakour tried hard to distance himself from his birth name, Troy, the streets of Camden, New Jersey, never seemed to let him live it down. When he found out a nigga from Jersey hurt Shaahir's man, Champ, he got right on the phone, tracked the nigga down, and put Shaahir onto where the nigga Sab was staying. He even offered to have it taken care of, but Shaahir told him the family had to handle it because it was personal.

"What's up, beloved brother?" Shakour said, noticing Shaahir's voice.

"Aw man, you're what's up. I got your messages. I've been a little busy, but we can talk about it over dinner tonight if you're not busy," Shaahir said, not wanting Shakour to know that he was knee-deep in the streets again.

"Brother, I was starting to think that you didn't want to be bothered by your poor little brother from Camden," Shakour said with a chuckle.

"Stop that, brother. My love for you is pure. Pick a restaurant and I'll be there."

"How about T.G.I. Friday's on Route 38?"

"The little dusty jawn next the Loews movie theater in Cherry Hill?"

"Yup, that's the one. How about around eight p.m.?"

"I'll be there."

"I'll see your there. *As Salaamu Alaikum.*"

147

"*Wa Liakum Salaam,*" Shaahir responded, then hung up.

"Damn, talking to Shakour made me realized how far off track from my original plan I am. I was supposed to be in and out. I was supposed to make some real paper real fast and get out," Shaahir said to himself, looking in the mirror.

He knew that Shakour was firm about leaving the streets. Shakour had a lot of legitimate plans and enough New Jersey politicians in his pocket to make them come to life. He promised Shaahir he would pull him in on some very lucrative deals, but Shaahir had to promise him that he was done with the streets before Shakour would let him invest in anything. Shaahir replayed in his mind over and over again how he got so deep so fast until a knock at the door startled him.

"Who is it?"

"It's us, nigga," Micky yelled from the other side of the door.

Shaahir unlocked the door to let his little homie in.

"What's up, little niggas?" Shaahir said, as Micky and Toot walked in.

"Ain't shit but the same shit," Toot said, shaking Shaahir's hand.

"Still my peoples, though. Love when I see you, though," Micky said, as always to Shaahir, quoting the Young Guns.

"What's good with y'all? Do y'all want something to drink?"

"Naw, I'm good homie," said Micky.

"Me too."

Shaahir didn't want to beat around the bush, so he told them to have a seat and got right down to it.

"Yo, the nigga Raheem might come out of hiding, and I don't want y'all to be running around slipping while he tries some dumb shit with y'all. Ducky already knows what's up, so he'll be laying low. Y'all are the only two out and about, so I wanted to let y'all know to be on y'alls p's and q's," Shaahir said, looking from Micky to Toot; then from Toot to Micky.

"Man fuck Raheem. I'm dying to catch up with his bitch ass. I just told Ducky the other day that we're running around like he's got us shook and I'm not with that," Micky said, mad about all the hype around Raheem.

"I feel like you. Fuck him. I'm not shook, but the nigga is crafty. Besides, I was just putting y'all on point because somebody knocked on his grandma's door and shot his aunt," Shaahir said, not taking credit for his shooting.

"Damn, that will definitely bring a nigga out," Toot said, now going into Shaahir's refrigerator to get a Pepsi.

"Who told you that?" Micky asked, playing dumb, knowing damn well Shaahir used the address that he provided him.

"It was on the news."

"Oh, well fuck it. I guess it's on then," Micky said, wanting to get this nut shit over with.

"Yeah, fuck it. I can't wait to dump this clip in that nigga's face," Shaahir said, exposing the 40 caliber Smith & Wesson Sigma with the extended 17-shot clip hanging out of it on his waist.

"Yo, I don't know what got into Raheem," Micky said to no one in particular.

"Fuck what got into him. He better worry about what's going to go into him," Toot said, patting the gun under his shirt.

"Yo, I'm just putting y'all on point. I don't want y'all to try to fuck with Raheem. He's too advanced. I told Weezy and Dawud the same shit, but they were hardheaded. If they would have just called me instead of trying to handle this nigga by themselves, he would never have gotten a chance to pull that shit off on them," Shaahir said, saddened by the thought of Dawud and Weezy's murders.

"No disrespect big homie, but we are a little more advanced than Weezy and Dawud. Y'all giving this cokehead ass Raheem too much credit. I got to be honest, if I see him I will call you, but only after I air his punk ass out," Micky said, tired of being underestimated.

"Micky, I'm not going to go back and forth with you. I just need y'all to watch yourselves and to let me get at this nut-ass nigga.

"Cool, we'll watch ourselves," Micky said, ending the meeting and trying to get away from Shaahir, so he and Toot could put their game plan together.

"I'm not playing with y'all, Micky."

"We'll watch ourselves, big homie, you got my word. We'll give you a call later. We got some work to move," Micky said, shaking Shaahir's hand.

Toot followed suit, shaking Shaahir's hand before they left.

~~~~~

Bingo was really gearing up to step aside and let his little brother take over. Teddy had proven that he was more than capable of running a crew and dealing directly with the connect. Since Bingo only dealt with Teddy, life was so much easier, and he had more time on his hands to spend with his wife.

Aside from the bullshit that Nino and Raheem had been pulling, Bingo was at ease; and his operation with Teddy as the head of the crew was running smoothly. He had a meeting with Ducky and Teddy to let them know they were the ones responsible for handling Raheem and Nino. Although Ducky was Champ's main young boy and Bingo didn't have a business rapport with Ducky, Bingo watched as Ducky came up through the ranks. Besides, Bingo was Ducky's oldhead, too, because Champ and Bingo's crews were basically like family; so Bingo had the right to advise Ducky, and Ducky respected Bingo's advise.

Bingo was confident that Teddy and Ducky had the Raheem and Nino situation handled. He decided to fall back and watch how the two new bosses would handle the fact that their old friends were drawing on their business and showing them up in the street. His main focus was to see if Teddy could put his feelings for an old friend aside and handle his business. This would be the very thing that would insure him that he could leave the street shit to Teddy unsupervised. He lay in the bed with thoughts of how he would spend all his free time with his girl. His thoughts were interrupted by Thelma's loud coughing and gagging.

"Boo, are you okay?" he yelled from the bed.

"Yeah, I'm all right," Thelma said, as she opened the bathroom door.

"What, did you eat something bad? It sounded like you were throwing up."

"I was throwing up but I didn't eat anything bad. I can't keep anything down and my period is about a week late," Thelma said, rubbing her stomach, hoping that she was pregnant because she knew how badly Bingo wanted to have a child with her.

"Boo, stop playing like that. You're saying that because Wanna and Rhonda are pregnant, or did you really miss your period?" Bingo said wide-eyed and hyped.

"Baby, I wouldn't play like that, and the only thing I ate that was bad was this," Thelma said smiling, flopping down on the bed and grabbing Bingo's dick.

"Damn, I might be a daddy. Let's go get one of them home pregnancy tests from Rite Aid," Bingo said, his dick getting hard from Thelma's caresses.

"We'll go after you give me some of this dick daddy," Thelma said, as she began sucking his dick, which was fully erect and sticking through the slit in his drawers.

She was sucking his dick slowly and licking all around the head. After about seven minutes, she began sucking his dick longer and harder with a deep throat motion.

"Ah baby, this shit is the best," Bingo managed to say between clenched teeth and a shortage of breath.

Thelma was always turned on by sucking her husband's dick, but as of late, she'd been extra horny. While she continued sucking his dick, he started stroking her wet pussy with two fingers. Thelma turned her body slightly to give Bingo full access to her pussy as she continued to shove his dick deeper into her mouth. Bingo inserted his fingers deep inside her pussy. She was so wet that they glided right in. Her moans of pleasure made him continue to stroke her pussy faster and faster.

"Suck this dick mommy, I'm about to cum. Suck this dick," Bingo moaned, on the verge of cumming.

He released his load into Thelma's mouth as he continued stroking her pussy. She had an orgasm from the way he flicked his fingers inside her. As her juices dripped down his hand, she continued to suck and lick his dick until it was fully erect again. She pulled his fingers out of her pussy slowly before inserting them into her mouth. She seductively licked every drop of her juice from his fingers. She spread his fingers with her tongue and licked her moisture from between them. Bingo immediately imagined a fantasy of two women being together. His body shivered as Thelma murmured, "Uh-hum," because she knew exactly what her husband was thinking.

"Damn babe, you know I like that nasty shit."

Thelma lay on her back and opened her legs. She licked her lips and looked at her husband with eyes that begged him to fuck her. Bingo put the head of his dick in and out of her pussy teasingly at first. She craved his whole dick. She begged him to put it inside her. She was so eager that she took his ass cheeks and forced him inside of her. Her pussy began to explode around the shaft of his dick. Bingo long-dicked her to the point that her screams were louder than ever before. Her moaning and screaming stroked his ego and brought him to his climax.

"I'm cumming, mommy, I'm cumming!"

"Cum in this pussy, daddy, cum in this pussy," Thelma answered, as she straddled her legs around his waist, locking him inside of her warm pussy as she gyrated her ass.

She began shaking and cumming all over her husband's dick. They laid there with his dick still inside her, although it was now soft. They both dreaded having to get up and go to the store for a home pregnancy test, but their curiosity gave them the energy they needed to do it. They agreed that if she were pregnant, they wouldn't reveal it until the baby shower next week, which Sharon had arranged for Rhonda and Wanna. They drove to get the test and went back home to see if they had a bundle of joy on the way.

~~~~~

Raheem was furious that Shaahir shot his aunt in broad daylight. He didn't know for sure that it was Shaahir, but he knew that it came from Shaahir or Ducky, so he was going to get at both of them or whomever he could get to first in their crew. The pain of his aunt getting shot and the death of Nay caused him and Nino to start getting higher than they normally did. Although their relationship with Nay started off just getting high and fucking, after awhile Nay grew on them and basically became part of the crew. The only difference was that Nay had a pussy that both Raheem and Nino fucked sometimes together and at other times on the solo tip.

"Damn, these niggas don't know they crossed the line. I'm killing any of them pussies on sight," Raheem said to Nino, standing in the living room of their Jenkintown apartment with the whole duffle bag of guns he had taken from the stash house he shared with Ducky.

"Real rap, dawg. I'm fucked up about Nay. If they did that nut shit to her, I'm not sparing any of them niggas. I'm shooting young ones, old ones, bitches, and niggas, whoever, whatever," Nino said, doing what he did best, snorting coke.

"What the fuck do you mean, 'If'? You know like I know that little nigga, Toot, did that shit to Nay."

"Yeah, I know she was supposed to meet him, but I didn't see him pull the trigger and neither did you," Nino said, snorted out of his mind.

"Fuck them niggas. If I say they did it, then motherfucker, they did it. Fuck all of them pussies. It's on," Raheem said, reaching for the bag of coke Nino was snorting from.

"Nigga, what the fuck are you getting mad and yelling at me for? I'm with you. Let's go put this work in now if you feel that way, my nigga," Nino said, car keys in hand, tired of all the pre-hyped shit Raheem was going through.

"First let's stop by to see Ms. Bernadette so I can check on her. I have to give her some money so Smoking Jay can move Nay's shit out of her apartment."

"Alright my nigga. We got to get at these niggas and go to that 'quiet town and tie it down,' " Nino said, quoting Beanie Sigel's rap.

They left the crib and drove down to Ms. Bernadette's. Nino parked at the top of the block. They both got out and walked down the street to the house. They could see the door was open as they walked up the steps. To their surprise, Detectives Starks and Hutson came walking out.

"Ms. Bernadette, give us a call if your hear anything," Detective Hutson said as he walked out, not noticing Nino and Raheem.

Ms. Bernadette closed the door just as Hutson reached the bottom of the steps. Starks went right into action and began fucking with Raheem and Nino.

"Goddamn, you motherfuckers ain't dead yet?" Starks said with a smirk.

"Dead? I think y'all will check out before us," Nino said, showing no fear of the two detectives who have picked on him for the majority of his life.

"Yeah, well, word is that y'all only have about a week to live. We have some of the most reliable rats in the world, and they told us that Ducky, Champ, Bingo, and Teddy are very displeased with you two maggots," Hutson butt in.

"Yeah, well tell your rats to tell all them punk-ass niggas that we said to kiss our asses after we take a shit. Now, if y'all don't mind, we got to go," Raheem said, as he walked up the steps toward Ms. Bernadette's door.

"I hope y'all don't think we're going to investigate your murders if you end up dead," Starks said, irritated by Raheem's last statement.

"Y'all don't never get shit right anyway, so if we die let our murders be because I'm sure you'll have the wrong nigga locked up for it," Raheem said, as he began knocking.

"Hey Hutson, lets leave Champ and Bingo's kids alone for now. We'll catch them slipping then we'll book 'em. Bye-bye bitches," Starks said, pulling his partner away as Ms. Bernadette opened the door.

Raheem and Nino were so mad that they almost forgot the two were cops.

"Hey fellas," Ms. Bernadette said, breaking their train of thought and letting them into the house.

Ms. Bernadette had become familiar with them because Nay had frequently invited them over.

"Ms. Bernadette, are you okay?" Raheem asked, as they sat down on her couch.

"I'm okay. You boys need to be careful though. Them police just left here asking a ton of questions about you guys, Toot, and the rest of the neighborhood guys whose names I can't quite remember but whose faces I know."

"Yeah, they're always running around harassing people," Nino said.

"Did they have pictures?" Raheem interrupted.

"Yeah, they had a big old book full of pictures. They said my Nay was at the wrong spot at the wrong time and that it was a hit for one of you two that went bad," Ms. Bernadette said, her eyes welling with tears at the mention of Nay's name.

"I don't know what they're talking about, but I do know they are full of crap. Them cops is always trying to stir something up," Nino said in a hateful tone.

"I just want you boys to be careful. Let the police handle their job, and the Lord will work everything out."

"Ms. Bernadette, we'll leave it all up to the Lord," Raheem said, as he dug in his pocket. "Here's the money and we'll see you later."

Raheem knew damn well he didn't believe in God; he just wanted to get out of there, especially after eyeing the baby shower invitation Sharon had left. Ms. Bernadette took the money, and they said their good-byes.

Once inside the car, Nino went straight for the bag of coke stashed in the ashtray. He took the first snorts while Raheem drove. Raheem took his snorts at stop signs and red lights.

"Damn my nigga, this shit is getting crazy. The rats done put Starsky and Hutch on us. How the fuck did them peckerwood-ass cops know all that shit they were saying?" Nino said, ready to get this street shit over with before the cops closed in on them.

"They know the same shit that the streets know and that is that we don't fuck with our old crews no more. They got that from the rats, but just like the rats, they don't know any details," Raheem said, hitting the coke.

"You're right, but I don't trust Starsky and Hutch."

"That's why we got to handle this shit and keep it moving," Raheem said, thinking of how sweet the invitation that Ms. Bernadette had on her table made his job.

"What's up with Ms. Bernadette? Do you think she said anything about us to the police?" Nino asked, now buzzed off the coke.

"No, I don't think she said anything about us because the old, horse-faced bitch don't know shit about us."

"Oh, because we can shoot her old ass, too," Nino said, looking spaced out with his wide-open eyes.

"Man, let's get at these niggas and then go get at this paper."

"Okay my nigga. Where are we going now?"

"We're going past Shaahir's Sea What It Is to see what it is," Raheem said with a wicked smile.

They drove Uptown to the seafood store. It was crowded out front, but there was no sign of Shaahir or anyone from Ducky or Teddy's crews. Raheem told Nino to get behind the wheel and drive back by the store slowly. When Nino pulled up, Raheem leaned out the window with his Baby A-R and shot the store up including any of its customers he could hit. At the sound of the gunshots and the glass windows breaking, people started running and screaming in panic. A few people were hit, which meant Shaahir's business would get a whole lot of unwanted police attention. Raheem got his message across; it's on.

Chapter 12

Micky and Toot were on point. They weren't scared of Raheem or Nino, but they respected their gangster. They knew if they were caught slipping, it could cost them their lives. Raheem and Nino weren't like the other niggas they had put work in on in the past. Everyone in Ducky and Teddy's cliques knew when Raheem was on his war shit he was hard to handle. They also knew that Nino would only add to Raheem's arsenal.

Shaahir, Ducky, and Teddy had a meeting about Raheem and Nino the day Shaahir's store was shot up. After the meeting, Ducky called Micky and Toot to tell them to stay off the streets until Raheem and Nino were handled. Micky let Ducky say all he had to say without interrupting him.

Once Ducky was finished, Micky looked him in the eye and said, "Nigga, I'm Little Ern. Ern's blood runs through me. Fuck Raheem and bitch-ass Nino. Y'all got me fucked up if y'all think I'm hiding from them or any other nigga. In fact, I'm dying to see both of them cocksuckers."

Ducky was shocked by Micky's words, but he could hear the reality booming through his voice and respected where Micky was coming from. He even began to believe that Micky and Toot could handle Raheem and Nino. Everybody from both cliques knew it would get worse before it got better. There was no talking it out. Somebody had to die.

Micky wasn't trying to convince Ducky that he and Toot could handle the beef with Raheem and Nino; he just decided to try to catch up with the niggas on his own time. He made Rhonda move in with his mom until he could find them a home. He knew Raheem knew about the loft, so it was best that he move Rhonda in with his mom and abandon the loft. Although neither Raheem nor Nino made any threat toward Micky, the fact that they were beefing with Ducky and Shaahir made it his beef as well.

"Damn Micky, these niggas won't let us chill and just get this paper without all the bullshit," Toot said, driving his truck back from Delaware.

They went to get the last of Rhonda's clothes from the loft and take them to Sharon's house.

"Toot, all of this shit comes with the lifestyle we chose. It is what it is," Micky said, as he leaned back in the passenger seat.

"I just want to get this shit over and go back to this paper and the little dick-suckers that be screaming our names," Toot said, getting off at the Island Avenue exit.

"Yeah little nigga. I've been making you look good out here with these little hoes," Micky said, joking with Toot.

Toot was really like a brother to Micky.

"Nigga, I be putting you on the hoes," Toot protested, smiling and thinking about all the little chicks they fucked.

"Yeah main man, we got to handle these niggas and get back to doing us."

"What do you think Champ would have done in this situation?"

"I think he would have put Ducky and Raheem on it. The only problem is that we don't have Champ and Raheem is the problem. Ducky's the new Champ, but he don't have that swag like Champ. Unc always made the most complicated situation look simple," Micky said, thinking of how good shit was when Champ was running the show.

"Yeah, I agree. Champ was the poster child for solving problems. I miss Unc myself. When we talked to him the other day I thought it was going to be about what's going on in the street; but he talked about everything but the street stuff," Toot said, thinking back on the meeting they had with Champ a few days back.

"Yeah, he had me fooled, too. I thought he was going to be on some wanting to hear what was happening in the streets type stuff; but every time I tried to bait him into asking me what was happening in the streets, he brushed it off."

"Yeah, Micky, Unc is really into his Islam."

"I know Toot, but Shaahir knows more about that religion than him, and Shaahir is not so hard on himself that he isn't still out here getting this money."

"Micky, I don't know enough about Islam to speak on it. I just miss Unc in these streets with us."

"I don't know enough to speak on it either, and I miss Unc too. It seems like Raheem and Nino got Ducky, Shaahir, and Teddy a little shook. I know all of them bust their guns, but they know how crazy and retarded Raheem can get; so it seems like they are being extra careful with this nigga," Micky said, speaking his mind to Toot, knowing that it wouldn't go any further than the two of them.

"Damn Micky, I didn't want it to seem like I thought they were bitching, but I was thinking the same thing. They all talking about they got people on it and shit. How long does it take to get at these two clowns? Shaahir got Weezy and Dawud popped messing with these two niggas," Toot said with anger in his voice, feeling as though Shaahir didn't move out for Weezy and Dawud like he should have.

"Toot, to be honest, I think they are just hoping that this will all go away. Baby boy, at the end of the day, we're all we got to handle this. I know these niggas ain't sweet, but I'm dying to see them. I'm tired of looking for them. When we locate these niggas, we're rocking out," Micky said with most serous tone of voice he could muster.

"I'm with you, as I've always been," was all Toot said.

They drove in silence for a while. They were both caught up with thoughts of how badly they wanted Raheem and Nino.

"What's up with Quiana? Have you talked to her?" Micky said, out of the blue, breaking Toot's thoughts of murder.

"Yeah, we talk here and there, but she won't let that shit go about the lipstick on my drawers," Toot said, thinking of how Quiana constantly brings up the incident, and how she breaks down crying about it.

"Toot, just give her some time and space and everything will be good."

"Man, all of this emotional shit is new to me. Sometimes when she starts that crying shit, I be ready to tell her fuck it and call it quits. I know I fucked up, but damn, if you're going to go, just go; and if your going to stay, let that shit rest," Toot said, meaning every word.

"Like I said, give her time. That bitch Muff knew what she was doing when she left all that lipstick on your drawers."

"I'll give it a little more time, but if she keeps pushing, I'm letting that shit go. As far as Muff's dusty ass goes, I don't even answer the phone for her anymore," Toot said, as they pulled up to 63rd and Vine Street and parked.

"Let me call this nigga so he can let us in through the garage," Micky said, dialing Ducky's cell number.

"Hello. Where are y'all at?" Ducky asked.

"We're out back. Open the garage, nigga," Micky said, hanging up before Ducky could respond.

Three minutes later, the garage door opened. They pulled in with the roof of the truck looking as if it would scrape the ceiling of the garage. Once they were in, Ducky hit the automatic garage button to close the door. When Toot and Micky got out of the truck, they could see that the truck had more than enough clearance from the ceiling.

"What's up, little niggas," Ducky said, shaking both men's hands.

After brief what's ups and hand shakes, they all went through the door that led to the basement and upstairs, which led them into Ducky's decked-out crib. Ducky learned about moving around in different cribs from Champ. Champ used to work out of several different cribs to keep stick-up kids and cops off balance. He always told Ducky that 'playing sitting duck will get a nigga stuck.' "

Ducky, just like anyone else who was around Champ, always took Champ's advice because Champ was, hands down, the smartest nigga they had ever seen play the game. Ducky had to admit that even the little piece of game Champ gave him about keeping it moving turned out to be a jewel; especially after Raheem broke into or firebombed all the cribs he knew Ducky either stayed in or worked out of. It didn't hurt Ducky's movement, though, because he had abandoned those spots once he realized Raheem was on some bullshit. He was working out of and staying in about four new spots Raheem knew nothing about.

"Damn Ducky, this little jawn is decked out. We got to party some hoes up in this jawn," Toot said, looking around at the newly shellacked hardwood floors throughout the living room and dining room.

A big, remote-controlled fireplace and 60-inch flat TV were built into the wall. A fish tank was neatly placed under the TV and built into the wall as well. The walls were painted a high-gloss tan. He had chocolate brown vertical blinds with tan Louis Vuitton LVs all over them. To top it off, he had a couch, love seat, and chair all in chocolate brown leather with the same tan LVs all over them.

"After we work out of here and I'm ready to move, y'all can bring all the freaks y'all want up in this jawn," Ducky stated, opening a big box on the floor and exposing the bricks he had for them.

"Nigga, you shouldn't want no freaks right now anyway after that bitch Muff left that lipstick on your drawers for your girl to find," Micky announced, pushing Toot in the back of the head playfully.

"Oh shit, you let a bitch get you with that lipstick on the drawers shit? Man, that's the oldest trick in the book," Ducky countered, laughing and enjoying the company of his two favorite youngins.

"Damn Micky, how you just going to put me out there like that? If Ducky wasn't family, you would have to box me for that," Toot said, laughing and swinging a bullshit combination of punches in the air.

"I'm just fucking with you, but Ducky's on some real shit. Where did you get this Louis furniture?" Micky asked, walking over to feel the leather couch.

"Man, the nigga Tuffy got Dapper Dan in his pocket. You know Tuffy is my boy, and he put me right in with Dap. If you want some shit done, we can ride right up New York and Dap will freak you some fly shit out. Dap is on some underground shit now because the feds tried to run down on him."

"When I'm ready, I'll let you know. I'm about to buy Rhonda a big crib, and I think I'll get tan blinds with dark brown LVs instead of the brown with the tan LVs and the tan leather furniture with the brown LVs."

"Micky, the nigga can do whatever."

"Fuck all of these couches and cute blinds. How much work do you have for us?" Toot said, cutting Ducky and Micky's conversation short.

"Nigga, I got a hundred for y'all," Ducky said, opening the flaps of the box so they could see the bricks.

"This nigga is hostile because he's in the doghouse," Micky said, causing Toot to smile and Ducky to burst out laughing.

"It's twenty-five bricks in each box," Ducky said, still laughing.

"Damn, that shit wasn't that funny Ducky."

"Yes it was Toot," Ducky said, closing the box.

"Yo, on a serous note, what's up with Tuffy? Did he say if he seen Raheem's bitch ass? You know Tuffy got a baby by Raheem's cousin Danielle," Micky said, getting serious.

"Micky, Tuffy is on deck with us. Me and Tuffy have a twenty-year friendship. He will kill Raheem and Danielle if it comes down to it. Raheem knows my relationship with Tuffy, so he won't contact Danielle. Tuffy got Danielle to call him a hundred times, and he won't answer; but Tuffy got his eyes open, and if he sees him, I know he'll handle Raheem on the spot."

"Okay Ducky, I just want to get this Raheem shit over so we can all rest easy and get this bread," Micky said, grabbing one of the boxes.

They all carried a box down to the truck. While Micky and Toot unloaded the bricks from the boxes and placed them in the stash box, Ducky ran upstairs and got the other box of twenty-five bricks for them. They all shook hands and promised to hook up later.

~~~~~

Detectives Starks and Hutson were getting a bit frustrated trying to sort out what seemed to be a drug war between old comrades. The loss of their closest informant was a real blow to their investigation.

Nay wasn't only vital in pinpointing what side of the drug war each dealer was on, but she also gave the detectives tips on who was dealing, where they were dealing, and whom they were dealing with. She had just started giving up info on her two closest friends, Nino and Raheem, around the time she died. She told the detectives about the drugs Nino and Raheem had stashed from the robbery they pulled off on Teddy.

The detectives now wished they had moved on her tip, but they were more concerned about the murders surrounding the crews. Because of these, they put the drug busts on the back burner. Besides, the chances of Raheem and Nino still having the drugs stashed in her apartment were slim to none. Plus, when the detectives went past there the night of the Nay's murder, they searched her house inside and out, and all they came up with were sandwich bags and a digital scale.

With the help of Nay and a few other rats the detectives had, they were able to put a chart together. It was labeled the Mantua Murder for Drug Proceeds Chart. The chart was almost accurate with the exception of two or three flaws. They were misinformed by their informants about Champ still running his former crew. They had Champ at the head of the chart as the boss with Ducky, Shaahir, Micky, and Toot under him. They had Bingo at the top of his crew with a picture of Teddy, Shiz, and Malik under him. The rats had no idea that Bingo didn't even know Shiz and Malik. They were Teddy's homies and muscle. The detectives also had Raheem and Nino as ex-crewmembers of each crew who turned into murder targets after messing up package money.

The rats almost got it right, but they were off on a few points which made putting the puzzle together a little stressful. Whenever the detectives were fortunate enough to get any surveillance on any crewmember from either crew, there was never any surveillance on Champ or Bingo. Phone records showed little or no correspondence from the two supposed bosses. Whenever they tailed Champ, it was to the Masjid or a construction site of some sort of business. Otherwise, they followed him out to eat with his wife and back to his crib.

Bingo was likewise tailed to a few business meetings and to his legit businesses. They had phone recordings of Bingo calling Teddy and Teddy calling Bingo, but there was no crime in two brothers calling to meet or check on each other. They came to the conclusion that the only way to get an indictment or an arrest on any of the crewmembers was to catch somebody slipping and try to make them do what niggas that don't want to go to jail do, snitch.

"Damn, these donuts are stale as shit," Starks said, parked in front of Albert Einstein Hospital.

They were waiting for Shaahir. Shaahir had been back and forth to the hospital checking on his store manager who was shot in the drive-by shooting at the seafood store. She was in stable condition. Shaahir came by regularly to bring her food and gifts.

"I told you to stop at Dunkin' Donuts on Fifth and Rockland, but you said the Chinese store on Broad and Olney got the best coffee. You forgot to say they had the hardest donuts on the east coast," Hutson said, tapping the hard glazed donut on the dashboard and smiling.

"Yeah, I fucked up on this one."

Before they could say anything else, Shaahir came out of the hospital entrance. They got quiet enough to hear a pin drop. The detectives watched as Shaahir gave the parking attendant his valet parking ticket. When the valet returned to the entrance with Shaahir's black Cadillac DST rental, Shaahir pulled off.

Starks followed him. He let Shaahir get about four blocks away before he put on his flashing light. They weren't intending to charge Shaahir with anything because they didn't have anything on him. They just wanted to pull him over, search his car, and shake him up. They hoped to find a gun or some drugs in the process, but if they didn't find anything, they would just be content with letting him feel their presence.

Once Shaahir saw the flashing light, he pulled over to the side of the road. Although he wasn't riding dirty, he was as shaken as any other hood nigga was when being pulled over by the cops. He didn't feel like dealing with all the bullshit.

Once he parked the car, the detectives got out and walked toward him. Starks approached the driver's side of the car from the street and Hutson walked on the pavement approaching the passenger side. Shaahir rolled down the window to see what the cops wanted.

"May I help you officer?" Shaahir said in his calmest tone.

"Yeah, license, insurance, and registration, and don't make any sudden moves," Starks said with his right hand on his gun.

Shaahir complied being sure to keep his hands in sight of the detectives. He handed Starks the paperwork and his license. Starks and Hutson took the paperwork back to their car as if they were going to run his paperwork. They waited a few minutes then walked back to Shaahir's car.

"Step out of the car, please," Starks said, with his gun drawn.

Shaahir got out of the car.

"What is this about?" he asked.

"Your car was reported in a shooting," Hutson butt in, lying through his teeth.

"A shooting?" Shaahir said, thinking there had to be a mix up. "I just left the hospital."

"Okay, sit in the back of our car, and if we search your car and there's nothing in it, you'll be free to go," Starks said, opening the back door of their unmarked car for Shaahir to get in before they searched his car.

Shaahir didn't resist because he knew he didn't have anything in his car. The cops searched his car as newsy bystanders looked on. After about a half hour of tearing up his car, the two asshole detectives let him go; but not before letting him know that they knew who he was and that they had heard of his involvement in the drug game.

"Damn, them cops are dickheads. Who the fuck is screaming my name in the streets? I got to tighten the fuck up. I need to kill Raheem and Nino's punk asses, get this money back straight, and get back to going to the Masjid," Shaahir said to himself.

He would go to *Jumu'ah* on some Fridays, but for the most part, he would stay away from the Masjid as of late. He felt guilty when he was around the Muslims who were really practicing the religion appropriately. He even stood Shakur up at T.G.I. Friday's because he knew Shakur was sincere about not messing with the streets. He knew that although Shakur was too modest to grind him up about playing in the streets, he would still see right through him. The streets tore Shaahir from his righteousness. He only felt good around the thugs and dealers as of late, but he had been trying to fight his demons and being confronted by Starsky and Hutch was even more of a wake-up call.

Chapter 13

Teddy was going to make his runs early. He had to meet Bingo to talk about some business, and he had to go meet his homies, Shiz and Malik, down 23rd and Jefferson Street at Blumberg Projects to take them some work and discuss Raheem and Nino's whereabouts. He also, like everybody else from their crew, had to go pick up some things for Rhonda and Wanna's baby shower.

It had been a stressful couple of months for Teddy just as it had been for everyone else. Teddy couldn't believe the nerve of Nino or Raheem. Raheem acting like a nut made Teddy mad; but Nino acting like nut hurt his heart. It was the ultimate betrayal, and he was dying to make Nino suffer. The fact that he always looked out for Nino made it hard for him to comprehend why Nino would turn his back on him. Teddy even paid for Nino's mother's funeral when Nino was a broke, little dirtball without a dime to his name. Teddy always made sure when he ate, Nino ate. Now that Nino betrayed him, all of his love turned to hate, and he wanted Nino dead. He daydreamed about how he would punish Nino when he caught up to him.

He was caught in his thoughts as he drove to Bingo's house when his phone rang. It actually startled him because he was driving without the music on.

"Yizzo," he said into the phone, as he stopped at a red light.

"Yo, pull over so I can holler at you," the familiar voice boomed through the phone.

Teddy pulled over and hopped out of the car. Micky and Toot hopped out of their truck. They all shook hands and said their what's ups. While Micky and Teddy stood on the corner and kicked it, Toot went into the store.

"Damn, I'm up early so I can get all of my business wrapped up and go to the mall to get some things for Rhonda and Wanna's baby shower," Teddy said, pulling out his pack of Newports and putting a cigarette in his mouth.

"That's what's up, Teddy. I appreciate that, but I called you and told you to pull over because I seen you drive by Lancaster Avenue and I busted a U-turn. I tailed you for five blocks before I called you and told you to pull over. Teddy you got to be on point while Raheem and Nino are on the prowl."

"Damn Micky, I was thinking about how dirty I want to do them pussies, so I wasn't thinking about being on point and watching out my rearview mirror," Teddy said, lighting his Newport.

"You know we're not dealing with no chumps, so one slip-up might be your last slip-up," Micky said naturally, sounding like Champ.

Teddy knew Micky was right, and despite the fact that Micky was younger than him, he respected Micky as a thinker.

"You're right, and I'm going to tighten up," Teddy said, blowing O's of cigarette smoke out of his mouth.

"Okay, I'll see you tonight at the baby shower."

They both shook hands.

Micky sat in the truck and waited for Toot to come out of the store so they could go get at their paper for today. Teddy drove over to Bingo's crib thinking of how smooth Micky was and how much his style resembled Champ's. It seemed like Micky grew up overnight, and it was easy to see that he had Ern's blood flowing through him by the way he moved and by how much swagger he had.

As Teddy pulled within three blocks of Bingo's house, he was really on point looking through his rearview mirror to be sure he wasn't being followed. He pulled onto Bingo's block, which sat in the back of Street Road in Bensalem.

Bingo lived in a ranch-style, single house. He bought it when he sold the pool hall and the tire shop. The only people that had been to his new crib besides Teddy were Champ and Wanna. Thelma had cooked a big meal there for Champ and Wanna because she wanted to show her appreciation for all that they did for her and Bingo when Bingo got booked by the feds.

Teddy pulled into the driveway. He called Bingo so Bingo could put his two filas out in the backyard before opening the door.

"Yizzo, put the big-ass dogs in the yard and come open the door," Teddy said, and hung up the phone without waiting for a response.

Seven minutes later, Bingo appeared in the doorway. Teddy got out of the car and followed Bingo into the house.

"Damn, Sis is making me want to move in," Teddy said jokingly, once he smelled the breakfast food Thelma was cooking.

"Nigga, your hungry ass ain't moving in here," Bingo said playfully, mugging his younger brother in the head.

"Sis, can I get a plate," Teddy yelled to Thelma, who was in the kitchen already preparing his plate along with Bingo's.

"I got you a plate right here, baby bro. Bingo told me that you was on your way, so I made enough for you too," Thelma said, putting the rest of the food on his plate.

She appeared in the dining room with their food on a tray. She put each man's plate in front of him. She had cooked cheese eggs, cheese grits, turkey bacon, turkey sausage, and whole wheat pancakes.

"Damn Sis, I'm glad I'm your favorite brother," Teddy said at the sight of the food.

"You are my only brother, but you don't have to brown-nose me for no food," Thelma said in a joking manner.

Bingo laughed so hard that Teddy had to laugh himself.

"I'm glad she busted you."

"Damn Thelma, I thought you was my sister."

"I am, but you know I got to keep it real," she said, as she placed juice in front of them before leaving the room so the men could be alone.

After they finished eating, Bingo went right into what was on his mind.

"Yo, on Monday I'm taking a page out of Champ's book and will be really done with this shit. You've really held this shit down and allowed me to stay under the radar while you took care of the street shit. Even though I'm not feeling how the Raheem and Nino situation is playing out, I'm happy with your overall performance," Bingo said, wiping his mouth with a napkin.

"Don't worry about Raheem and Nino. I'm going to handle these clowns before the weekend is over."

"They should have been dealt with already. Anyway, I'm taking you directly to the connect on Sunday, then I'm done."

"Damn! What, Champ got you about to take *Shahadah* too?"

"Naw, I'm not taking *Shahadah* yet, but I made my money. I can use the piece of mind that Champ has been enjoying, plus I got a child on the way," Bingo blurted out unintentionally.

"Damn, I knew Thelma was getting a little thicker. Damn, I'm about to be an uncle. I got to pick her up something for the baby shower," Teddy said with excitement.

"Slow down. You can't tell nobody yet because she wants to break the news tonight while everyone is at the baby shower. You don't have to pick up a gift for our baby just yet because tonight is Rhonda and Wanna's night. Thelma will have her own baby shower in a few weeks," Bingo said, getting up from the table.

"Okay big bro. Where do you want me to drop the paper off tomorrow? By tomorrow morning, I'll have everything wrapped up from that last load," Teddy said, now standing as well.

"Just hold it until Sunday, and when I go meet the folks, you can bring the paper with you."

They kicked it for a little while longer then Teddy left to meet up with Shiz and Malik. On the way, his thoughts of getting at Nino and Raheem were overtaken by thoughts of having a niece or nephew. Ever since their mom died of an overdose, it had been only Bingo and him. He was excited that there would be another person running around with the Grant bloodline. He hoped for a boy, but even if it were a girl, he would spoil her just as much.

Once he reach Shiz's project, he called Shiz on the cell phone so that he could come out to meet him. Minutes later, Shiz and Malik walked out of the building and over to Teddy's car. As they approached the car, Teddy got out to speak to his boys.

"What's up baby boy," Shiz said, as he gave Teddy a handshake and hug after which Malik followed suit.

"Ain't much. How's things coming along with that line on getting at that faggot-ass Nino?" Teddy said, as he looked around aware of his surroundings.

"Don't worry about his bitch ass. Like I told you, if he's in the city, we'll have him by the end of the week," Shiz said, gesturing toward Malik, who was standing off to the side.

Shiz and Malik were like night and day. Even though they hung together every day, their actions were total opposites. Shiz was the negotiator and people person. Malik, on the other hand was the enforcer and the quiet one. They were both cold-blooded killers, though, and together they were one hell of a team.

"I know what you told me, Shiz, but these niggas are getting in the way of this money. The connect is about to open up, and I need this shit taken care of," Teddy said.

"We on it, baby boy. On another note, what's up with that work you was suppose to bring," Shiz said, nodding his head at Malik to let him know it was cool to get the money for the new work out of the crib.

"Yo, when all's said and done, our squad and Ducky's squad will be the only ones in the city moving work," Teddy said, as he finished getting the last of the bricks out of the stash spot.

Malik came back out of the building with the money. He got into the back of the car, and they made the exchange. Before they left, Teddy let them know this would be the last time they would do business in front of the projects. It was understood that from here on out they would meet in traffic. The projects just weren't a safe place to do business.

~~~~~

Since Sharon and Thelma were in charge of throwing the baby shower, they arrived at Belmont Mansion an hour early to make sure everything was in place. They wanted everything to be perfect.

Thelma went over the menu with the head caterer to be sure that all the food that was ordered was there in abundance. Sharon was talking to the decorator, making sure everything was to her liking. Although the decorator was a professional, Sharon still wanted to put her personal touch on it. She wanted to make sure that all three hundred pink and white helium balloons were in place along with the pink and white place settings for the tables.

"Bitch, stop eating the shrimp. Come over here and help make sure the open bar is set up right," Sharon joked, as she walked into the room and caught Thelma grubbing.

"Girl, this shit is going to be the bomb. I can't believe that both of our girls are pregnant," Thelma said, licking sauce off her fingers.

"I can't believe I'm going to be a grandmom and an aunt at the same time," Sharon said, while thinking of how much she had been through with Wanna over the years together.

Sharon and Wanna were more like sisters, which is why she went all out without worrying about the cost of the event. She didn't even bother to let Champ pay for the liquor.

Upon seeing the cases of champagne, Thelma blurted out, "I see you went all out. We even got cases of Crystal."

"Bitch, you didn't read the label on this Ace of Spades. You ain't hear what Jay-Z said? We don't fuck with Crystal...they are some prejudice mutha-f'ers," Sharon said, holding up a case so Thelma could see.

"I don't give a fuck. They both have gold bottles, shit," Thelma said, doing a little dance while Sharon busted out laughing, seeing how silly Thelma was acting.

Time flew by before they knew it, but not before they had everything in place. The food was in order, the servers ready, the open bar and buffet were set up, and DJ Baby DST had the music blaring through the speakers from the sound system he had set up.

"Corey, put on 'Cater To You,'" Thelma said, calling DST by his real name. Just like any other event, no one was on time. The first two to arrive were the women of the evening, Rhonda and Wanna. Both girls were in awe of how glamorous the place looked. They couldn't believe the trouble the girls went through to make this night so special for them. Both girls had tears in their eyes.

"Girl, thank you, thank you so much," Wanna said, hugging Sharon, not even attempting to wipe away the tears that started pouring down her face.

"Girl, don't thank me. You're my sister. Do you know how much you've been there for me over the years? I wanted to curl up and die after Ern died, and you encouraged me to live," Sharon said to Wanna, as both women turned to Thelma and Rhonda.

"Come here daughter, and give me a hug," Sharon said to Rhonda.

"I appreciate this so much. Thank you," Rhonda said, returning the hug.

"You don't have to thank me. I've never seen my son so happy since his dad died. Thank *you*," Sharon said.

"All you bitches are real emotional now. You can tell y'all are having babies," Thelma said, making all the ladies laugh at her crazy self.

Before the women knew it, people started showing up in droves. If one didn't know any better, they would have thought a famous star was in town throwing a party. Everybody that was somebody came out to celebrate the new additions to an already prosperous family. The outside of the mansion was looking like an expensive car lot. There was every kind of car; from S550s to Bentley GTs, and even a couple of Phantoms were there.

As the shower got underway, the men started showing up one by one. The first to show were Bingo and Teddy baring gifts in both hands just like everyone else who came through.

Sharon was on point when it came to the gifts. The mansion was paid for until the next afternoon, so the gifts were secure. She paid for two U-Haul trucks to pick up the gifts and drop them off at two different storage bins; one for Wanna and the other for Rhonda.

As the night wore on, everybody was partying and enjoying themselves and stopping in on the women to congratulate them. This was basically a family affair, so everyone was mingling with each other.

Although it was Rhonda and Wanna's night, just like any other time when he stepped into the room, all eyes turned to Champ when he arrived. He had a fresh, bald head and a neatly trimmed beard. His black throbe draped over his Prps jeans, which were hemmed right above his ankle exposing his Louis Vuitton boot shoes. Champ, and only Champ, could make Islamic attire look so fashionable. He came in with Micky by his side looking more like his son than his nephew and with Toot in tow looking like secret service.

DJ Baby DST, upon seeing his childhood friend, immediately put on Jadakiss' song "The Champ is Here." Upon hearing the music, Champ approached his wife smiling and showing his pearly white teeth, blushing and enjoying the feeling of old times.

"What's up pretty girl," he said to Wanna, kissing her on the lips.

"Hey daddy, about time you showed up. I was wondering if you was even going to show up," Wanna said, swatting Champ on the arm.

"I wouldn't miss this moment for the world. Oh! Come here sister, and give me a hug. Thanks for putting this together for the girls," Champ said, hugging Sharon, and kissing her on the cheek.

"I wasn't the only one who made this happen," Sharon said, looking at Thelma.

"You sure wasn't," Thelma said, cutting Sharon off before she could go any further.

"Let me give this girl a hug and some props too, before she has a heart attack," Champ joked, as he hugged his favorite cousin.

"Now that's more like it," Thelma said, smiling and loving Champ's attention.

Champ felt good being among his peers, and he took time out to talk to everyone even if it was only for two or three minutes. Ducky, Micky, and Toot felt great to have Champ with them all for the first time in a long while. After the greeting cards were read and the gifts opened, Champ got a chance to talk with the person he really wanted to talk to.

"Shaahir, *As Salaamu Alaikum,*" Champ said, waving Shaahir over to where he was sitting.

"*Wa Laikum Salaam,* brother Saleem," Shaahir said, addressing Champ by his Muslim name.

The two men hugged each other with a tight embrace. Shaahir was thinking about how far Champ had come in Islam and admiring his loyalty to the religion. Champ was thinking about how he could get Shaahir back on track practicing the religion. That was the least he could do for the man who taught him the religion. Champ knew that Shaahir loved the religion and was just caught up.

"Damn Shaahir, I miss you, *akh.* I don't see you around the Masjid anymore. I'm not knowledgeable enough in the religion to admonish you, and this is not the place to do so anyway, but I just want to say that you taught me about this beautiful religion, and it hurts me to see you falling off. Regardless if you get mad at me or not, I love you enough to let you know how I feel," Champ said, not knowing how Shaahir would react.

"I know, Saleem. I got to get back to remembering Allah if I want Allah to remember me. I'll never get mad at the truth, and you have spoken the truth," Shaahir said, all choked up from the lump developing in his throat.

They kicked it for a while until Thelma's voice came out of the speakers.

"Excuse me. I have two announcements to make, so can I have y'alls attention, please."

Once all the chitchat and whispering stopped, she continued.

"The first thing is that Quiana couldn't make it, so she sent gifts with Micky. He left the card in the car, so I don't know what she said in it, but that's our girl, and we know it was all love. Moving right along to the news of the night...Wanna, Rhonda, and Sharon, y'all can open them checkbooks, and everybody in here needs to get back to the mall because me and my B I N G O are expecting a baby too," she said, spelling out Bingo's name and looking at him.

Teddy jumped up and led the applause. Everybody was clapping, screaming, and shouting. Thelma was smiling hard when Wanna, Sharon, and Rhonda all ran over to her and gang-hugged her. Champ, Toot, and Micky all commended Bingo for joining in on becoming a father. When everybody calmed down, Thelma couldn't continue from the excitement of sharing her secret.

Sharon stepped in, thanking everyone for coming out and making it a joyous night. Everyone was saying good-bye and exchanging numbers with one another. Sharon, on the other hand, was making sure the servers and caterers were putting away the food and cleaning up while DST was breaking down his equipment.

The parking lot looked like Greek night; traffic was crazy. Champ and the guys were waiting for the women to come out, so everyone could go their separate ways for the rest of the night.

All Champ wanted to do was get home and make love to his wife. Wanna and Sharon were the last to come out and walk to the cars where everyone was standing.

Boc...Boc...Boc...Boc...Boc!

The sound of automatic gunfire broke through the festive atmosphere followed by the sound of screeching car tires. These were the only sounds that could be heard before people started to panic.

"Damn, you see the way I had that A-R spitting? I know I hit like ten of them pussies. I was aiming for Champ's bitch ass the most," Raheem said to Nino, hyped from all the coke they were snorting.

"I know that shit sounded like a train running off track. You see how everybody was trying to run and hide?"

"Fuck them niggas. I hope I hit all of them, so I can piss on all their graves. Make this left so we can get out of this dumb-ass park and jump on the expressway," Raheem said, as he was breaking down the gun to put it away in the stash box in their A-Team van.

Their plans were to make it back to the stash house to switch cars before grabbing their money and coke so they could leave town for a while. Raheem thought he had the perfect spot for them to relocate to get their chips up because he knew the city would be on fire after tonight. With all the trouble Raheem and Nino caused, they knew there would be many sleepless nights to come.

Chapter 14

"Oh shit. What the fuck was that? Is everybody all right? Anybody see who the fuck was shooting?" Micky asked, pulling himself up off the ground with his gun drawn.

"Naw, I didn't see who was shooting, but whoever the fuck it was is a dead man walking," Ducky said, looking around at the chaotic scene.

He noticed Champ, Bingo, and Wanna standing over top of someone. When he got close enough, he saw it was Thelma on the ground moaning and holding her stomach with her shirt full of blood. He heard several people screaming, "Call an ambulance!"

He could tell Thelma was in bad shape by how quickly her shirt was filling up with blood.

"Fuck an ambulance! Somebody help me put her in the car!" Bingo yelled.

Champ and Teddy quickly followed his command.

"Somebody help me too! I need help over here!" Micky screamed at the top of his lungs.

Ducky ran over to Micky weaving through the crowd.

"What's wrong Micky."

"It's Toot. He's been hit and hit bad," Micky spat, his eyes wide open.

When Ducky looked down at Toot, he almost threw up all the food and liquor he had in his stomach. Toot must have caught the first and most of the shots. His face had blood on it from the bullet that grazed the side of his head. One bullet went in one side of his mouth and came out the other side shattering his teeth in the process. He was also hit in the stomach and in the chest. He was in bad shape.

"Help me put him the car," Micky said to Ducky, upon seeing Champ and Bingo put Thelma in Bingo's car and speed off.

"Don't move him. It's too risky," Rhonda said, sitting on the ground next to Toot with her jacket propped up under his head and talking to him even though he was unconscious.

She was devastated by what happened at her baby shower. She hated to see Toot like this because she loved him like a little brother.

"Hold on, Toot baby. Just hold on. The ambulance is coming," Rhonda whispered in his ear, as the sound of the sirens became clear.

Minutes later, the ambulance and the police pulled up. Rhonda rode in the ambulance with Toot while Micky and everyone else followed them in their personal cars. Two other people were shot as well and were taken to the hospital by ambulance although their wounds weren't life threatening. Micky and Ducky drove together following the ambulance.

"Yo Ducky, on some real rap, this was some bullshit Raheem and Nino pulled off, and I swear on everything I'm going to make them pay."

"Micky, how did them niggas know we was even out here?"

"I don't know, but I swear I'm going to rip them niggas' heads off. Them pussies busted guns at my mom,

Aunt Wanna, Aunt Thelma, my baby mom, and even Uncle Champ. They hit my nigga Toot up all crazy. It's the fuck on," Micky said, with bloodshot red eyes.

"Don't worry about it. We going to get them niggas if it's the last thing we do."

"Fuck that. We let them get away with too much shit already and look what happened tonight, Ducky. No disrespect, but I feel as though y'all getting soft because of this money we making, but not me," Micky said to Ducky, not really caring how he felt about the conversation they just had.

When Micky and Ducky looked up, they were nearing the hospital. The ambulance took Toot to HUP on 34th and Spruce not only because it was close, but also because it had one of the best trauma units in the city, and if anyone could help Toot, it was this place.

Rhonda couldn't control herself in the back of the ambulance because they lost Toot twice in transit.

"Stay with us, Toot. We need you, brother. Micky needs you. Somebody fucking do something!" Rhonda shouted, as they opened the back doors to pull the stretcher out.

Doctors were already curbside to rush Toot straight into surgery. The doctors had to stop Rhonda and Micky at the door because they were trying to stay by Toot's side.

Bingo and Champ beat them there, and they were already in the waiting room waiting for a doctor to let them know how Thelma was coming along. When they first entered the hospital, Quiana just happened to be finishing her lunch break. Once the doctors took Thelma in the back, she got to ask the guys what happened.

"How'd this happen to my girl, Bingo?"

"I don't know. I should have been there to protect her. I fucked up," Bingo said, with a spaced-out look on his face.

"She's in good hands. We just got to pray," Quiana said, as Sharon walked up and told Champ that Micky and the others were downstairs.

Champ couldn't believe his little cousin was shot, and he couldn't do shit about it.

If Champ and Bingo knew that their youngin was downstairs clinging to life, it would only have added to the dread they were already feeling.

Quiana told everybody that she'd inform Micky and whoever else was downstairs that Thelma was in good hands. Upon seeing Rhonda when she got up front, she noticed all the blood that was soaked into her dress.

"What happened, Rhonda? Where did all that blood come from?"

"They...they...they shot him."

"Shot who? What are you talking about?" Quiana said, not quite understanding what Rhonda was trying to say.

"Toot...they shot Toot," Ronda said, wiping her nose and eyes at the same time."

"Not my baby. You're lying. You're fucking lying! Where is he?" Quiana questioned, not believing a word Rhonda was telling her.

"How you let him get shot, Micky? How you let that happen?" Quiana said, walking up to Micky, crying and making a scene.

She was causing such a scene that some of her co-workers came out to make sure she was okay and to see what was going on. One of the head doctors came out of the back to take control of the situation.

"Ms. Derkits, what seems to be the problem out here?" he asked, addressing Quiana by her last name.

"My boyfriend just came in with GSWs. I need to get in the back so I can help Doctor Cho."

"Now you know we don't let family work on family. It would be too emotional for you."

"I promise it won't. I just want to be there for him," Quiana said to Dr. Cho, trying to calm herself down.

"Get yourself cleaned up and meet me in OR 4 so we can make sure your loved one pulls through. It's going to be a long night," Dr. Cho said to Quiana, hoping to be of some help to her because he considered her one of his best nurses.

Teddy, Micky, Ducky, and Rhonda went to look for everyone else so they could console one another. When they found them, they couldn't even get peace of mind before Detectives Starks and Hutson started with their bullshit.

"Well I'll be damned. If it ain't Mr. Champ and Bingo. Tell me which one of you wants to make a statement first," Detective Hutson said, being sarcastic without knowing the severity of the situation.

"We don't make no fucking statements, so take your cheap-suit wearing ass and your partner and get the fuck away from me and my family. I'll make sure you get a statement when whoever did this gets what's coming to them," Champ said, stepping up into the faces of both detectives.

"Y'all must not have been feeding the dogs lately. You know what they say; an unfed dog will bite its owner," Starks said, adding to the fire that was already brewing in the room. "If you change your minds, here's a card to get in touch with either one of us," Starks continued, trying to pass the card to Bingo.

"Fuck you two faggots. I'll go to hell and call the devil before I call y'all clowns," Bingo said, tearing up the card in front of Starks' face.

Hutson saw that the rest of Champ's friends and family were stepping up ready to take a stance against the detectives, so he decided to call it a night.

"It's been a long night, and I know everyone is a bit emotional, so we'll be leaving now, but we will keep in touch," Hutson said, pulling his partner by the arm.

~~~~~

The next morning Raheem was up early. He decided against leaving Philly last night once he and Nino got into the house; he figured the cops would be all over the place. He told Nino that it was best that they leave in the morning, and Nino agreed. The first thing he did was turn on the news. He wanted to see what was being said about the shooting that he and Nino pulled off last night. When the news anchor came on the TV, he turned up the volume.

"Last night, this was the scene of a drive-by shooting. One woman and four men were shot. No names have been released as of yet. What we do know is that one of the men is in extremely critical condition. The police have no motive and no witnesses. In fact, one police source, who wishes to remain anonymous, said that the family and friends of the victims are very uncooperative. We'll keep you updated on this savage shooting, which occurred here last night in the Fairmount Park section of Philadelphia at

Belmont Mansion as the story unfolds. For 'Eyewitness News,' I'm Kate Brown."

"Damn, we hit a bitch too," Raheem said to himself, as he got up to wash up and get dressed.

He stopped in Nino's room on his way to the bathroom.

"Get the fuck up, nigga. We got to blow town for a while. We done made the news, my nigga."

"Damn nigga, I'm tired. I feel like I just laid down," Nino said, sitting up in his bed.

"Nigga, we can sleep when we die," Raheem said, walking away without letting his homie reply.

When he got to the bathroom, he washed his face and looked at himself in the mirror. This morning was the first time he looked at himself in a while. After really examining himself, he realized how badly the coke had torn him down. He was losing weight fast to the point that he was starting to look like a different man. He couldn't even remember the last time he or Nino sat down and had a nice meal.

Raheem knew he made some drastic decisions in the last couple of months, ones that changed his life forever. He knew he had to clamp down, get his shit together, and help his homie, Nino, pull himself up as well. Raheem knew that his new move was for the best. They just couldn't move around the city anymore because of last night's shooting. Nino, on the other hand, just didn't give a fuck. His main concern was getting his next high.

"Yo nigga, you up yet? We need to get shit moving while time's on our side," Raheem said, coming straight out of the shower into Nino's room.

"I'm up…I'm up. Damn nigga, you loud as shit. Why we got to be up so early," Nino protested, reaching for a bag of coke so he could get his day started.

"See, that shit right there's going to be the cause of us making a mistake, and now is not the time to be making any mistakes," Raheem said, referring to the bag of coke.

"All of sudden you better than me like you don't be putting nothing in your nose," Nino said, not liking the way Raheem was trying to play him.

"You're right. Let's just get this shit packed up so we can get out of here within the next hour or two. You grab the coke and the guns and make sure they are secured in the car while I call this chick and let her know we'll be there in the next couple of hours," Raheem said to Nino, trying to throw water on the fire before things got out of hand; now was not the time for it.

While Nino secured their things in the car, he started to let his thoughts get the best of him.

"This nigga sweet-talking me like I'm his child or something. When we get to where we're going and shit gets right, I got something for his ass. I'm going to help him take over this town then I'm going to get rid of his ass and keep everything for myself," Nino muttered under his breath, waiting for Raheem to come out so they could be on their way.

When Raheem finished talking on the phone to his female friend, he grabbed his bag of clothes and made his way to the car. When he got in, he tried to apologize to Nino by explaining to him that he just wanted them to be on the same page. He didn't know it was too late and that Nino was already in his feelings. Raheem shook Nino's hand and proceeded to put in Tupac's *All Eyez on Me* CD.

He turned down the volume so they could make plans before they made it to New Jersey.

Once they arrived in Willingboro, the first thing they decided to do was scope out the town to see where it would be best to move their work. Raheem called his female friend to let her know they were there. She didn't believe him when he said he was coming out her way because he'd been telling her this for a while. Karla let her phone ring three times before she decided to answer it.

"Hello Karla, what's up? I just made it to town. I need your address so we can come through," Raheem said into the phone, while watching his surroundings and noticing how different things looked compared to Philly.

Nino was in his own thoughts; he also considered how shit looked different. He just wanted to get things underway so they could start making the money they knew they always deserved to make.

As Raheem pulled the car up to the address, Karla was already out on the steps waiting for their arrival. This was the perfect time to keep his feelings under the rug.

"Damn, this little bitch got a body."

"I told you the broad had a body. She's just not a looker."

"Shit, that body makes up for a whole lot. A nigga like me is more concerned about the body than the face anyway, homie," Nino said, as they both exited the car.

Upon seeing the men coming up her driveway, Karla ran down the steps and gave Raheem a hug.

"I told you ya' boy was going to come out here and kick it with you for a while. Oh! I didn't mean to be rude. Let me introduce you to my homie. Nino, this Karla, and

Karla, this is Nino," he said, getting both of them acquainted with each other.

"Grab y'alls things out of the car and come make yourselves at home," Karla said to both men, as they made their way into the house.

Once inside, she showed Raheem and Nino a room where they could put their things away.

"Aye, what's up with your little cousins you been telling me about; the ones out here doing their thing?"

"Oh, they're probably down at the barbershop. That's where they be hanging out sometimes."

"Y'all got a barbershop around here? That's what's up. Niggas need a haircut anyway," Nino said, cutting in on the conversation while rubbing his hand through his beard.

"As a matter of fact, let me show y'all around a little so y'all can be familiar with getting to where y'all have to go in town," Karla said to both men, as she tried to light her blunt.

"Yo! You might got yourself a winner here," Nino whispered to Raheem.

"I know. I was thinking the same thing. We should have been made this move out this way," Raheem said, smiling up at Karla who was coming back from the kitchen.

On their way to the barbershop, they were all kicking it, laughing, joking, and getting to know one another. Karla promised Nino that she would hook him up with one of her girlfriends, Sabrina, later on that day so he could have someone to chill with while they were in town.

As they pulled up to the barbershop, Karla called Roach to come out front to meet Raheem and Nino.

Roach was a good hustler who was really up and coming; all he needed was someone who could keep him supplied with coke. Karla had been telling Roach for a while that her friend, Raheem, might be the supplier he needed to take his game to the next level.

Karla got out the car first, leading Raheem and Nino to where Roach was standing. She ran up to Roach and hugged him.

"This is my favorite cousin, Roach, and this is Raheem and Nino, my Philly boys," Karla said, blushing as she looked from Roach to Raheem.

They all shook hands and said their what's ups.

"I'll be back to get y'all in a few. Take care of my peoples Roach, and be sure that Randy gives them a sharp haircut," Karla said, hugging her cousin and walking away.

Raheem and Nino followed Roach into the barbershop. The shop was a nice sized shop to be in the hood. It had mirrors on every wall. In the back, there was a pool table with two vending machines alongside the back wall. There were four barber chairs and a shampoo station in the front. Randy, Roach's oldhead, was not only a barber but also the shop's owner, so his cutting station was the most spacious.

He put Roach in the drug game when Roach was a young bull. His whole crew was indicted four years ago, but Randy managed to avoid being charged. The situation was a wake-up call for him, so he decided to leave the game alone. It was rumored that he cooperated with the feds, but there was never any paperwork produced to prove the accusations. When people brought the accusations about Randy to Roach, he would tell them to produce the paperwork or get the fuck out of his face with the gossip.

Randy was really like a big brother to Roach. Roach stayed around the shop with his homies, playing pool and Madden on the Play Station 3 and just hanging out. Randy only requested that Roach never deal drugs in his shop, and Roach respected Randy's request.

"Yo Randy, this here's Raheem and Nino. They are Karla's peoples from Philly," Roach said, as he walked over to Randy's station with Raheem and Nino.

"What's up y'all? Any peoples of Karla crazy ass is peoples of mine," Randy said, shaking both the men's hands.

"You think we can get some cuts?" Raheem asked, running his hands through his nappy bush."

"Yeah, I can get y'all after I finish with my other two clients," Randy said, pointing in the direction of the seated clients.

They ordered pizza, played pool, got their haircuts, and kicked it with Roach until Karla came and picked them up. They liked the little town so far, and they had big plans.

Chapter 15

A week went by, and the shooting at Belmont Mansion was still the talk of the streets. Everyone knew that Raheem and Nino were dead men walking after pulling the stunt they pulled. Everyone had eyes wide open and was ready to cash in on the $100,000 that Champ promised to anyone who gave him their location. The money wasn't for their murders; it was just for their location. The murders were personal and would have to come from someone in their crew.

While Raheem and Nino were busy starting their new lives in Jersey, they couldn't imagine the lives they destroyed back in Philly. Thelma was physically in stable condition, but mentally she was in critical condition. She was still in the hospital because the doctor wanted to run more tests on her to make sure she was okay and healing from her surgery. He also wanted to make sure she was mentally stable and well rested before he released her.

They had removed the bullet from her stomach with no problem except that it punctured her baby's sack. The baby inside her was dead before she got to the hospital. All the blood that soaked her shirt and pants was the blood of her unborn child. When the pain medications didn't have her sleeping, all she could think about was how someone could take her world and crush it by killing her baby. She wanted to know who did it and where they were, so she could get revenge for the death of her baby.

Bingo and Champ kept all the street shit away from the women in their lives. Bingo acted as if he didn't have a clue; and Champ did the same. Rhonda, Wanna, and Sharon really didn't know who was responsible for the shooting, but one thing they all knew was that someone would pay and pay dearly.

Thelma was up early waiting to see if she was going to be released. She knew she would have to convince the doctor that she would rest and take her medication. She already convinced Bingo that she would do whatever she was asked to do to get better. She told him to be at the hospital early this morning so he could help her convince the doctor to release her into his care. She was dying to get home, but not because she wanted to rest or take no damn medication; she wanted to find out who shot her so she could get revenge.

She was thinking of how she was going to get even with the nigga that shot her when she heard a knock at the door. Bingo walked in with a get-well teddy bear and a dozen pink, long-stemmed roses.

"Good morning, baby girl. How are you doing?" he asked with concern evident in his voice.

"I'm okay. I'm just ready to go home," Thelma said, thinking of how soft Bingo was to be at the hospital with the bullshit-ass gifts instead of being in the streets killing the nigga that killed their baby.

"Baby girl, I just seen the doctor in the hallway. He said that he's going to go over your chart and come right in to see us."

"That's good because I need to get back home. I hate this place."

"Boo, I hate this place too, but until they release you, what can we do?"

"I guess all we can do is be patient," Thelma said, trying her best to hide how turned off she was by her husband.

She began to be turned off by him because she thought that he wasn't doing anything about the shooting. Little did she know, he had plans on getting revenge for her and for their unborn child, and his plans were full of murder. He hadn't felt this violated in his whole life. This was personal to him. He wasn't getting soft; he just stuck by the old rules of not putting your women in your street business.

Thelma couldn't comprehend any of the street laws. All she knew was that somebody killed their baby and hurt her, and her man stood by and didn't move a muscle. In her mind, nobody had suffered yet for their loss and it'd been a week. She didn't know it had been a restless week for both Champ and Bingo's crews.

The other night, Bingo caught himself before he cursed her out for questioning his manhood. She asked him if he was scared and why he was always at the hospital when the person who killed their child was out in the street. He was furious; not only because of her statement, but also because he'd been back out in the streets alongside Shaahir, Teddy, Champ, Ducky, Micky, Shiz, and Malik. They weren't always together literally, but they were all in the streets busting guns and shaking down anyone who had any type of relationship with Raheem and Nino. Her statement was a low blow. He was just as much out of the game as Champ until this shooting, and the minute that the shooting took place, he jumped back in the street head first, just like Champ. They both felt that, retired or not, if they let this slide without getting involved, it would come back to haunt them.

Bingo and Champ both knew Teddy and Ducky had tried their best, but they couldn't handle the Raheem and Nino situation; and they refused to let it get anymore out of control than it already was. Both Ducky and Teddy could handle Nino and Raheem without a doubt, but they just needed to be told how and when to bust their moves. Champ and Bingo earned their leadership roles; however, Ducky and Teddy were handed theirs. A person who earns a position is more equipped for the position than one who is given it without merit.

Had Champ and Bingo considered that Thelma and Toot would be lying up in the hospital because Ducky and Teddy were not suitable for positions as bosses, they would have stayed in the streets or folded their operations entirely. Bingo was feeling the wrath of Raheem and Nino's shit getting out of control. He didn't care how the situation got to this point, he just wanted to kill the motherfuckers who caused him so much pain.

The way Thelma looked at him of late pierced through him like a sword. When they talked, she stared blankly at him with her face balled up. Even her fake smiles had a bit of fury behind them. He was relieved when the doctor came into the room.

"How are we today, Mrs. Grant?" The doctor said, smiling as he looked at Thelma.

"I'm fine doctor. I just want to get home so I can get better," Thelma said, letting him know that going home was the most important thing to her at the time.

"Ah yes, I was going to get around to that. I went over your chart and you're healing at a rapid pace, but I need you to stay over the weekend because I want to keep an eye on your wound. The bullet was nasty and you have a slight infection. I prescribed antibiotics that you'll need to take three times a day. The nurse will assist you. I want you to get some rest, and I promise you will be discharged on Monday."

"Doc, can't she just take them at home? I can keep an eye on her."

"No. Unattended, the infection can spread and could prohibit her from ever having children."

"I'll stay, doc," Thelma said plainly.

The doctor stayed around for a few more minutes to answer some questions then left.

"Boo, you got seventy-two hours, and then you'll be back at the crib. I know you think I'm not on top of this shit, but trust me, I am. I can't go into what's going on, but I got this, boo."

"Okay Bingo. I trust you," she said dryly, not trying to hear shit, especially since she had to stay in the hospital for a few more days.

~~~~~

Quiana had love for Toot and was worried about him just like everybody else. What made her different was that she had worked in the ER of HUP for years and had seen too many victims die of gunshot wounds. Although it was her job to tell the families of other victims that things would work out and to focus on the positive, she could not fool herself with that textbook bullshit.

She knew Toot was in terrible shape. She would talk to him and read to him sometimes during her eight-hour shift even though he was in a coma. Some nights, she would stay in the room overnight just to be with the man she loved. There were so many things she wanted to say to him, so many things she wished she had said while he was conscious. She practically moved into the hospital. Rhonda, Wanna, and Sharon came to visit Toot frequently, but not nearly as much as Quiana, who was there all the time.

Ms. Gail would make sure to bring the girls some home-cooked food after she closed the breakfast store for the day. She remembered Micky and Toot as young teens coming into Champ's breakfast store before school. She watched them grow up and was very fond of them. She also checked in with them every day to see if they needed anything.

Quiana didn't know Gail very well, but any family of Wanna and Rhonda's was family of hers. Everybody was pulling for Toot. Quiana constantly studied his charts to see if he was improving.

She made sure she was made aware of Toot's progress through Dr. Cho, who promised her that if there were a God-given chance, he'd do whatever it took to get Toot back on his feet. All the specialists were given the green light to share any and all information with Quiana regarding Toot's health.

Quiana knew the hospital inside out from working there so long. She also knew that if Toot weren't one of her people, the doctors wouldn't be fighting so hard to give him a chance to live. Quiana wouldn't let them slack one bit. HUP had some of the best doctors, but the average hospital would let this seriously injured, young, black male die. Despite how dark and slim Toot's chances were, Quiana was there with him every step of the way with hopes of him pulling through.

Today she was going to tell Toot the good news she had received after talking to Dr. Cho. She went into his room and began cleaning him up a bit. Although the nurse in charge of him kept him clean, Quiana always felt the need to wipe him down once more. She carefully washed his face with a warm rag and applied Vaseline to it.

"Baby, I talked to the doctor. He said that the neurologist checked your x-rays from yesterday and reported that the swelling on your brain is rapidly going down. I know you hear me, big head. I think we are going to be okay. You better not stop fighting, boy. Everybody misses you."

She sat on the edge of the bed and grabbed his hand.

"Micky is supposed to come by and see you later. He's not taking this very well. He really hasn't been himself lately. He comes past here in dickies and sweat pants. You know you and that damn boy don't wear no damn dickies. Y'all think y'all are too fly for that."

Quiana laughed at the thought of them walking the streets in such attire.

"Rhonda, Wanna, and Sharon have been like sisters to me."

She paused for a moment. She thought about the fact that she was upset with him and could possibly never get the opportunity to make amends. What seemed like a good reason to throw her man out before now seemed petty and foolish.

"They stop in every day to see you and Thelma. I know you have a few little girls you run around with, but at this point, I don't care. I know I was tripping about that lipstick in your drawers, Toot, but I've never ever loved a man like I love you. You are my world, so when I saw that lipstick, my whole world came crashing down. I didn't know how to handle it."

Tears began to well up in her eyes. She cleared her throat and gained her composure. She refused to cry in front of him because she had to be strong for them both.

"Baby, I panicked and lashed out. I figured one day, when I got past the pain, I'd get back with you. I didn't want to break up. I just wanted you to miss me. I have so much to tell you. I have so much I want to experience with you. I feel like I'll suffocate without you. I now know that I can't breathe without you. You are my air. Just like I told you last night, I'm not going to sleep in my bed until you can sleep with me," Quiana said, kissing Toot on the forehead, as a single tear forced its way through her emotional barricade.

Although he couldn't respond, she was sure he could hear her. She left him with the promise of coming back in an hour. On her way out, she ran right into Micky in the hallway.

"What's up little brother?"

"Nothing much. I wanted to come and see Toot before I started running around. How is he?"

"He's okay, but he's got a lot of fighting to do, and I'm here to fight every step of the way with him."

"That's why I love you sis, because I know you really got Toot's back."

"And his front too. Go talk to him. He can't respond, but he can hear you. I'm about to go get some coffee."

"Okay sis, my mom and Rhonda are in Thelma's room."

"Okay, I'll get them some coffee and go kick it with them."

Quiana gave Micky a hug and walked to the elevator. Micky always had to pump himself up before going into Toot's room. He couldn't stand seeing his main man like that. They had been through it all. Toot turned his back on his own family when it came to Micky. Micky trusted him and thought of Toot as his brother. Seeing Toot in this unresponsive state hurt his heart. He knew that Toot was hurting and hurting bad. There was nothing he could do but wait and hope he got better. He tried to pray for Toot the other day, but he didn't know how to pray. Micky wasn't big on religion, but he knew that there was a God. All he wanted was for God to bring Toot back to life.

He walked into Toot's room after he got his heart up to see his man. Toot was still lying on his back unconscious with tubes connected to different machines in his mouth and nose. Although Micky didn't know how to operate the machines, he knew that they were keeping Toot alive. He phased out the beeping of the machines and stared at Toot.

He was being as strong as possible, but it was really crushing him to see Toot like this. He could see the lipstick that Quiana left on his forehead. She had planted a kiss in the center of his swollen face. Smiling at the lipstick, Micky thought back to how freak-ass Muff left that lipstick on Toot's drawers.

"Damn playboy, you still can't get away from that lipstick, huh? I told you Quiana would come back to you, my nigga, but I didn't want this to happen in order for that to happen."

Micky paused for a moment then the smile disappeared from his face.

"Damn my nigga. They say things happen for a reason, and I really believe that, but I don't understand the reason for this shit. I hate to see you like this. You can't go out like this. I need you homie. Who the fuck can I call when it's time to put some work in? Who the fuck can I call when it's time to party the little bitches?"

He looked at Toot again. He wanted his brother to wake up and tell him that everything would be okay. The fact that Toot didn't respond made Micky angry. He became frustrated and began to yell as he nudged the bottom of Toot's foot.

"Dawg, if you leave your brother like this, that's some sucker shit. Nigga, I know you hear me. I wouldn't leave you like this my nigga. Plus I got to tell you about the work I put in for you the other day when I seen Nino's Uncle Kenny coming out of Club Plush on Eighth and Callowhill. Besides, my first child is supposed to be your godchild."

Micky had to calm himself down.

"Nigga, my first child is supposed to be your godchild," he whispered as the tears streamed down his face.

This was some hard shit for him to do. It felt like he was talking to a corpse. He knew he had to be strong, but how could he stay strong when he felt so helpless? Seeing Toot like this made him want to hurt any and everything that Nino and Raheem loved. He would have killed Raheem's cousin, Danielle, last week if it weren't for Champ. Micky noticed her in the car with Tuffy and was ready to bust his gun on sight. Champ tried to negotiate with Micky since Tuffy was in the car. Micky didn't give a fuck about Tuffy's relationship with Champ and Ducky, all he cared about was airing the bitch Danielle out. When Champ couldn't reason with Micky, he had to physically restrain him from blasting the car. It was at that moment that Champ realized how hard Micky rides.

"Yo, I'm about to go and talk to Aunt Thelma. She got hit too. She lost the baby she was so proud to be having."

He paused for a moment and smiled, eager to fill his homie in on what was going on.

"Yo, I wish you could see how Uncle Champ and Bingo have been wilding out. All that retirement shit is down the drain. They done gave us the green light to fuck this whole city up. Unc is even out in the battlefield himself. He's been riding with me every night. I know he's surprised at how I bust my gun, but I'm surprised at how hard Unc rides too. I hope niggas don't get that getting money shit twisted thinking Unc is soft. Unc is a Gee for real."

Micky took pride in how hard his family was riding to rectify the situation. His mood was lightened as he explained everything to Toot.

"You be having me on some crying shit when I come visit you, but it feels good to see you."

Micky sat and talked to his unconscious play-brother for a little while longer then went down to Thelma's room with the girls. He knew Thelma was feeling better because he could hear her voice across the room. She was louder than everyone else. As soon as he walked in, big smiles instantly formed on the faces of his mom and Rhonda.

"What's up y'all?" Micky said, hugging his mom and Rhonda.

"You better bring your little, handsome ass over here and give me a hug too," Thelma said smiling.

"I see you're feeling a lot better by the sound of your voice booming all the way out in the hallway," Micky said, walking over to give Thelma a hug.

"So what. They need me to liven this place up," Thelma said, causing the girls to laugh at her crazy self.

Even Micky had to laugh.

"I guess you're right."

"What's up with you son? Where have you been?"

"Mom, I've been cool. I just left Toot's room and he doesn't look too good. He actually looks better than the last time I seen him, but he still looks bad. He got all of them dumb machines hooked up to him, beeping and stuff. I hate to see him like that. This is the first time in years that he needs me, and I can't help him," Micky vented to his mom.

All the women were quiet for a few minutes because they knew Toot was in bad shape, and they knew how much he meant to Micky.

"Micky, you know Toot is like a son to me, and I love him dearly. He's strong. He'll pull through. We just got to wait and pray for him. Quiana is on top of the doctors. They know Toot is her people, so he is getting the best treatment possible. She just left here with all of these charts with Toot's name on them. That girl loves that boy so much; if she had to take her own heart out to put it in him, she would. So don't stress yourself out. Just keep going to see him and talk to him. I'm going to walk down there with Rhonda after we finish messing with this crazy girl," Sharon said, pointing at Thelma.

"Boo, are you coming in early tonight?" Rhonda asked, cutting in on the conversation.

"Yeah, but then I'm going back out for a couple hours."

"Okay, but be sure to get back in the house because I won't go to sleep until you're back," Rhonda said, giving Micky the eye but not wanting to go too deep into the fact that Micky had been coming in around 3 a.m. every night.

Rhonda knew that she had to let Micky be a man, but she didn't want to lose him or want him to get in trouble.

"Be easy sweetie. I'll be in at a decent time."

Micky stayed and kicked it with his mom until it was time to go meet up with Champ and Ducky.

Chapter 16

Everything in Philly seemed to be spiraling out of control. The streets felt the after math of Raheem and Nino's actions. There was an instant drought. Champ told Ducky that all dealing was on pause, and Bingo told Teddy the same thing. The only place niggas were able to get work was in the Badlands, and that was run by the Puerto Ricans. The Puerto Ricans, for the most part, didn't trust the blacks, so when there was heavy traffic in the Badlands, they would shut down shop.

A few niggas had coke, but for the most part, it was bone dry. The party scene had even slowed down because of the shortage of cash flow from the hustlers. Philly was in a big slump. On the other hand, Willingboro was on the rise. All the little hustlers were getting money in abundance. The drug scene in Willingboro was up; it hadn't been popping like this since Sab came through there hustling under the name Apache. Sab really left his mark on the small town, and they still talked about him to this day.

Naturally, now that Raheem and Nino were out at the clubs partying and balling out, the hustlers began to compare them to Apache. There were many rumors about what happened to Apache. He only hustled in Willingboro for a short period of time, but they grew to love him there, and he was the closest thing Willingboro had to a street legend.

Raheem couldn't believe some of the stories. He knew the rumor that Apache moved to California was a lie because he was there alongside Ducky and Toot when Micky killed Sab (Apache), but he would never tell anyone; not even Nino even though the two of them had put in a lot of work and killed a few niggas together. He knew that speaking about old bodies could come back and haunt him because there was no statute of limitations on murder. He just let the Apache fans live with their stories and their legend. He wasn't there for the comparison; he was there to get money and to lay low from the heat and the war zone he and Nino left back in Philly.

Things were picking up, and the twenty bricks they came to Willingboro with were halfway gone. Roach did most of the footwork and serving. The only other person that Raheem and Nino dealt with directly was Roach's brother, K-Reem.

K-Reem was from Willingboro, but he was raised in Camden, so he had that little extra swag that Roach lacked. Roach had most of the customers because K-Reem didn't fuck with too many niggas, but the niggas that came to cop from K-Reem were solid, and they would get at least a half of brick. Roach sold everything from eight-balls on up to nine ounces.

Raheem was trying to get with his man, Spanish Richy, so he could see about buying some more work. He had a twenty-year history with Richy; they had known each other since high school, and he always kept niggas off Richy's ass. He knew that Richy was probably the only nigga he could trust right now.

He knew that Champ would have everybody in the city looking for him and Nino. When he read in the paper that Thelma was one of those shot at Belmont Mansion and that she lost an unborn baby as a result of her wounds, he knew that Champ and Bingo would come back in the streets and that they had endless resources and money.

He and Nino decided that they would stay in Willingboro for about six months, get their money all the way up, and then move to Baltimore, Maryland. The biggest problem at the moment was finding somebody they could trust; and no matter how much they wracked their brains about who to cop off of, they kept coming up with Richy.

They both had cut down on using coke. They were damn near back to their old selves, and they had this little town under their feet. Karla was loving her some Raheem, and Nino had turned Sabrina out. Sabrina liked the way Nino moved his little dick up in her, but she really loved the way he ate her pussy. Both Nino and Raheem played their parts in taking over the little town, and things were looking up for them.

"Yo, when Karla gets back from her mom's house, I'm going to get her to take us to Fifth and Rockland to see if Richy is at his tire shop," Raheem said, sitting at a table in Karla's crib, smoking a Newport.

"So you're not going to call or nothing? You're just going to pop up?" Nino said, reaching his hand out to Raheem, indicating that he wanted to smoke some of the Newport.

"Yeah, we're just going to pop up. I don't want to call him because I don't know if Champ got his bitch-ass on some looking out shit."

"Damn, I didn't think of that."

"What's up with your cousin's boyfriend?"

"Who...Tuffy?" Raheem asked, to be sure who Nino was referring to.

Nino nodded.

"I don't trust that nigga right now. He's down with Champ on the low. Plus he is Ducky's right hand," Raheem said, taking his Newport back.

"So what, are we going to cop off of Richy, or do you want to rob his bitch ass?"

"We are going to feel him out first. I'm going to set up a fake meeting to see if he tries to sell us out to Champ and them. If he tries to set us up, we'll rob him and kill him. If he don't try no tricky shit, we'll cop off of him until we find a new connect, and then we will rob him anyway."

"Now you sound like the Raheem that I know and love."

They shared a laugh. They talked about their game plan until Karla came in. As she entered, she was smoking a blunt and talking on her cell phone. By the time she was done with the phone conversation, Raheem and Nino had smoked up her blunt.

"Y'all owe me a bag of purple, niggas," Karla said, referring to the purple weed that they just smoked.

"That shit tasted like some brown, regular shit," Raheem said, causing Nino to burst out laughing.

"Y'all can laugh all y'all want, but when we come back from over Philly, y'all better get my weed."

"We got you, homegirl," Nino said, still chuckling.

Karla went to use the bathroom before they left. They stopped by Sabrina's mom's house so that Karla could let Sabrina hold her Neiman Marcus charge card. Afterward, they jumped onto the expressway, and Raheem gave Karla directions.

Once they reached Fifth and Rockland, Raheem told Karla to pull into Richy's tire shop. He wanted Richy to see what he was driving, so when he came back to cop, Richy would be expecting him to be in the same car.

Richy was taken by surprise when Raheem stepped out from behind the tinted window of Karla's Buick LaCrosse. He rushed Raheem back into his office.

"What's up Raheem, my man?" Richy said, sitting behind his desk.

"What's up Richy, my man? What's good with you?"

"Raheem, people come by here and call me asking if I seen or heard from you. The black guys have been coming down here and over the Badlands robbing my peoples, and a lot of them come by asking to buy coke. The word is that your man, Champ, and Ducky are looking for you to blow your head off. They sent me a message telling me that, if I just let them know where you are, they will give me $150,000. Of course, I said I don't know where you are," Richy said, filling Raheem in on what was happening.

"Yeah Richy, they got my name in a bunch of bullshit, but I don't give a fuck about Champ or Ducky. Before I let them send me to hell, we will all go together. What did you tell them, and do you plan cashing in on the $150,000."

"Raheem, I don't have anything to do with y'all's war. You're my friend, and I'll never sell my friend out for money. Plus you know $150,000 isn't a lot of money to me. I bet that type of money on chicken fights. I don't want trouble from Champ though, so you can't be seen here. What do you need, my friend?" Richy asked

Raheem, wanting to hurry Raheem out of his shop before anybody saw him.

"Richy, I need a good price on twenty bricks, so I can go to Delaware and get my paper right," he said, spinning Richy off to Delaware in case Richy was trying to set him up.

"Raheem, that's good you're hustling outside of town. Keep a low profile because $150,000 is a lot of money to some people. I'll give you twenty for $350,000, and that's only because you are my friend."

Raheem knew that was a sweet price, so he didn't even try to talk Richy down. He promised that he'd be back in two hours. He left feeling good about the price, but he didn't trust Richy with his life. He knew Richy had a lot of money but didn't know if Richy would sell him out for the extra cash. He knew that he would not only sell Richy out for $150,000, but he would do the actual hit on Richy if there were $150,000 on his head.

Once they got back to Willingboro, he called K-Reem and Roach. He got them to follow him back to Philly. He drove alone in the car with the stash box, but had Nino, Roach, and K-Reem follow behind him in Karla's car. He knew if Richy sold him out to Champ, Champ and his crew would go after Karla's car.

When they pulled up, he told them to park in front of the shop. He called Richy's phone so that Richy would know he was outside. When he saw Richy come out carrying the car stereo box housing the bricks and head toward Karla's car, he rode up on Richy with the window down.

"Get in here, Richy."

Richy got in and Raheem pulled in front of Karla's car.

"Damn, I thought you was in that car you drove earlier," Richy said, placing the box on the back seat.

"Yeah, I'm getting them to tail me back to Delaware so that no cops get behind me.

"Oh, I see."

They made the exchange, and Raheem was on his way back followed by Nino, Roach, and K-Reem. Raheem had his shit planned out well. If Champ and his boys had come and killed the occupants of Karla's car, he would have pulled off and left them. He figured that he would still have been on top because, if Nino had been killed, he wouldn't have to split his money with anyone, and he would have just kept it moving. Nino, Roach, and K-Reem had no idea they had just been used as crash-test dummies. Raheem was a true piece of shit, and he was full of bad blood.

~~~~~

Wanna was deep in thought and full of fear. Her thoughts of losing Champ caused her to be fearful of her world crumbling down around her. Champ was her everything. The baby she carried only made her love him that much more. She wanted nothing more than to just serve her Lord, love her Champ, and have him around to help her raise their child. She hated the fact that Thelma was shot and felt bad about Thelma losing her baby. Wanna couldn't imaging losing her child. She knew that it could easily have been her who got hit that night. She thought of being in Thelma's shoes, and the thought of her losing her child made her sick to her stomach.

She knew Thelma was more like a daughter or sister to Champ than a cousin. It was evident that her being shot in

Champ's presence was tearing him apart. He wasn't himself. He was back in the streets, often not coming home until the middle of the night. He tried to be gentle with Wanna and let her know that his being back in the streets was temporary, but she feared the worst.

She watched the news every night hoping and praying that Champ wouldn't be on the news getting arrested or, even worse, shot. She fully understood that the niggas who violated Champ's family and crew had to be dealt with. She figured that the niggas who shot up the baby shower had to have big balls to shoot while Champ was present. It was a foolish move because shooting at Champ was like signing their own death certificate.

She wasn't tripping about Champ and his crew going to put in the work and kill the cowards who violated them. As far as she was concerned, it had to be done. She just wanted it done and over with so she could get her life with her man back.

Champ had just led her in the *Fajr Salat* (morning prayer). She loved praying with him because he was always there to lead her in the *salat*. No matter what he was out doing with his crew, he still managed to make it home before the sun came up.

She was downstairs making breakfast while he was upstairs washing and dressing before he hit the streets. She made cheese-grits, turkey bacon, scrambled eggs, whole-wheat pancakes, and wheat toast.

Champ came downstairs just as she was setting the plates. He watched her. She had on a pink, lacy boy-short and bra set from Victoria's Secret, and pink Gucci house slippers. Wanna was still one of the baddest all-around chicks in the city. She was still pretty with the little weight she picked up from the pregnancy. She still turned

Champ on, and he wouldn't trade her in for any other chick in the world. Although it was his religious right to take on more than one wife, he hadn't even thought about getting a second wife. Wanna wasn't just all he wanted in a wife, she was all he needed.

"*As Salaamu Aliakum*, Fatimah."

"*Wa Liakum Salaam*, Saleem."

They greeted each other as always, using their Islamic names.

"You always cook like you're feeding an army up in here," he joked.

"I'd rather my husband have too much than not enough," she said, placing his orange juice in front of him.

He sat there eating his food while Wanna sat next to him eating toast and drinking hot tea. He could feel her watching him out of the corner of her eye. It was obvious that she wanted to talk about him being in the streets; he'd been preparing to have this talk for the last few days. He knew that he'd been out in the streets far too much since the shooting, but he truly believed the shit with Raheem and Nino would only get worse if he didn't get involved. He wanted to be in the house spending time with his wife just as much as she did.

He ate his food in silence knowing after he was done eating he could just peck her on the lips and run out the door without giving her a chance to vent. That wasn't his style, though. He always wanted his wife to feel like everything would be fine. He was mindful of her feelings, and although he knew that she would try to talk him into leaving the street shit alone, he still opened up the floor for conversation.

"Fatimah, what's on your mind, sweetie?"

219

"Saleem, there's a lot on my mind."

"I have to run out to meet with Ducky and Shaahir, so I can't talk about everything right now, but tell me what's bothering you the most. When I get in tonight, you can tell me the rest."

"Okay Saleem. I hate that you're out in the streets at all times of night. I know you have to do what any man would do if someone violated his family, but how long will you have to be out there putting your life on the line? I don't know and I don't want to know who shot up the baby shower, but how long will it be before you will have all of this handled?" Wanna said, tears running down her face.

She was crying because the reality of Champ sacrificing himself and all that they built was starting to hit her as she was talking. He sat there quietly and collected his thoughts as she vented.

"Fatimah, you know I distance you and all the family members, especially Thelma, away from the streets. I'm out of the game, but the streets won't let me rest. Boo, we were enjoying ourselves and celebrating the fact that we are having a child. Niggas who ate off *my plate* came by and shot guns at an event that my wife and unborn child, my family, and real friends were attending. What is a man to do?"

Champ was getting angry and Wanna could tell because the vein in his forehead was bulging.

"Baby, I'll never tell you how to be a man, and I'll never tell you how to handle your business, but this is stressing me out. When is it going to be over? What about Allah? What about Islam? When was the last time that you lead me in the night prayer? I'm always thinking about you and thinking about something happening to you."

She paused for a moment.

"Saleem, you have been putting it all on the line your whole life. When are you going to leave Champ totally alone and be Saleem regardless of what's going on?" Wanna was now crying out of control.

Champ remained patient and quiet. Although Wanna was upsetting him by her line of questioning, he knew she was right.

"Fatimah, this will be over soon. I am Saleem, but when niggas cross the line like them chumps did, I have to put on my Champ suit. I'm not going back and forth with you. I know how you feel. I see where you're coming from, and, for the most part, you are correct, but please let me just handle this situation. I need you to be patient with me," Champ said, kissing her on the lips passionately.

He grabbed his keys and was gone. Wanna looked out the window as Champ pulled off.

"Oh Allah, please watch after my husband while he's in them streets," Wanna quietly said to herself.

She went upstairs, showered, got dressed, and went to meet Thelma so they could go meet Rhonda and Sharon at the hospital. She called Thelma once she pulled up to her house so Thelma could come out. Three minutes later, Thelma came out of the house and got into the car.

"What's up girl?"

"What's up Thelma? How are your doing?"

"I'm cool, Wanna. I'm just trying to take it one day at a time," Thelma said, as Wanna drove en route to the hospital.

Thelma had lost weight from not eating, and she had bags under her eyes from lack of sleep. All she thought about was the unborn child that had been taken away from her. She wished that she could get her gun and ride with Champ to find the nigga who shot her.

"Wanna, did Champ find out who shot me yet?" she asked in the calmest voice she could muster.

"Thelma, you know that he would never discuss that with me or you."

"I know he call himself protecting us, but I want the nigga who shot me to die."

"Thelma, the nigga will get what's coming to him. Believe me, Champ is in the streets all the time handling whatever it is that needs to be handled."

"I know my cousin be on top of this shit. I be telling my pussy-ass husband that he don't be out there enough looking for the nigga who shot me. I'm about to move with y'all soon," Thelma said, thinking of how out of hand the arguments with Bingo had become of late.

"Thelma, you should just let them do whatever they need to do without pushing them because you're pushing them. If you push to hard, someone could get hurt or land in trouble."

"Wanna, a nigga killed my baby, and my husband didn't protect me," Thelma said, thinking that Bingo really was the blame.

Wanna remained quiet. She was thinking about Thelma's ignorance. She wanted to lay Thelma out, but because she knew the pain Thelma was going through, she chilled.

"Thelma, sweetie, I can only imagine what you must be going through. I promise you, if Champ, Bingo, me, or anybody else from among our family and friends could have prevented you from getting shot, they would have. I've been falling apart about Champ coming in the house in the middle of the night, but I know that a nigga violated him as a man by shooting in his direction and the direction of his wife, friends, and family. I know it hurt him twice as much that you got shot on his watch."

Wanna got stuck at the light right before the hospital's entrance. She turned to Thelma with a look of confusion on her face. As she cleared her throat and managed a smile, Thelma could tell that her friend was politely holding back. Thelma tilted her head, assuring Wanna that it was okay to speak her mind honestly.

They were friends, so the ladies knew that being frank with each other was a sign of respect and that there would be no animosity as a result of doing so. As the light changed, Wanna continued.

"As far as Bingo goes, if he could have jumped in front of that bullet, he would have. When I talked to him outside your hospital room, he was crying physical tears. I never seen a grown man cry like that. Thelma, cut him some slack. Be thankful for your health, and try to have another baby," Wanna said, as she pulled up to the hospital.

They sat in the car for a minute while Thelma gathered herself together and wiped away her tears. Wanna made her see her loss and pain from a different angle. She began to feel better knowing when she took that loss and got hurt, everyone took the loss and was hurt as well. Once Thelma got herself together, they were off to see how Toot was coming along.

Chapter 17

Micky was torn between putting in work to revenge Toot and Thelma and trying to please Rhonda. Rhonda was a more emotional than usual due to her pregnancy. She was constantly in Micky's ear about spending so much time in the streets. He loved Rhonda and was excited about her carrying his first and only child, but it was important to him to get at Raheem and Nino. He was determined to flush them out of hiding even if it meant that he had to hurt each and every person he thought they loved. Micky was heartless when it came to avenging somebody he loved.

Although Ducky and Champ told him to spare Danielle because she was a female and she was Tuffy's girlfriend, Micky still doubled back and shot Danielle in the face and chest. Tuffy was broken up about that, and so was Raheem when he read about it in the paper. Despite that, Raheem still didn't come out of hiding.

Danielle's death was the one that made the cops turn up the heat. She was on the front page of all the Philly newspapers as the poster child of innocence. She was a pretty girl and a law-abiding, tax-paying citizen. The papers ran with the story that she was caught in the middle of a drug war.

The public began to cry out for help from the police. The mayor gave the okay for a special task force consisting of narcotic and homicide detectives. The task force was named Operation Pressure Point. They were running down all drug houses and street-level dealers; pressuring them into talking about the murders.

Although Champ hadn't been selling drugs and hadn't allowed Ducky and his boys to sell any, that didn't stop the rats caught by the task force from saying their names.

Champ asked Micky if he killed Danielle, and for the first time, Micky lied to the man he looked up to. He didn't feel sorry for Danielle, but he regretted lying to Champ and causing all the heat from the police. They couldn't apply more pressure to the hood. Champ told everybody to fall back for a while until the police presence cooled down; however, Micky was still in and out of the hood, busting his gun at any and everybody tied to Nino and Raheem.

Last night he was in a high-speed chase with the police after he shot Spanish Richy in front of his tire shop. The cops jumped right on Micky's tail after they heard the shots and saw him speeding away in his black Chrysler Charger. He was fortunate enough to have a supercharged, hemi engine. That along with a few skills, allowed him to ditch the police and get away without having to shoot it out with them. After last night, he decided he had to play by the rules and do what Champ said because Champ never steered him wrong.

Rhonda was going to ride to the hospital with Micky. She had a prenatal appointment at the same hospital Toot was in, so Micky was going to drop her off to her appointment before he walked over to Toot's room to see him. He told Rhonda that he had some running to do with Champ and Ducky, and he would pick her up when he was done with them. She agreed to stay at the hospital, see Toot, and kick it with the girls. She knew Wanna, Thelma, and Quiana would be at the hospital, as always.

"Come on boy, before you make me late," Rhonda yelled up the steps to Micky who was upstairs getting his car keys. Micky came downstairs smiling at Rhonda who was standing there looking at him, trying her best to look mad with her face balled up.

"Ain't nothing funny, punk," she said, as she punched Micky in the arm.

"Girl, let's go. I never had your swollen ass late yet," Micky said, playing with Rhonda, lightly pushing her in the back of her head.

"This big-head baby you put in me got me swollen," Rhonda said, hand on her hips.

"Get in the car, girl."

They jumped into his Maserati. He hadn't driven it in a while because he couldn't put work in driving such a flashy car. He'd been driving rentals for that. It felt good to be in his real car after driving the rentals.

Rhonda put in a CD of mixed slow jams. She quietly watched Micky as he drove. She couldn't help but think of losing him to jail or death. She had plenty of conversations with Wanna lately about how to deal with him being in the streets. Wanna told her that things would work out, and he would be back to normal again. She knew that Toot getting shot hurt Micky, so she really tried to stay out of his way. She did her best to let him be the man.

"Ernest, when will all of this BS be over?" she said, addressing Micky by his real name.

"Soon, I hope. We just have to do what it takes to get this street shit taken care of," he said with his eyes on the road.

"So, in the mean time, I have to wait and see what happens to you? I have to wait and see if you'll be free or, better yet, alive for the birth of your child? I'm trying to understand, but at the end of the day when I add it up, I keep coming up with bullshit. I know you love Toot. Shit, I love him too, but no matter what you do in them streets, nothing will change what happened that night. I need you to be around, Ernest."

"I'll be around, and I'm not doing anything in the streets."

"I don't know the details, and I don't want to know them, but I'm not as naïve as you think I am."

"Rhonda, we done had this conversation about a hundred times. I'm burnt out on it. Let me handle my business."

"There's no fucking business in them damn streets at one and two o'clock in the morning. I was on the phone last night with Wanna, and Champ stayed in the house last night. If he can take a day to be with his pregnant wife, why the fuck can't you? Oh, I get it…you're a black-ass, ghetto superhero."

Her words cut through Micky like a razor. He was steaming about the way she compared him to Champ and clocked his moves.

"Bitch, listen, and listen close. I know it's obvious that I look up to Champ, but my dad is dead and I'm grown. I don't have to be in until I fucking feel like it. I don't give a fuck if Barack gives a worldwide curfew…I'm coming in the house when the fuck I want to come in, so don't tell me what the fuck time Champ was in the house. I'm Micky, not Champ," Micky said angrily, now pissed off at Rhonda.

Rhonda couldn't believe Micky called her a bitch. She could tell by his tone she had upset him, but he hurt her feelings by calling her out of her name.

"Micky, I'm not a bitch. I'm not your bitch or anybody else's bitch."

"You're whatever I call you," Micky spat, still upset and knowing that if she wasn't pregnant, he would have smacked the shit out of her.

"Micky, I think I'm going to stay with my parents until you sort out what's going on in the streets and get back to your old self. I'm tired of staying in that house by myself. Your mom is hardly there. She's been back and forth to Ms. Bernadette's and stays over her new friend's house."

Micky was quiet, and although he didn't want Rhonda to go anywhere, his pride and the fact that he was upset made him say, "Fuck it."

He drove to the hospital caught up in his thoughts. He was wondering why his mom was fucking with Ms. Bernadette so heavily, and who the fuck was this new boyfriend. He made a mental note to question his mom when he ran into her.

When they pulled up to the hospital, he walked Rhonda to her appointment.

"I'll call you when I get to my father's house. There's no need to come get me when you're done running around."

"Okay, call me," is all he said.

He was mad and really wanted to say a lot more, but he elected not to. He walked down the hall to see Toot. When he got to the door, he saw that Quiana was already in the room. Quiana was cleaning Toot up, as always, and talking to him as she did every time she visited.

Micky stood in the doorway and let her do what she was doing. He had a new respect and love for Quiana because of how she had been riding for Toot ever since he was shot. Micky knew that Quiana and Toot were on the outs when he was shot, but ever since he'd been in the hospital, she'd been riding hard for him. It was easy to see that she loved him, and she was really pulling for him. She had been practically living in the hospital.

A couple of days ago, Wanna and Rhonda had to damn near drag her out of the hospital. Wanna treated her to a mani-pedi and a hairdo. She really needed the pampering, but she wanted to be by Toot's side. Once they got her groomed, they tried to take her out for brunch; but she was not having it. They knew she would catch a cab back to the hospital if she had to, so they all went back to the hospital and had Ms. Gail bring them some homemade soul food. That was the longest she stayed away from the hospital since Toot had been there.

Micky just sat there staring at Quiana for a while.

"What's up sis?" he said, startling Quiana who was busy cursing Toot out as if he could argue back with her.

"Nothing brother. I'm just trying to get this damn boy to wake up. He needs to get the hell up. He's being stubborn. I was just telling him that if he's trying to scare me into coming back to him, he did it already."

"I know. He got me scared as shit too."

"He's going to pull through, and that's when I'm going to sock him in his eye for scaring us like this."

"Yo, don't say that old-ass word, sock, no more. Nobody uses that any more," Micky joked.

"Well, that's what I'm going to do him."

"Ain't nobody socking my brother but me," Micky said playfully, winging a punch in the air.

"Where's Rhonda at?"

"She's down the hall. She had an appointment. We're going through it right now."

"Micky, life is too short to be on the outs with the one you love. Look what happened with me and Toot. I may never get to say the things that I need to say to him."

"You right, but she has been on some nagging shit."

"Work it out brother. I'm telling you, work it out."

Beep...Beep...Beep...Beep...

Toot's machine started beeping like crazy before they could finish their conversation. Doctors and nurses started rushing into the room.

~~~~~

Raheem was hurt by the fact that Danielle was killed, and he was pissed off that Richy was shot. He knew that both Danielle's death and Richy's gunshot wound were because of him. Now that he tasted a new level of money and was the man, for once, he wished he didn't have the beef with Ducky and them lingering over him. He knew it wouldn't be long before he would either have to address the beef or get far away from the tri-state area.

Although Willingboro was a low-key spot, and it was a sweet takeover, Raheem knew it was still too close to Philly. He also knew that Champ was too strong, and he knew Champ knew too many people. It wouldn't be long before Ducky and the rest of Champ's crew would be directed toward his little gold mine in Willingboro.

He often read the Philly newspapers, and he talked to his little cousin, Marty, at least once a week. Marty was only sixteen years old, but he was street-smart, and he understood what was going on. He understood that he couldn't let anyone know he was talking to his cousin on the regular. Marty didn't hustle, and he went to school, so he was able to fly under the radar without anybody from Champ's squad feeling the need to get at him.

Raheem's thoughts of Danielle being unrecognizable came from the vivid picture Marty painted when he reported in graphic detail the way Danielle looked after she was shot.

Marty also told him that he had seen Ducky and Micky in a car, squatting outside of the funeral, and Teddy and Bingo in another car. What he didn't know was that Shaahir was out there as well as Shiz and Malik. Although cops were all over the place, it was understood that if Raheem was spotted by any of the men, they should start busting on the spot.

When Marty told Raheem that he saw the niggas outside the funeral, Raheem knew that had to be Ducky's plan because Champ would normally be against something so reckless.

Raheem sat in Karla's bed reading the obituary. He had fucked Karla, and she went to work about an hour ago. He wanted to stay in bed a little bit longer, but he had to pick Nino up from Sabrina's crib.

He got up and put the obituary back on the dresser, where he kept it ever since he got it in the mail from Marty. He got himself together and left to pick up Nino so they could meet Roach and K-Reem at the barbershop. He stopped at the newsstand and picked up the *Philadelphia Daily News*. He always wanted to know what was going on in Philly. When he got to Sabrina's spot, he called Nino. Nino came out and jumped right into the driver's seat, noticing that Raheem had climbed over to the passenger side to read his newspaper.

"Whats up my nigga."

"It ain't shit Nino Brown," Raheem said, calling Nino by the New Jack City nickname he always used.

Nino was also fucked up by what happened to Danielle. He felt bad when he saw Raheem crying the other day when Danielle's obituary first arrived. Nino had his own plans on getting at Raheem because of the way Raheem talked down to him about his cocaine habit the day they fled Philly to hide in Willingboro, but he decided to adjust his plans.

"Oh shit, this nigga's ass is out," Raheem said after reading the article in the paper.

"What happened? Who's ass is out."

"The nigga Tuffy. It say's right here that he got caught with five bricks of coke and $269,000."

"Damn, he's going straight to the feds."

"I know, and you know they are not giving him no bail because he's on state parole. Damn," Raheem hissed.

"At least he's out of the way," Nino said, pulling onto the block where the barbershop was located.

"I wanted to rob and rock that chump-ass nigga. He let them pussy niggas kill Danielle, and he didn't do shit about it. I don't care if it's twenty years from now, I'm going to kill that nigga," Raheem said, closing the paper as Nino parked.

"Do you really think he knew they were going to rock Danielle?"

"That was his girl, and he didn't bust a move on them niggas behind her death, so I'm holding him responsible too."

"I'm with you on that, but you got to admit, the only two niggas that's crazy enough to go right at Ducky and them is me and you. Maybe Tuffy wanted to bust a move, but didn't have the balls."

"I didn't look at it like that, but I'm still going to deal with him if the opportunity presents itself," Raheem said, hopping out of the car with Nino following.

K-Reem and Roach were right in front of the shop talking when Raheem and Nino walked up. They all exchanged handshakes, hugs, and what's ups. Raheem went right into the reason he called this little meeting.

"Yo, as y'all know from us all talking, we left some uncooked beef back in Philly. They just crossed the line by killing my female cousin, so now is the time to go address this shit. I'm bringing it to y'all because we can use the manpower. It will just be the four of us. When the shit is wrapped up, we can continue to eat out here and go back to Philly to take that shit over too. I just need to know if y'all are all the way in."

There were about four minutes of silence. Roach was known to bust his gun if he had to, but K-Reem was known as a vicious freak for gunplay. He put in a lot of work down in Camden until his squad was locked up. His oldhead had come home not long ago, but he wasn't fucking with the game anymore. K-Reem respected his oldhead's wishes and just kept getting his money in Willingboro.

"I'm with it," Roach said, after giving it some thought.

"Count me in too. Who is the niggas? What's the plan, and where are they?" K-Reem said with a straight face, ready for whatever.

Raheem filled them in on everything. They agreed that if they killed Champ and Bingo, everybody else would fall in place. They were going with the old kill the head and the body will fall train of thought. Since Champ and

Bingo were the heads, Raheem decided that they would be the targets. They planned to catch up with them in a couple of days.

~~~~~

Shaahir was lying in bed with his new chick. He was on the outs with his wife because of his constant chase after the almighty dollar. His love for the dollar had not only caused him to distant himself from his religion, but it caused him to lose his wife as well. She was tired of him not being around and indulging in things that went against their beliefs.

When he was home, his phone rang constantly. Although his wife was a good Muslim, she was far from naïve. She knew that all the calls in the middle of the night were from women. She loved Shaahir to death, but she couldn't take the heartache he brought to the table, so she asked him for a divorce. He knew he was hurting her, so he agreed to let her go.

Last week, when Shaahir was leaving the hospital after seeing Toot, he ran into Sharon. They kicked it in the lobby, and Sharon told him how fucked up she felt about Toot and Thelma being shot at the baby shower she coordinated.

As Shaahir told her she was not responsible, he did a little venting himself. He let her know that he was coping with the separation from his wife. Before they knew it, they were in the Martini Bar in the Old City section having drinks.

Sharon was impressed with Shaahir's intelligence and smoothness. She hadn't slept with a man since Tone and was turned on by Shaahir's overall swag. They ended up leaving the bar and going to Shaahir's crib. Shaahir fucked her so well she didn't want to leave in the morning. Every night since then, she'd been staying over Shaahir's crib.

Sharon had made some bad choices in her life, but she was still one of the baddest bitches in Philly. She had her own, and she was fly as all outdoors. The fact that she was pretty and had a bad body also raised her stocks. Shaahir was really feeling Sharon. The pussy and head were crazy too. Their only problem was that neither one of them wanted to hurt Micky by letting him know they were messing around because they didn't know how he would take it, so they decided to keep their relationship a secret.

Sharon came out of the bathroom and into Shaahir's room with nothing on but one of his T-shirts and jumped into bed. The sight of Shaahir in his boxer briefs and the Maxwell CD playing in the background set the mood. Sharon jumped on top of him and kissed him on the mouth.

Sharon really turned Shaahir on, and he had her sprung as well. His dick got hard as she kissed him and rubbed his chest. She slipped the oversized T-shirt off, revealing her perfect C-cup titties. She started sucking on his chest while he fingered her soaking-wet pussy. She pulled his drawers off and began licking the head of his dick with long wet licks.

"Damn S-Dot, this shit feels good," he moaned between clenched teeth, calling her by the nickname he gave her.

She licked up and down the shaft of his dick before taking it in her mouth, sucking it softly and slowly. Shaahir was losing his mind. His dick was brick-hard now. She began deep-throating his dick with passion and aggression. The combination made him release in her mouth. She sucked and swallowed every bit of his cum.

After a few minutes, he got himself together and laid her on her back. She spread her legs, exposing her bald, freshly shaven, pink pussy. Shaahir spread her pussy lips and started licking her clit. Sharon loved when Shaahir ate her pussy because he was a pro. He knew right where her buttons were and how to push them. He started licking the inside of her pussy while finger fucking her with his middle finger at the same time.

"Oww daddy, right there. Don't stop. I'm about to cum," Sharon panted.

Shaahir stroked her pussy harder. When her legs started shaking uncontrollably, he knew he hit the spot.

"Please don't stop," she said, holding his head until she completed her orgasm.

Once the oral was done, it was time for the pipe game. He loved the noises she made when he long-dicked her. He climbed on top of her while she was still on her back. He held her face, kissing her while sliding his eleven and a half inch dick back and forth inside her. Sharon felt herself falling for Shaahir, falling hard, and she didn't want to fight the feeling.

"Oww, this dick feels so good up in this pussy, daddy," she moaned.

"Whose pussy is this, huh?" Shaahir asked, thrusting his dick in her harder.

"It's yours, daddy. It's yours."

Shaahir flipped her over onto her stomach, put his dick in her from the back, and closed her legs while his dick was in her. She loved this position because it allowed her to feel every inch of his dick. He had one hand on her hip and the other tangled in her hair. He was fucking her long and hard; the way she loved. He made her have two more orgasms before he busted his other nut and came inside her. They went to sleep with her head lying on his chest.

Chapter 18

Champ had just finished breakfast and was prepared to get his day started. He'd been coming in a little earlier since it was too hot to be in the streets. Between Starsky and Hutch and the new task force, Champ and his crew's names were in heavy rotation. He wasn't in denial. He always faced reality, and the reality of anyone in the street was that they ran the risk of getting killed or locked up. Even though he knew that it was too hot to be in the streets, he knew that it was too risky to leave the beef unsettled. It was obvious that was exactly where Ducky and Teddy went wrong and was part of the reason Thelma and Toot were shot.

Champ refused to let any more of his loved ones get hurt. He often wondered how Raheem could go against the grain. He was more than fair to Raheem, and before he retired, he instructed Ducky to follow his lead. As far as he could tell, Ducky had everybody eating and was being fair. If there was ever a possibility that Champ could bring Raheem and Ducky together before and patch up their break up, it was far too late now. Raheem crossed the line when Thelma and Toot were shot.

Champ wanted Raheem and Nino dead, and he was frustrated having to chase after them. It seemed as if they fell off the face of the earth. No matter how much money he spent and how much manpower he used, he still came up empty.

He was getting out early today to get with Ducky and Shaahir. He grabbed his keys and headed toward the door with Wanna following behind him.

"Be careful. I'll call you later," Wanna said, between kisses.

"I'm good, baby girl. I love you," Champ said, and headed out the door.

He was driving a rental, a tinted-out Buick LaCrosse. He was listening to the *Blueprint 3*. Jay-Z was his favorite rap artist, and his music always seemed to hit the spot. It was as if Jay's lyrics always related to what Champ was going through.

As he raced the rental down the expressway grooving to the music, his cell phone rang.

"*As Salaamu Aliakum.*"

"*Wa Laikum Salaam.* You left your other cell phone on the table and it keeps ringing," Wanna said.

"Damn, take it to the hospital when you go down there. I'll swing by there and get it from you. What name came up?"

"C-Law."

"Okay, just call me when you get to the hospital. I'll come in the hospital. I want to see Toot anyway."

"Okay. *As Salaamu Aliakum.*"

"*Wa Laikum Salaam.*"

They hung up, and Champ turned his music back up. His thoughts were scattered. He knew that he put Bingo's name in that prepaid phone under C-Law, which stood for cousin-in-law, not wanting to use his real name or nickname. They used the prepaid phones to keep in touch and to keep each other posted on the Raheem and Nino shit. Although prepaid phones were a way to keep the feds from tapping their phones and recording their conversations, they still kept their airplay to a minimum.

Bingo was already on top of his game, but being around Champ during this crisis with Raheem and Nino made him even sharper. Bingo was smooth, but Champ played the game effortlessly; he was a natural. So if you placed Bingo next to Champ, there was no comparison. There was no one as smooth as Champ.

His cell phone rang again.

"Yizzo," he said, noticing that it was Micky calling.

"What's up Unc? Where are you at?"

"I'm on my way to the car wash."

"Okay, I'll be right up there," Micky said, knowing that Champ was talking about Duck'y car wash, which had become their meeting spot ever since Ducky reopened it.

Champ drove the rest of the way to the car wash listening to Jay-Z and thinking. When he pulled in, Ducky and Shaahir were standing outside.

"*As Salaamu Aliakum.*"

"*Wa Liakum Salaam,*" Shaahir returned Champ's greeting with a smile.

"What's up Ducky-Raw?"

"You're what's up, big homie," Ducky said, hugging Champ.

They all walked into the reception area of the car wash. No one else occupied the spacious reception area since most of the customers dropped their cars off and came back to pick them up later.

"Yo, did anybody hear anything on Pinky and the Brain?" Champ joked, talking about Raheem and Nino.

"Naw, them niggas are hiding under a rock for real," Ducky said, turning the TV to "Sports Center."

"We got to track these niggas down so we can go back to living," Champ said.

"I don't know about y'all, but I'm living my life. Fuck them niggas. We can't fight a ghost, so I'm living my life," Ducky said, looking at the highlights from the 76ers versus Atlanta Hawks game.

Champ couldn't believe how lightly Ducky was taking this shit. He always advised Ducky to take everybody as a potential threat and never underestimate an opponent. It really bothered him that he was taking Raheem so lightly. Champ knew Raheem could be, and was, very dangerous. He knew of the missions Raheem and Ducky went on when he had any problems when he was in the streets. He even witnessed some of the gunplay Raheem and Ducky put in back then.

"So after we groomed Raheem into being a cold killer, you're just going to take him light. If I'm not mistaken, taking him light is what had him pop up at my wife and Rhonda's baby shower and let off about thirty shots. He killed little cousin's baby and damn near killed Toot. What could you or anybody tell me if my wife had gotten killed or Thelma or anybody in our circle?" Champ spat in a smooth, but stern, tone.

Ducky was caught off guard, but he knew Champ was speaking the truth. He admired Champ and would never go back and forth with him.

"I hear you, big homie, but what are we supposed to do, be scared of them niggas?"

"It ain't about being scared. It's about never underestimating any nigga in these streets. The littlest nigga can push your head back. And how could you underestimate Raheem of all people? Y'all done put a ton of work in together. Ducky, I'm not coming down on you. I just want this shit over."

"Champ I hear you, and I want to get it over as soon as possible."

"I want to handle this shit without any of us getting killed or going to jail behind these ungrateful chumps," Champ said, thinking of how he had extended his hand to Raheem over the years.

"They got to come out one day," Ducky said, walking in the back to answer his office phone, which was ringing off the hook.

"What's good with you Shaahir?" Champ said, as Ducky walked into the back.

"Nothing main man, I'm having my grand reopening of Sea What It Is tomorrow. I want everybody to be there."

"I know your grand reopening is tomorrow. You got the fliers posted all around the city."

"Well, I got to promote the reopening hard. I need to make the money back that I put into the renovations."

Shaahir lost some paper on rehabbing his store. He thought he could get away with only replacing the windows that were shot out, but L&I was on his ass making sure everything was up to code. They were really busting his balls because of the shooting outside of the seafood spot.

"I'll be there, without a doubt."

Champ got quiet. The distinguished look on his face let Shaahir know that he was in thinking mode.

"What's on your mind, Saleem?" Shaahir said, calling Champ by his Islamic name.

·

"Shaahir, I feel like a hypocrite knowing that everything we're doing goes against the religion. What's crazy is that, no matter how pious I want to be, I can't let this shit ride. Them niggas really crossed the line. I know you've been Muslim longer than me, and you are far more knowledgeable than me, so can you explain how I can put my religious beliefs on hold to attend to this shit?"

"I'm going to tell you like this. You've been Champ for thirty-plus years, but you haven't been Saleem for more than a year. When you were violated in the manner that those clowns violated you, it's only natural for you to react the best way you know how, and the best way for you is Champ's way. Maybe later on in life, Saleem's way will prevail."

"So because I haven't been Muslim that long, it's okay?"

"No, it don't make it okay, but Allah didn't create you as an angel. You are human, and no matter how good of a human you are, you aren't exempt from making mistakes," Shaahir said, looking Champ in the eye.

Champ respected Shaahir's knowledge, and when he could pick Shaahir's brain for some of that knowledge, he did. After Shaahir was done talking, Champ felt better. He vowed to get the situation with Raheem and Nino taken care of and to get out of the streets.

"Yo, that was Tuffy. He's booked in Philadelphia F.D.C. He said he's cool and that the niggas in there with him have a million different stories floating around about what's going on out here. He couldn't say but so much on that jail phone, but he said he would send me a message through his little sister, Indira, when she comes to visit him," Ducky said, walking back into the room.

"Damn, Tuffy is my man. I feel sorry for him. His bitch got killed, and then he got grabbed by the feds. I know the nigga got some major paper put up, but if he needs something, tell his sister to tell him to let me know," Champ said, thinking of all the shit he did with Tuffy over the years. Tuffy was one of the few niggas outside of his team who he considered to be a friend.

"Okay. When I meet his sister, I'll tell her what you said," Ducky said to Champ, while looking at Micky who just strolled through the door.

"What's up with y'all? What it do?" Micky said, shaking hands with all three men.

"What's up with you, nephew?" Champ said, grabbing Micky by the shoulder.

"Nothing much. I just wanted to swing by and see what's the latest on them two dickheads," Micky said, referring to Raheem and Nino.

"It's the same thing. They're ducking and dodging."

"Let me hit the nigga Raheem's little cousin, Marty. I think that will bring him out."

"Micky, your little ass is trigger happy. We are not doing no more of that shooting up their people to bring them out shit. It hasn't worked. The next time we bust these guns will be right at them two niggas. They can't hide forever," Champ said, looking at Micky.

"Okay Unc. I'm about to go down the hospital and see Toot."

"Damn, we all might as well ride down and see him," Ducky said, wanting to see Toot with his eyes open.

"Yeah, that sounds like a plan because I got to pick my phone up from Wanna anyway," Champ said.

They all drove to the hospital in two cars: Champ and Micky in one, Ducky and Shaahir in the other.

245

~~~~~

Raheem was chilling in the crib with Nino waiting on K-Reem and Roach to come over. They were supposed to be back from Camden half an hour ago so that Raheem could go over the final part of their plan.

Raheem and Nino heard about the work that K-Reem put in from the little niggas at the barbershop and out at the clubs in Willingboro, but last night they got a chance to witness the little nigga in action.

Some Trenton niggas came through the bar that they were hanging in. The niggas started getting drunk, and that's when the shit hit the fan. One of the niggas started shaking up a bottle of champagne and it squirted all over K-Reem. K-Reem nicely asked the dude to watch the champagne. Between dude being drunk and the Trenton niggas thinking that all the Willingboro niggas were soft, K-Reem didn't stand a chance of getting a respectful apology or a simple my-fault. Instead, the dude told him that he could squirt his champagne where he wanted and when he wanted. K-Reem cracked him over the head with a half-full Corona bottle, which started a big bar fight. At the end of it all, K-Reem waited outside the bar, and when the Trenton niggas exited, K-Reem started chopping at them with a Mac 90.

Raheem was in awe of how well K-Reem handled the automatic rifle. The work K-Reem put in at the bar reassured Raheem that he wanted K-Reem on the team when they went over Philly to kill Champ and Bingo.

"Yo, them little niggas are pulling up now," Raheem said to Nino, who was rolling up a dutch.

"About time."

"Nino, did you see how that little nigga was dumping with that big-ass gun last night?"

"Yeah, he was relaxed, and he worked that thing like a pro."

"The gun was bigger than his little ass," Raheem joked, as he let K-Reem and Roach in.

They exchanged what's ups and all the fly handshakes. Nino sparked up the dutch.

"Yo little nigga, you are wild as shit," Raheem said, looking at K-Reem.

"Naw, that nigga was crazy for talking crazy to a nigga he didn't know. I was trying to rip that nigga's whole face off," K-Reem said, puffing the dutch Nino handed him.

"Them niggas aren't going to come back through here with that bullshit no more," Raheem said, reaching for the dutch.

"What took you little niggas so long?" Nino said, wanting Raheem to get on with the plan, so he could go over Sabrina's and get some pussy.

"My oldhead had a lot of rap for us," K-Reem said.

They engaged in small talk until the dutch was gone. Raheem went into the dining room, got a manila envelope with a flier and pictures inside of it, and brought it back into the living room. He passed the pictures around. There were ten pictures, and the only people in the photos were Champ and Bingo. He wanted the images of Champ and Bingo's faces to be burned into K-Reem and Roach's minds. He wanted them to be familiar with their targets.

"Yo little homies, these two niggas are the niggas that we have to put the dirt on. The nigga with the beard is the infamous Champ. He's the more powerful of the two. The other one is Bingo. He's powerful too, but he's not quite on Champ's level. However, I want both of these pussies dropped at the same time. We can't miss."

Raheem turned to focus on K-Reem.

"K-Reem, I want to assign you to get up on Champ and blow his motherfucking head off. Roach, I need you to be up on Bingo, so that when you hear K-Reem's first shot, you'll already be in position to kill Bingo, who I know will be panicking at the sound of gunshots. By the time their niggas get on point, y'all should be able to blend in with the crowd that will surely be running for the door trying to avoid getting hit. Once we see y'all come running up, we'll start dumping these A-R 15's at everybody else," Raheem concluded, then waited for a response.

"I love the plan. I'm with it. This is my type of shit," K-Reem said, seeming excited about the gunplay.

"What if they peep the game and start dumping on us?" Roach countered.

"Nigga, stop bitching. They won't peep the game. They don't know us. We'll blend in just like everybody else," K-Reem snapped at his younger brother.

"Okay, fuck it. I'm riding dawg," Roach snapped back, letting the crew know he was down.

After a little back and forth between the brothers, Raheem took the floor again.

"This is where they're supposed to be tomorrow. This is their man Shaahir's goofy-ass seafood store where they're having a grand reopening," Raheem said, holding up the flier that Marty had mailed to him.

The flier had a picture of the store on it along with a list of the grand reopening specials.

"We can't just walk in there. As soon as they see us, it will go down on the spot. K-Reem chirp me right before you're about to shoot Champ in his fucking head. We'll be parked on Mustgrave Street on the side of Dunkin' Donuts. When I get the chirp, we will start walking up the block. If the timing is right, we should be able to catch the crowd running out. Once y'all are in the clear, it's on," Raheem said, loving the thought of Champ getting shot in the head.

He knew K-Reem had what it took to slide up on Champ and kill him in cold blood. The bad blood in him had him smiling at the thought.

"And after we give these faggots a dirt nap, what are we going to do then?" K-Reem asked with a wicked smile on his face.

"I told you, I'm going to put y'all all the way on. We're even going to take some parts of Philly too."

"Damn Raheem, I love the sound of getting money," Roach cut in.

"Well little nigga, get used to it. Tomorrow night at seven thirty sharp, we are pulling off from here."

Everyone was on the same page. Roach and K-Reem headed to the barbershop to see what was being said about the bar shooting. Raheem was taking Nino to Sabrina's to drop him off, and then he was going to pick Karla up from her mom's house.

"Yo, you are going to get them little niggas killed. There's no way they will be able to make it out of that store if they so much as raise a gun at Champ. Think about how on point them niggas are going to be," Nino said, trying to understand Raheem's crazy-ass plan.

"I know it's risky, but it's the most promising chance we got at getting at these chumps. When I get the chirp from K-Reem, we will run to the corner and see if they made it out. If they do, we'll start blasting until we can all get back to the car. If we don't see them, that means they got their shit pushed back. We'll go back to the car and do a drive by. As long as them little niggas kill Champ and Bingo in the midst of getting themselves killed, who gives a fuck."

"Oh, I see. We'll put them at risk. If they make it, we're good...if they don't make it, we are still good," Nino said, thinking of how much of a piece of shit Raheem was.

"Yeah, as long as we're safe and Champ and Bingo get what they deserve, it don't matter how it goes. If K-Reem and Roach make it, we'll put them on, and if they don't, we'll get some more soldiers and eat regardless."

"That's a hell of a plan, my nigga," Nino said, smiling and thinking, after this, the Champ and Bingo shit would be over, and then he was going to go ahead with a plan of his own. He planned to put the dirt on Raheem, take all the money, and bounce to Minnesota with Sabrina.

Raheem dropped Nino off and went to get Karla.

~~~~~

Toot had been on a tug-of-war ride between life and death. Although everyone hoped and prayed he would make it, at one time or another, they all thought that he would die. Quiana and Micky got the scare of a lifetime when his machines started beeping the other day. At that moment, they thought they had lost him.

It was a heartwarming surprise to see his eyes open. Micky and Quiana were both more surprised and shocked than happy. Once they realized what was happening, the joy began to set in and erase the shock. There were at least a dozen nurses and doctors surrounding Toot's bed within thirty seconds after the machines started beeping. At the sight of the medical team surveying and working on Toot, Quiana began to unknowingly repeat, "He's alive, my baby is alive."

From that moment on, her whole life changed. She was on a mission to get Toot all the way back to health and back to her home where she felt he belonged. She was fighting an uphill battle, but she was prepared and up to the challenge. Toot was conscious, but he was still in bad shape. He was in critical but stable condition. He had a trach in his throat to help him with his breathing, and he had several open wounds. He was put on liquid steroids because his lungs had collapsed. He would need intense physical rehab to learn how to walk again.

The biggest plus was that, although he could not talk because of the trach, he still seemed to have his memory. When the doctor called Quiana over to the edge of his bed to see if he would notice her, he just stared at her as if he blocked out everyone else in the room. She told him to squeeze her hand if he knew who she was. He complied and gave her a weak smile. She quickly called Micky over.

Once Toot saw Micky, his smile got bigger. Through his eyes, which had become glassy, anyone in the room could tell Toot was happy to see Micky. If eyes could tell a story, Toot's told a novel and a half.

The doctors noticed Toot was using a lot of energy trying to talk with his wide-open eyes. They told Toot that Micky and Quiana would be allowed back in after they ran some tests; he was also instructed to avoid trying to talk.

Ever since he gained consciousness, there was hardly a moment during visiting hour that he didn't have a visitor.

The doctors and nurses knew that Toot was loved by his family and friends because of the strong support they gave him. His room was full of stuffed animals and all sorts of flowers.

Quiana and Micky were at his side more than anybody. The first couple of times he visited, Micky cried while talking to Toot. Now, he just went into Toot's room and vented. He laughed and joked about the things they used to do and will do. Toot just smiled and looked at the man he loved like a brother.

Today, Micky brought Toot a treat. He came to visit with Ducky, Shaahir, and Champ. Although each of them had been there before, they never all came at the same time. Together they all laughed and joked and assured Toot that everything was going to be okay. When they left, they all had heavy hearts and felt bad for Toot. Champ got his prepaid cell phone from Wanna. He called Bingo, who gave him the best news that he had received in a while.

Chapter 19

Wanna has been doing a great job being patient with Champ and all that was going on around them. She was raised around Champ, and as she surveyed his past relationships, she saw that the women in Champ's past went wrong by trying to control him. She knew that there was no controlling a man like Champ. He was a made man, who was in control of everything around him. To try to control a man of his measure would only cause friction, and she didn't want any friction with her husband. He was her everything, so she decided to wait it out.

She felt a little better because he had been coming in earlier of late. She was pleased with just being able to lie in bed at night with him hugging her and watching "Sports Center" on ESPN. More than anything, she was happy that he had been home to lead her in the night prayer. His leadership in prayer and in life was important to her. He was a natural at leading. His crew loved him like a father or an uncle because he never asked them to do anything he wasn't willing to do. He was always thoughtful of his crew's well-being.

Before Champ and Wanna began messing around, she used to hang around him on the play-brother and sister tip, and she noticed back then how he would put his crew before himself. His heart was made of gold. He never ever said no when a family member or friend called on him for financial support. Wanna was always attracted to his physical features; but when she found out how amazing he was as a human being, she set out to make him hers. Once she got him, she vowed never to let him go.

She was patient, but she still disliked the fact that Champ was out on the front line of this bullshit. She thought Ducky and the others should be able to handle whatever was going on. She didn't understand, after all the years of feeding and leading them, why he had to come out of retirement to rescue them once again. She was disgusted that he had to play hero time and time again for his crew, but she would never voice her opinion to Champ. She did not want him to think she was questioning him, so she kept her thoughts to herself.

When Champ was out in the streets, she hoped and prayed that he was okay. She would often tell herself not to worry, but she couldn't help it. With Champ in the streets with his life and freedom on the line, she felt her whole life was on the line as well, so how could she not worry? He was her world. She just wanted whatever was going on to be over.

She left the house right after Champ. She was on her way to meet Sharon, Thelma, and Rhonda at the hospital. The hospital had become the girls' second home. They ran around and handled their business throughout the day, then went right back to the hospital to make sure Toot was good. Quiana was happy to be a part of the girls' lives. She loved the bond they all shared. They were like sisters to one another, and they accepted and treated her like a sister.

Once Toot introduced Quiana to Rhonda, she started bringing Quiana around the girls, and it's been love ever since. Everyone was there for each other, and they were all pulling for Toot. Wanna drove down I-95, listening to Trey Songz's CD. She was thinking of how life would be once she had the baby.

She had been looking at floor plans for houses in Charlotte, North Carolina. She talked to Champ about moving down to Atlanta when all of the street shit was over. He said Atlanta was out of the question because that's where everybody from Philly has been moving to, so they agreed to move to Charlotte. In the middle of her thoughts, her phone rang.

"What's up crazy lady?" she said, seeing it was Sharon.

"No hello or nothing for your sister, huh? Where they do that at?" joked Sharon.

"What's up girl? I feel you beaming through the phone."

"Wanna, what I'm about to tell you is between me and you. Don't tell your husband, and please don't let my wild-ass son find out. I got to tell somebody about this shit, and you're the only somebody I can think of to tell this juicy shit to."

The phone line was quiet for a few minutes.

"What is this juicy stuff about, and who's the nigga?" Wanna said, knowing her girlfriend like a book.

"I think I'm in love. The nigga is thorough. He got his own, and the dick is crazy."

"Yeah, well, why haven't none of us met this dude?"

"See, that's the problem. I can't expose the nigga, at least not now anyway."

"When did we start holding secrets from each other?"

"Oh, I'm going tell you right now, but you can't tell nobody. I've been fucking with Shaahir. Girl, he is the bomb, and his dick be blowing up right in this thing."

"All the stuff about his dick is too much information. I like him for you. He is thorough and fly."

"Wanna, he is a sweetheart. I've been putting this pussy all on his fine ass too. The only thing is that he really has love for my son, and he don't want our relationship to come between their friendship. I told him Micky is not my father...I am Micky's mother. He asked for some time to work it out, so I got to hide it a little longer."

"Yo, to be honest with you, I don't think Micky will have a problem with it. Now that I think about it, when we ran into them all last night in the hospital, I seen you and Shaahir with the eye contact thing."

"Damn, it was that obvious? Micky should be cool with it...he will have to be."

"Girl, I'll see you at the hospital."

"Okay, but this is not no hospital rap."

"I know girl." Wanna said, laughing and hanging up on her friend.

She turned her music up and drove to the hospital lost in thought. When she got to the hospital, the first person she saw was Rhonda.

"What's up Aunt Wanna?"

"What's up niece? Look at you getting all big. Are you sure it's only one in here?" Wanna said, rubbing Rhonda's belly which was sticking out like a beach ball.

"It better be only one. Aunt Wanna, you are pretty big yourself," Rhonda said innocently.

"So how did you make out with the conversation you had with Micky?"

"I made out good. He told me to get my behind back to his mother's house and that things will get better."

"I told you to just talk to him and let him know you got his back and everything would be okay. Remember to always let the man be a man. I know you get frustrated and feel as if you know what's best for him, but just let things work themselves out."

"You're right. Thanks for always having my back, Aunt Wanna."

"You are my favorite niece, Rhonda, and it's duty to have your back," Wanna said, as Quiana approached them in her nurse's uniform.

"What's up yall?" Quiana said, hugging both girls.

"How is my nephew doing?" Wanna asked, after she and Rhonda both said their what's ups.

"He is doing good. He's literally getting stronger by the hour. I thank God every day that he gave my boy a second chance."

"Toot's a good kid and he's loyal, so he deserves a chance. I just want him to get all the way back to health so we can shake this damn hospital. They're about to start charging us rent for all the time we spend up in this joint," Wanna joked.

Rhonda and Quiana laughed.

"Can we go and see him?"

"Sure, y'all can go see him. He was asleep when I left him."

"We'll just go and look in on him for now. If he is asleep, we can come back later when he's awake," Wanna said, walking behind Quiana who was leading the way to Toot's room.

When they got to his room, he was still sleep. They stood there for a little while then left. When they got to the lobby, Sharon and Thelma were there. The girls kicked it with Quiana for a little while, then Sharon and

Wanna left to go to the bank with promises of coming back to see the girls and Toot.

When they got into the car, they kicked it about everything going on with the fellas and about how this whole situation had brought them all closer. Sharon went on and on about Shaahir and how much she loves him. Wanna was happy to see her girlfriend so radiant about life. She looked as if she had found herself again. Wanna wanted nothing but the best for her girlfriend, and she thought Shaahir was a good look for Sharon and encouraged her to keep seeing him.

"Sharon, if he makes you this happy, I'm all for it."

"I just want Micky to be for it too."

"Micky should understand that you've been through a lot. I know if he sees that Shaahir has bumped this much life back into you, he'll be all for it."

"You're right. He did bump life back into me," Sharon said, humping the air and laughing.

They went to the bank then headed back to the hospital as they promised.

"You know Shaahir is having the grand reopening of his seafood store tonight?"

"Yeah Sharon, I heard, but Champ told me that we wasn't allowed to come down there when me and Thelma asked about it last night."

"I'm sure he got his reasons, so I'll pass too. I'll be at Shaahir's house waiting for him to come in," Sharon said, laughing.

"Girl, you are too much."

Sharon was happy to be laughing and joking again. Wanna was happy about that as well. It felt like old times.

~~~~~

It's been a long time coming, but today was the day Raheem intended to even all scores with Champ, Ducky, Shaahir, Micky, or anybody else that got in his way. He even promised to shoot at bitches if they got in his way. The day was moving slowly, so he got Nino to start snorting with him. They weren't completely drug-free, but since they had been in Willingboro, they had slowed down on the snorting. Today they were getting ready to make the craziest move they had ever made in their lives, so they decided to use the coke to get them through the day. They were snorting some of the raw fish scale they had taken from one of the bricks they had in the truck.

It was six thirty in the evening, and they had already snorted about a quarter ounce of the raw coke. They both felt good, and they were convinced that killing Champ was going to be a walk in the park. They thought K-Reem would be able to get next to Champ and had the heart to blow Champ's head off. Now that they were snorted up, they felt unstoppable and ready to get the shit moving.

"Yo, if I have to run up in that store myself and get killed, I'm killing Champ tonight. That pussy must have forgotten who put all of that work in over the years for his bitch ass. He knew Danielle was my heart, and he gave authorization for them pussies to kill her. This nigga is a dead man walking. I swear on everything I love I'm going to kill this nigga," Raheem said, his eyes bulging wider than usual.

"Be cool my nigga. Let's stick to the plan. I really think that our little niggas can pull this shit off. I'm with you, homie, and I'm riding for Danielle too. Your folks are my folks. It's me and you against the world, homie," Nino said, snorting the coke and feeling like Tony Montana.

"I just want to get at these niggas. You're right though. I'm going to stick to the plan. Where is K-Reem and Roach at?"

"It's only six fifty. They have forty more minutes," Nino said, checking his watch.

"Damn, it seems like time is in slow motion."

They sat there and kicked it until K-Reem and Roach got there. Once they did, they didn't waste any time. They loaded the guns into the car and headed over to Philly. Each man had his game face on. K-Reem was so caught up in his thoughts Raheem had to shake his leg to get his attention.

"Yo, what the fuck are you zoned out about? I need you to be on point. This is a sweet plan, but the niggas ain't sweet. If you slip up, they will kill you. K-Reem, do you think you can handle this?"

"Them niggas ain't going to kill shit. You're fucking right I can handle it. I *do* this shit. I really get my nut off with this killing shit. Some niggas kill, but I'm a real killer," K-Reem said in an even tone with a cold look in his eyes.

Everyone in the car could hear and knew the seriousness of K-Reem's statement.

"Well, I guess you're going to get this shit done tonight?"

"Just get me to where the niggas are at, and let me handle the rest. Roach, you just handle your target because mine don't stand a chance. Champ, Chump, or whatever his name is, will get all he's looking for today."

"That's what I'm talking about. I love this little nigga right here," Raheem said, looking at Nino.

"Yeah, you got to love him," Nino said, thinking what a piece of shit Raheem was.

They drove the rest of the way in silence. Each man was caught in his own thoughts. When they pulled up to the store, it looked more like a car show or grand opening of a club than a seafood store. It was dark out, but the lighting in the store showed it was packed inside.

"These pussies are living it up, and they got my family grieving over Danielle. It's the fuck on," Raheem said, as he pulled up the street and into the dark Dunkin' Donuts parking lot.

"Don't worry main man. You won't have to worry about these niggas after tonight," Roach said, letting Raheem know that he had his back.

"Yo, hit me on the chirp, and we'll come jogging around the corner with the AR's in our gym bags. Remember little niggas, we are all we got," Raheem said, letting K-Reem and Roach out of the car.

When they were out of sight, Nino broke out the bag of coke, and Raheem began to roll up a dutch, so they could get prepared for war.

"Sprinkle some flour in this weed, Nino."

"'Okay, hurry up and spark that shit," Nino said, pouring some coke on top of the weed Raheem was holding. Fifteen minutes later, Raheem's phone chirped.

"It's K-Reem. We got to move out," Raheem said, grabbing a gym bag from the back seat. Nino grabbed the other one.

They walked quickly to the corner and made a left, walking toward Shaahir's store.

Boom...Boom...Boom!

Shiz and Malik stepped out from behind the parked cars Raheem and Nino had just walked past. Nino was hit and his bag fell out of reach. Shiz and Malik were still shooting at Raheem who was trying to get the AR-15 out of his gym bag. Before he could get his gun out, a minivan pulled up with the slide door open and a hail of bullets rained in his direction sending him flying to the concrete.

Micky and Ducky stepped out of the minivan driven by Teddy and looked down at their old friend squirming on the ground. They opened fire on Raheem from point-blank range. He was hit at least twenty times. He was a done deal.

Nino was getting it just as bad. Shiz and Malik stood over him doing him dirty. He took about the same amount of shots as Raheem. Ducky's crew made a clean getaway. As Raheem and Nino lay motionless on the ground, K-Reem and Roach drove by them in the car with K-Reem's oldhead, Shakour, from Camden.

"Damn, them niggas caught a bad break," Roach said, peering out the window at the dead bodies as they drove by.

"Fuck them niggas. They was trying to send us into a deathtrap. When you got that bad blood in you, you always catch a bad break."

"I taught you that a long time ago, little homie. We all we got, for real," Shakour said smoothly.

"Yeah, that's why when these new clown niggas were talking about they wanted me to kill a nigga for them, and they hardly even knew me, I had to come holler at you. Although you're not hustling anymore, I knew to run it past you before I got in too heavy with them clowns from out of town."

"Yeah, and it just so happens that they were trying to get you to hit my peoples," Shakour said, heading toward Willingboro to drop K-Reem and Roach off.

They promised to link up with Shakour the next day. They couldn't believe Shakour didn't want any of the coke or money that they were going to take out of the stash box in the car Raheem left at Karla's house. Raheem had gotten too lazy and comfortable around K-Reem and had shown him how to use his hydraulic stash box. Roach and K-Reem were sure to be the toast of Willingboro with all the money and bricks they came up with, and Shakour was going to plug them in with Bingo.

The whole crew was happy that Raheem and Nino were out of the way and that it was done by their immediate circle, but no one was happier than Bingo. He had lost his baby because of Raheem and Nino's recklessness, and he was on the verge of losing his wife.

When he got the call from Shakour that they needed to meet, he thought Shakour wanted to meet him to get some work so he could get back in the game. Shakour was cool with Bingo; they had met through Shaahir at F.D.C. Shakour stayed in touch with Bingo when they got out.

Shakour was notified about the dumb shit that Nino pulled off the last time he saw Shaahir outside the Masjid. Although Shaahir knew that Shakour was done with the streets, he still felt the need to keep him updated with what was going down. Shakour was happy to see Shaahir but also troubled that his brother in Islam was going through such turmoil. Shaahir promised to get with Shakour once the bullshit going on in the streets was over.

Shakour tried to call Shaahir first when K-Reem told him about Raheem and Nino, but Shaahir didn't answer so he called Bingo. Bingo was forever grateful to Shakour for that phone call. He offered Shakour money, but Shakour declined. He only asked Bingo to be sure to look out for K-Reem and Roach when all was said and done.

Bingo promised to take the youngins under his belt if they led him to Raheem and Nino.

K-Reem and Roach took it a step further and brought Raheem and Nino to them. Bingo was relieved. Thelma had been taunting him about not being able to catch up with Raheem and Nino ever since she heard they were the ones that shot her. Bingo loved his wife and hoped that the deaths of Raheem and Nino would be the start of rebuilding their life together.

Chapter 20

The double homicide on Chelton Avenue and Mustgrave Street was the talk of the town. It was on every news station in Philly and the main topic in every barbershop. There were many rumors surrounding the killings. As in every hood, people adjusted the truth and put their own spin on it. The newspapers called it the Chelton Avenue Overkill. They reported that the person or persons responsible for it should get charged with abuse of a corpse along with murder charges because they were shot at least ten extra times apiece after they were dead.

Starsky and Hutch were on at least three different news stations talking about the murders. They attributed the double homicide to a nasty drug war, but at the end of the press conference, they were sure to say they had no motives and no suspects. Although they had a hunch about where it came from, they didn't go public with it. They knew that Champ had one of the best lawyers in Philly and that Fortunate Perri would tear them new assholes if they made those kinds of accusations about his client in public.

Thelma was up early after hearing about Raheem and Nino. She watched Bingo lying in bed as if he didn't have a worry in the world.

"So you heard what happened last night to them niggas that shot me?" she asked him.

"Naw boo. What happened?" Bingo said, with a groggy voice and a crooked smile.

Thelma knew when he was lying.

"So you don't know that Raheem and Nino got killed down the street from Shaahir's store last night?"

"Naw boo. That's good news to me though. Fuck 'em."

Thelma got the picture. She understood her husband didn't want to discuss murder with her.

"Okay daddy, but I want you to know that today is the first time in a long time that you look sexy."

"Damn, that was cold, but I'll take what I can get for now."

"You can get it all, daddy. I'm sorry I acted like an ass toward you, but I couldn't take them bastards walking around after they did that nut shit to me."

"It's cool sweetie. That shit is a dead issue now."

Bingo and Thelma talked a little while longer before he left to meet Champ at Champ's breakfast store. They were going to discuss a few things before Champ left to go to South Beach to relax with Wanna for a few days. It had been a long time and being back in the streets drained both men.

When he pulled up in front of Champions, Champ was standing out front talking to Micky and Ducky.

"What's up y'all," Bingo said, as he approached the men. Everybody said what's up before going inside the store. Ducky and Micky stayed up front to kick it while Champ and Bingo went into the back.

As always, Gail came and waited on Champ and his guest. Once she got them squared away, she left them in the back and went to go wait on Ducky and Micky.

"What's your next move Bingo? Are you staying around here, or are you and my cousin moving away?"

"I don't know. Right now, I'm undecided. I am tired of this lame-ass city."

"I'm flying out tonight to ease my mind with my wife, and I'm coming back with preparations to move out of this city."

"You know what? I'm going to see if Thelma wants to go up New York and stay for the weekend. I'll see what she wants to do as far as moving," Bingo said, now wishing he was going to South Beach with Champ and Wanna, but he didn't want to draw on Champ and Wanna on some double-dating shit.

"I'm telling you now to get out of Philly before it's too late. Although we claim not to be doing anything, when they see Teddy, they think of you. When they see Ducky, Micky, and Shaahir, they think of me. The only thing you are going to do in this city is get indicted," Champ said, drinking his iced tea.

They kicked a little longer, and Champ promised to get with him when he got back to from South Beach.

~~~~~

Wanna was going to see Toot before she left for South Beach. When she got to the hospital lobby, Sharon was already there.

"What's up girl?"

"Nothing. Did you see the news?"

"Yeah, I seen it."

"Yo, somebody did Raheem and Nino dirty."

"That's crazy. They won't be doing all that crazy stuff out in these streets no more."

"You got that right. I stayed at Shaahir's last night, and we talked throughout the night. He is what I need right now, so I'm just messing with him. We both agreed not to tell Micky just yet."

"Sharon, I'm with whatever makes you happy. Let's go upstairs and see Toot so I can get out of here and go to South Beach and relax with my husband."

"Make sure you go to Big Pink on Second and Collins Avenue and get one of them big, sloppy-good turkey burgers."

"You are greedy. All you think about is food," Wanna said, leading the way to Toot's room.

"Wrong. All I think about is Shaahir."

"You are pipe-riding now."

They both laughed.

Toot was sitting up in bed smiling at the TV when they entered. He was enjoying the show so much he didn't even bother to look up to see who walked into the room. When Wanna and Sharon looked at the news, Raheem and Nino's pictures were on the air. Toot was laughing at their murders. Toot couldn't talk because he still had the trach in his throat, but he could understand and respond by shaking his head yes or no.

"Are you laughing at the news lady's hairdo?" Wanna questioned Toot.

He shook his head no.

"Were you laughing at her clothes?"

He looked at Wanna and shook his head no again, and then he pointed at Raheem and Nino whose pictures were still on the news.

"Oh, you're happy to see Raheem and Nino on TV."

He shook his head no and puckered his lips so she could read them.

"Dead. Did you say dead?"

Toot smiled and nodded his head.

"Oh, you are happy that they are dead?"

Toot smiled even harder and shook his head yes.

"Boy, you are crazy. We can tell that you are going to be up and running in no time," Sharon finally cut in on the conversation and gave Toot a kiss on the cheek.

They both stayed for a while and kicked it with Toot. He was always happy to see his peoples. They were the only family he had, and they always looked after him. The whole time they were there, all he did was smile and shake his head yes or no. They each kissed him on his cheek and said their good-byes with promises of coming back to see him soon.

~~~~~

Roach and K-Reem had underestimated how much money and coke Raheem and Nino had in the stash box. They knew Raheem and Nino were rolling heavy, but never in a million years did they think they were rolling that heavy. All together, the coke and the money totaled to about $485,000. They were up damn near a free half a million dollars. The thing that made it even sweeter was that they didn't have to worry about anyone coming after them about the paper. They were more than capable of running their whole town with that type of money; especially with the right connect.

K-Reem knew that if Shakour said Bingo was good people and could supply them, then that's what it was.

K-Reem had known Shakour all of his life and Shakour had never steered him wrong. Roach didn't care about all the detail shit. He just knew that they were up crazy. He had never seen that much money, let alone owned that type of money before. He was just following K-Reem's lead on all the getting the connect shit. When K-Reem explained that Shakour was going to get them a connect, Roach simply said that he was down with whatever.

They sat in the apartment they shared, counting the money. When they finished counting, they put the coke in the drop ceiling and the money in the refrigerator. K-Reem left $50,000 out and put it in a shopping bag.

"What's that for?"

"It's for Shakour."

"He said that he didn't want anything."

"Yeah, you're right, he did say that...but he said that meaning that he wasn't going to charge us anything for putting us in position to get away with this paper. That don't mean we can't show our appreciation. I don't care how much money a nigga got, everybody can use a free $50,000. Now if he declines the paper this time, we'll put it to good use," K-Reem said smiling.

"I'm with you player," Roach said, grabbing his car keys off the table.

They were on their way to meet Shakour in Camden. They listened to Young Jeezy's *The Recession* CD at low volume.

"Yo, them niggas did Raheem and Nino dirty. Shakour said that these niggas are peoples, and they will treat us like family as long as we don't cross them," K-Reem said, as Roach pulled onto the highway.

"Man, I'm just trying to get this money and lock this shit down to the point that there won't be a need for any out-of-town nigga to come through here trying to get money. We got real dough now, so why would we cross a nigga?"

"You're right. We got real dough and Willingboro is ours. Nobody is going to come through here selling shit. It's either buy our coke or there's no coke at all."

"I like the sound of that K-Rizzo," Roach said.

"Did you see the look on Raheem's face when he was laying there on the ground?"

"To tell you the truth, I wasn't even trying to see their faces after seeing their bodies twisted all up on the ground like that," Roach said, pulling onto Haddington Avenue in Camden.

"It seemed like, when we rode by, Raheem was looking at me with that help-me look on his face although he was already dead," K-Reem said, pulling out his cell phone to call Shakour to let him know they were there.

Shakour came out and they headed to Philly to meet Bingo.

~~~~~

Micky and Ducky had been together all day. They were relieved that the bullshit with Raheem and Nino was over. They went by the barbershop on 40th and Lancaster Avenue to get haircuts and to see what was being said about Raheem and Nino. They both had a silent understanding that they would be all ears and no mouth in the barbershop where the murders of Raheem and Nino were the main topic.

Everybody had their own version of the story and what happened. Nobody knew the truth except the two men that were quietly listening to the men coming in and out of the shop gossiping like a bunch of bitches. When they left the shop, they talked about all the gossip going on. They knew that the streets had the story about Raheem and Nino's murders twisted, and they intended to keep it that way.

They left the barbershop to go to the hospital. When they got there, they ran into Starsky and Hutch in the lobby. They would have preferred to run into anybody but them. Starsky and Hutch were some real assholes, and they hid behind their badges.

"Look what we have here. It's two of the gangsters we've been looking for," Detective Starks said, pointing at Micky and Ducky.

"Man, we ain't no fucking gangsters. The gangsters are on TV. You know, like Nino Brown, Bump Johnson, Frank White, Tony Montana, and the Tony Soprano's of the world," Ducky said, looking Detective Starks in the eye.

Starks turned red after Ducky played him in the lobby in front of a crowd of onlookers.

"Listen here, you little fuck. This is not a movie. This is real life. When people die in the streets, it's not for entertainment. They can't come back from that shit," Detective Starks said, all up in Ducky's face.

Ducky wasn't backing down. He was tired of this punk-ass cop.

"Fuck them people. I have no idea what or who you're talking about. If I'm not mistaken, y'all motherfuckers should be out in the streets investigating. Do me a favor; don't accuse me or my peoples of shit. When y'all feel as though y'all have enough evidence to arrest any of us, just come and lock us up. Until then, stay the fuck out of my face and the face of my peoples. Now, if you'll excuse me, I have to visit my little cousin," Ducky said, stepping around the two detectives and heading toward the elevator with Micky following.

Detective Starks stood there staring at them as they got on the elevator. Detective Hutson held his partner's arm to prevent him from following Ducky and Micky upstairs. He knew that his partner could get crazy at times, so he prevented him from making a bad move in the hospital in front of hundreds of spectators.

Ducky and Micky got off the elevator on Toot's floor.

"Yo, that cop is a dickhead. I'm tired of that pussy."

"Well, let's kill his bitch ass. I'm down for whatever," Micky said with a smile, but meaning every word.

"Champ would never give us the go-ahead on that."

"Who said we have to ask Champ?"

"Micky, you're crazy. We're not ready for that," Ducky said, letting Micky know that killing a cop was out of the question.

"Well, what should we do?"

"Stay out of their way."

"Okay, I'll stay away from them," Micky said, thinking that once Toot got back on his feet, they were going to kill a few niggas, and Starks was at the top of his list along with Marty.

When they stepped into Toot's room, Quiana was sitting in the chair next to Toot talking to him. When she saw them, she let him know they were there and promised to come back later. She hugged them and said what's up to both men on her way out.

"What's up, playboy? What it do? You're looking good. Quiana said the doctors are talking good. She also told me she had to get the doctors to run nut-ass Starsky and Hutch up out of here for trying to talk to you in your condition. You know they are two dickheads without balls," Micky said to Toot, who sat there smiling and nodding his head.

"Yo little nigga, we can't wait until you come home. We miss you. That little bitch, Tanya, keeps asking about you...the one you fucked the night we was in Scooters. She was trying to come up here and see you, but I know Quiana be up in this jawn all the time, so I told her your room was under heavy security and that she would have to see you when you get home," Ducky said, looking at his little homie propped up in the hospital bed smiling up at him.

It hurt him to see Toot like that, but the fact that he was alive and stood a chance at a full recovery brought joy to his heart.

"Yo, you need to hold onto Quiana. She rode this shit all the way out with you. That's my real sister now. There wasn't one time that I came through this jawn that she wasn't around. Yeah, and them niggas Raheem and Nino caught a bad break. Somebody did them two faggot-ass niggas dirty," Micky said with a sarcastic smirk on his face.

Toot was already smiling about Quiana holding him down, and he began smiling even harder hearing about Raheem and Nino's fates.

Micky and Ducky felt so much better knowing that Toot was happy about the murders of the niggas who hit him. They kicked it with Toot for a while and rolled out. They were happy that they put a smile on their homie's face; but they couldn't imagine the joy they put in his heart by always coming through letting him know that, even during the rough times, they still loved him and he was their family. The support they gave Toot made him understand that some friends could prove to be more like family than family.

~~~~~

Teddy was relieved that the circus shit with Raheem and Nino was over. The shit exhausted him as much as everybody else involved. He met up with Bingo and was happy that his big brother was happy. He knew how much of a burden the cat-and-mouse shit with Raheem and Nino was on Bingo. When he talked to Bingo this afternoon, he could see that the pressure was off him. He was laughing and smiling like his old self again. Even Thelma seemed to be happy again.

Bingo was talking that retirement shit, and Teddy didn't mind that; but he was talking about packing up and moving out of town. That got Teddy thinking. He didn't have any plans on moving out of town; Philly was all he knew and all he wanted to know. Although Ducky, Micky, and their crew would still be in town, and he knew he could call on them if he needed them, nobody could be there like his brother. Bingo raised Teddy and he was everything to Teddy. He was his brother, his friend, and his father figure, and he was always a phone call away. He pleaded with Bingo not to move out of Philly; but after a while, he could see that Bingo's mind was made up, and he let it alone.

Bingo told him the connect was going to deal with him directly, and all he asked was that he look after K-Reem and Roach. Teddy agreed. He went to meet Shiz and Malik at the basketball game at Gratz High School on Huntington Park Avenue where Shiz's daughter, Shakirah, was playing. She was co-captain of the team, and she was the starting guard. Shiz played in the drug game, but he was a family man and never missed any of the Shakirah's games.

When Teddy pulled up, Shiz and Malik were standing outside in front of the school.

"What's up my niggas?" asked Teddy.

Both Malik and Shiz responded with what's ups and handshakes. Teddy knew Shiz had to get inside and catch the tip-off to the game, so he knew he had to get right to the point. He just wanted to tell them face to face that everything was good. He didn't want to talk about it on the phone.

"Yo, I know you got to get in there to watch your daughter's game, so I'll get right down to the point. Thanks for getting that shit done. My brother is thankful. I just seen him, and I could see in his whole demeanor that them chumps being dead has taking a lot of stress off him. He gave me the connect to run with. He's done. Our circle will be just us and these two little niggas from New Jersey. I'm going to stand by my word. I told y'all that, once them two niggas was in the dirt, we're taking over. I'm only serving y'all and the two little niggas in Jersey. Y'all can get whatever y'all want, and I'm trying to get us the best price that I can get. It's on, my niggas," Teddy declared.

Malik and Shiz expressed that handling the Raheem and Nino situation was a pleasure. They also reminded Teddy that they had his back and his front on whatever. Teddy was happy that they were excited that he was staying true to his word and that they were on their way to getting that next level of paper.

Chapter 21

Three months had past since the deaths of Raheem and Nino, and it had been pretty quiet in the streets as far as the shootings and homicides were concerned. Shit basically got back to normal for just about everybody.

Starsky and Hutch were still being assholes, harassing niggas every chance they got. They tried to follow every lead on the murders of Raheem and Nino, but at the end of the day, they kept running into a dead end, so they decided to leave the murders unsolved.

Ducky was still running the detail shop and running what was left of the crew. He would only serve Micky and Shaahir. He was waiting until Toot got back to full health to serve him also; but outside of those three, he wasn't serving anybody else.

Shaahir's seafood store was still the spot to be. People came through his store in packs, especially on the weekends. Business was good for him at the store and on the streets. He linked up with some new young bulls from Uptown. Every hustler in Philly knew that, when it comes to that sweet paper, Uptown is where you want to be. He was still messing with Sharon, but they still kept it a secret.

He was getting with Shakour on the weekends. Shakour kept him grounded and was his silent reminder that, no matter what he did, he'd be okay if he reverted to Allah and repented.

Micky was back in the streets heavy. The old-time hustlers said he was the spitting image of his dad. He was sure to spend a lot of time with Rhonda. She was so big she looked like she was carrying twins. He bought the house that Champ and Wanna were living in from Champ. He was Champ's favorite, so, of course, Champ gave it to him for next to nothing.

Thelma and Bingo decided to move to Marietta, Georgia. They got good news from the doctor who told them she would be able to conceive again. Thelma's worst fear was that she wouldn't be able to have kids. When she heard that she could, she and Bingo went at it day and night trying to conceive another baby.

Teddy was moving smooth with his new crew. Shiz and Malik proved to be the best hustlers he had ever come across. They just needed a good nigga behind them with a good price, and Teddy proved to be that nigga. K-Reem and Roach also contributed to Teddy moving the bricks as fast as he was. They had Willingboro on lock, and the coke was moving super fast. The connect was pleased with Teddy, who was moving work at an even faster pace than Bingo used to move it.

Champ and Wanna purchased a single town house in Charlotte, North Carolina. Wanna was happy to have her man back by her side, and they were living their days and nights building their empire and pleasing Allah. Champ found a building in downtown Charlotte where he wanted to open a breakfast store. It was right beside the Masjid. He named it Halal Champions. He turned the breakfast store in Philly over to Gail. She cried and tried to decline taking it; but after he reminded her how much she'd done for him and that store over the years, she gladly accepted. He told the crew not to be strangers and that he wanted everybody to fly down Charlotte because he was throwing a big cookout in a few weeks.

Toot had come a long way in his recovery. He still needed extensive physical therapy to regain all of his mobility, but for the most part, he was okay. He walked with a cane for balance. Quiana moved him in with her. They were back together, and she waited on him hand and foot.

She was extremely happy that, despite the damage the bullets did, his dick still was able to get hard. She took him to all of his appointments to make sure he got all the treatment he needed. It seemed as if he wanted his dick sucked all the time, and she gladly sucked it. Anything for her man was her thinking.

Today was Champ's farewell party. Everybody was coming out to see Philly's Champion off. It was an event that nobody in Philly wanted to miss.

At first, he was going to have a private going away party with just his crew and close associates, but Ducky and Micky talked him into letting them throw him a big bash. They rented the African American Museum for the event. Sharon and Thelma decorated with a black and white theme. Baby DST was the DJ, as always. Shaahir paid for security. Although shit had been quiet, he didn't want to take any chances with laxed security.

The girls were to wear white and the guys were to wear black. Just as at the baby shower, it was open buffet and open bar; in fact, they hired the same caterers. A comedian from Philly named Buck Wild hosted the party, and there were live performances by Philly's own Musiq Soulchild, Jill Scott, and Jazmine Sullivan.

On the outside of the building hung a huge banner that read, "Damn, we are going to miss Philly's Champ." There were two tiger tamers outside with two white tigers in huge jail-bar type cages, one cage on each side of the entrance.

As expected, all the hot wheels were parked out front: Maybachs, Phantoms, Bentleys, and every style Benz and BMW to name a few. Around 11 p.m., the place became packed with people.

Ducky, Micky, and Toot were chilling in VIP. Quiana tried to stay up under Toot who was on a cane, but Micky convinced her that Toot was okay. She went over to be with the girls, but she kept an eye on her Toot.

Teddy came through shining with his crew. As soon as he got in the VIP, he ordered fifteen bottles and they were all ready to ball. They hooked right up with Ducky, Micky, and Toot. Teddy told Toot how happy he was that he made it out of the hospital and that he had something for him tomorrow.

Everybody was kicking it. Champ was all over the place. People were wishing him well; some even begged him to stay in Philly. It was his night, and he was enjoying it.

Wanna chilled with the girls. She teased Rhonda about how big she was. She congratulated Thelma on moving out of Philly and promised they would see each other at least every other weekend. She gave Quiana her props on how she rode out Toot's near-death experience. She told her how much she admired that type of loyalty. She had so much to say to Sharon that it would have taken days to get it all out, so she just told Sharon how much she loved her and how she was the sister she never had. The rest of the night, she teased Sharon about stalking Shaahir from across the floor.

"Let me find out you are really on that boy's head like that," Wanna whispered.

"Like what?" Sharon uttered back, not taking her eyes off Shaahir who was across the room talking to Champ.

"Like that."

Wanna pushed Sharon on the shoulder slightly causing her to stop staring at Shaahir and to start laughing.

After the artists' performances, DJ Baby DST stopped the music and turned up his mike.

"Yo...Yo...Yo...can I have y'alls attention for a minute. I know y'all want to get back to partying, but I have an announcement for the man of the night, Champ. If nothing else, I know everyone in this room agrees that you're the fairest dude in our town. If anyone ever had the right to be arrogant, it was you. But instead, you always remained the humblest dude around."

The crowd applauded at the statement until DST motioned his hands up and down to silence them.

"You've been good to everybody, even the haters. Half the people I've seen you help had me thinking, why in hell is he looking out for that dude, but then I think about it and realize that your heart is good, and you helping anybody is just Champ being Champ. I always told myself that, if I came across some big money, I was going to cut you a big check, but I never did, as you can see," he said, laughing before he continued.

"I always wondered, with you looking out for everybody, who looks out for you when you need? Anyway, I just wanted to personally and publicly thank you for all that you've done for this city and for me. No matter where you move, you will always be Philly's

Champ," DJ Baby DST concluded, turning the music back on.

The crowd broke into cheers. Champ and Wanna hit the dance floor alongside Micky and Rhonda, Thelma and Bingo, and Shaahir and Sharon. They were all in the crowd two stepping to Franky Beverly's "Before I Let You Go." Micky danced with Rhonda but watched Shaahir dancing with his mom. Sharon was smiling and having a good time. Micky honestly thought that kicking it with Shaahir was a good look for his mom.

The party was a complete smash. Champ and Wanna had a good time with their friends. It was the best time out they had had together in a long time. They would love to stay in Philly, but they really had outgrown it. No matter where they lived, Philly would always be their home, and just as the DJ said, Champ would "always be Philly's Champion."

TUFF INK PUBLICATIONS

Order Form
Tuff Ink Publications
P.O. Box 24540
Philadelphia, Pa 19120

Name:	
Address:	
City:	
State:	
Zip:	
Email (optional):	

AVAILABLE TITLES

Title	Quantity	Price	Total Price
Bad Blood		$15.00	
Bad Blood II		$15.00	
Jinxed		$15.00	
Sub Total			
Shipping & Handling			**$4.95**
Total			

Shipping via Priority Mail

Accepted Forms of Payment:
Certified & Institutional Checks & Money Orders
*** Place online orders on our website ***
www.TuffInkPublications.com